TAMESIDE LIBRARIES

3 8016 02102

KT-461-050

I LOST
YOU

www. **Tameside**.gov.uk

ASHTON LIBRARY

WITHDRAWN
TAMESIDE LIBRARIES

Met. She was co-founder of the Chipping Norton Literary Festival and now works for Oxford City Council. She lives in Oxfordshire with her family.

MERILYN DAVIES

WHEN I LOST YOU

arrow books

1 3 5 7 9 10 8 6 4 2

Arrow Books
20 Vauxhall Bridge Road
London SW1V 2SA

Arrow Books is part of the Penguin Random House group of companies
whose addresses can be found at global.penguinrandomhouse.com

Penguin
Random House
UK

Copyright © Merilyn Davies 2019

Merilyn Davies has asserted her right to be identified as the author of this Work
in accordance with the Copyright, Designs and Patents Act 1988.

First published by Arrow Books in 2019

www.penguin.co.uk

A CIP catalogue record for this book is available from the British Library.

ISBN 9781787461550

Typeset in 11.04/16.21 pt Times New Roman by Jouve (UK), Milton Keynes
Printed and bound in Great Britain by Clays Ltd, Elcograf S.p.A.

MIX
Paper from
responsible sources
FSC® C018179

Penguin Random House is committed to a
sustainable future for our business, our readers
and our planet. This book is made from Forest
Stewardship Council® certified paper.

For Mum and Dad. I wish the former was here
to read this, and hope the latter enjoys it.
Sorry for the Ryvita* crumbs.

* Other brands are available

Prologue

A screen sits to the left of the judge, and displayed on it is my child: a fragile, beautiful daughter, who had barely begun her life before the chance to live it was taken from her.

'Not lost,' the lawyer is saying, his wig a little frayed, in sharp contrast to the fresh youth of his closely shaven skin. 'Her life wasn't lost, it was *stolen*.' He emphasises the words, ones I've heard endlessly during the two-week trial, by looking in my direction. He doesn't linger, it's more a glance – the way a painter uses a gentle brushstroke to shape the outline of an image before colouring it in – but it's enough to make sure the jury remember I am the image he is painting: mother, killer, guilty.

I shift a little in my seat. The packed courtroom is hot and the white blouse I'm wearing sticks to my armpits, the polyester scratching against my skin. I see a juror glance in my direction and freeze; he's the one my lawyer warned me about.

'Third one from left, hipster beard,' he'd said in the cell as we waited to be recalled on that first day. 'Jeans and a tight jumper. He's got it in for you, so make sure you don't fidget too much or it makes you look guilty, but move a bit, because too little makes you look heartless.'

I am a trapeze artist – one wrong move and I fall into a cell, seven foot by nine. I steady my breathing and look down at my feet, concentrating on the new brogues I'm wearing, their brown shine complementing the sky-blue suit my husband bought me for the trial.

'Here,' he'd said, handing me the plastic bag he'd paid five pence for, then sitting down across from me in the noisy, smelly visiting hall. 'I'm pretty sure it's your size, but I kept the receipt just in case.'

I didn't remind him we had no time to exchange it. I just smiled my thanks and stuffed it by my feet next to the cooler bag full of fruit and biscuits. He took my hand. 'We'll get you out of here, my love,' he'd said. 'As soon as they see you, they'll understand, and then this nightmare will be over.'

I lost myself for a moment in his touch, the lightness of it, a soft caress. I marvelled again at how resolutely he'd stood by me. Against all evidence to the contrary, he'd refused to ever accept my guilt. But then his words returned – 'This nightmare will be over' – and they dragged me back to the bowels of the prison where the whispered threats told me otherwise.

Afternoon. I'm told juries are less focused after lunch, which would explain why the defence has called their next witness – a Thames Valley Police pathologist – because no one is going to fall asleep through her evidence. My heart is beating so hard, I'm convinced everyone can hear it as the woman walks silently to the witness box and raises her right hand. This is the evidence I've been dreading – the day my guilt is a medical fact, a not-to-be-questioned, scientific certainty – because who is going to question science? Certainly not the plumber sitting in the far right of the jury box, or the local-government worker sat two in from the left.

I reach to pick up my glass of lukewarm water – half empty from this morning – and sip at it. My hand is shaking and so, quickly, I lower it back down. I daren't look at the jury in case they are looking back at me, reading the shaking as a sure sign of my guilt. Then, as glass touches wood, the pathologist begins and each word feels like a nail in my jail cell door.

'The body showed signs of bruising consistent with being restrained.'

'Restrained? Can you describe why you concluded that?'

The pathologist raises her wrists. 'There was bruising on the inside of each wrist, inconsistent with normal movement.'

The barrister glances at the jury, letting them know this bit is relevant. 'And what was it consistent with?'

'Being restrained, and—' She opens her mouth to say something more but the barrister holds up his hand and whatever it was is lost, to become part of someone else's story, not mine. Because this is how my trial feels; I'm the lead in a story being written by this barrister as he deftly guides the jury down one plot line to another, each of them designed to get me fifteen to life.

'And how did the defendant seem to you when you arrived at the scene?'

'She seemed distant. She didn't speak.'

'Did she look at her daughter?'

The pathologist shook her head. 'No.'

'Not once?'

'Not once.'

'In your experience, did the defendant behave the way a woman who had just lost her child would behave?'

The pathologist paused and the barrister continued. 'If she hadn't killed her, that is.'

'You mean, if it had been an accident?'

'Yes, that sort of thing. A natural death.' Another glance to the jury and I dig my nails into my thighs.

'No, I would not say her behaviour was consistent with that of other mothers I have seen.'

The barrister nods, as if this alone is enough. I pick up the water again, not caring if my hand is shaking, and down it in one. I think of all my lost babies, the death of each as real as any scar across my skin, and wonder how it was we'd got to be here.

It took us years to get pregnant. If you added up all the money we spent on ovulation kits and pregnancy tests you could probably pay off the debt of a small country. So when at last we were, the joy was immediate. At least for the first one. We bought clothes, a pram, a car seat, and by twelve weeks we'd decorated the nursery in a neutral shade of green. We chose names – Jamie for a boy, Sammy or Ellie for a girl – and settled into our long nights dozing on the sofa waiting for whoever they were to arrive.

So when they'd arrived without a sound – when the second and the third babies did the same – we'd packed away the pram, the clothes, and painted the room magnolia; because there is only so much two people can suffer before the cracks begin to show.

The last was Charlotte. She'd taken root and we'd watched her grow, my stomach expanding with each week, our fear for her growing alongside it. But she'd come into the world mewing like a kitten and had curled up in my arms as if she'd always known she was meant to be there. And maybe she was, we dared to think. The day she died I'd been down at the bottom of the garden when my husband's yell came from upstairs. I didn't move; I think I knew it had always been too good to be true. I didn't kill that child, but after so many dead, no jury alive is going to believe that; even I don't, and I know it to be true.

The barrister has moved on to the crucial bit. I bow my head, not caring if it makes me look guilty.

'And when you tested the item you considered to be the murder weapon, did you find any evidence to suggest it had been that used by the defendant to kill her own daughter?'

The pathologist nods. I glance at my husband in the gallery and he gently shakes his head, so I look back at the tall woman in the box who swore on the Bible she would tell the truth.

'I found remnants of bone and blood from the daughter and DNA matches for the mother.'

There is a sharp intake of breath from the barrister but I barely hear it. The room has grown too hot; it starts to sway and I grab the wooden edges of my chair to steady myself. Not blood, not blood from my child.

'And the blood matches that of the defendant's daughter?' he continues.

I stare at him, then at my husband, then at my barrister. I turn to the jury. This can't be allowed. This is not the truth; the truth is I loved my child – all my children. I stand and see my barrister stand too. She reaches towards me, gesturing to the guard beside me but I push them off. Words that have been like fists thundering against the wall of my head are finally released into the room and I shout:

'I DID NOT KILL MY BABY.'

One

DS Nell Jackson looked up at the shabby white-fronted flats with her usual sense of déjà vu – after eight years with Thames Valley Police she felt she knew this stubby block of flats better than she knew her own. Even the fading light couldn't hide white paint peeling from window frames, or the makeshift clothes lines spanning balconies like decorations on a Christmas tree while toddlers' bicycles hung from walls in a desperate attempt to util-ise what little outside space there was.

'Morse, it is not.' DC Paul Mackintosh's tone was flat and Nell didn't bother to agree. Two weeks into a heatwave that smothered Oxford like a duvet, she saved her words for less obvious observations. Besides, she was long past being surprised by the city. At first, fresh out of Wales, she'd found it laughable drunks urinated in shop doorways on Friday nights past closing, when only the kebab vans remained open; that the homeless hung remnants of past lives in century-old doorways, grand pillars marking the boundary to that night's home.

She'd soon learned that Oxford's estates pumped out the same old crimes they had in Wales. Same problems, different view. So, Oxford for Nell was now not so much spires as shitholes. Populated not by worldly professors, but by people whose weekly income didn't even match what some students spent on a night out – all existing under the watchful gaze of Oxford University, which managed the city in a way that would have put the Corleones to shame.

Unbuckling her seat belt, Nell nodded towards an open door on the second floor. 'Best let's go up then.' Reluctantly tucking a dog-eared notebook in her back pocket, she prepared for a blast of late-night air and pushed open the door.

'Are the parents still in situ?' She slammed the car door and as the heat hit her she resisted the urge to take off her jacket. This wasn't the type of case you went into half dressed.

Paul nodded. 'Yep.'

'Any sign it's not natural causes?' Nell asked as they climbed the open-air stairwell, the smell of urine heavy around them, cigarette butts and broken bottles nestling at the edges of each step.

'Not yet, but the pathologist has only just arrived.'

She hoped it was Eve, then they might stand a chance of getting out of there before midnight. Fishing her warrant card out of her jacket, she flashed it at the uniformed officer standing discreetly beside the open door: 'DS Nell Jackson and DC Paul Mackintosh.'

The uniform nodded and tipped her head down the hall. 'Parents in the front room, second on left,' she said, her voice low. 'Deceased on right, directly across from them.'

'Pathologist?' Nell asked. Her heart pumped a little faster, adrenalin and nerves kicking in.

'In with the child.'

'OK, thanks.' She looked at Paul, who gave a weary smile.

'Child first, parents second, OK?'

He nodded, then smiling her thanks at the uniform, Nell said, 'Right, let's go and get this over with.'

In contrast to the hall – with its frayed pink carpet and tobacco-stained walls – the nursery was freshly painted, albeit unprofessionally. Despite the darkness – blackout blinds still down from the night before – Nell could make out paint spots on the carpet beneath a large cream cot; stuffed toys cramming the end of the mattress; a red blanket folded neatly over the wooden bars. And in the far corner of the room, a lone chair, next to which sat a bottle on a table, barely touched. There had been care given to this room, Nell thought; the best had been made of a bad job. So what had gone wrong?

Eve Graham was standing by the cot, gloved hands on the frame, staring downwards. The pathologist's short white hair caught the light from the hall, but her face – the wide cheekbones, thickly carved jawline – remained in the shadows. There was a stillness about the scene that Nell felt uncomfortable interrupting.

'Why hasn't she started?' Paul asked, voice low.

'She likes to get a sense of the scene before she starts, to take it in as it was, before we arrive and swarm all over it.' But Nell conceded the delay was unusual, even for Eve. She must have been there for half an hour at least.

At the sound of Nell's voice, Eve straightened, drawing in air as she removed her hands from the cot and turned to face them.

'Better late than never, I suppose.' Her gravelly voice betrayed years of late nights smoking Benson & Hedges while drinking whisky and wine. Her tone was light; there was no chastisement, rather a bored disinterest in their arrival. Nell relaxed. This was the Eve she knew.

Approaching the crib, Nell felt Paul hanging back. She didn't blame him. No reason they both had to see the body, not when statistics told her this was probably going to be a sudden infant death – a tragedy, but not a crime.

The baby was wrapped in a yellow polka-dot blanket and looked for all the world like she was sleeping but for the sense of absence, a feeling impossible to describe, but which was immediately felt.

Nell felt Eve's eyes on her and looked across at the pathologist.

'Have you met the parents yet?' Eve's blue eyes were hard, so Nell assumed she had and it clearly hadn't gone well.

'No,' said Nell.

Eve puffed her displeasure. 'Nasty man. Can see the control he has over the mother just from one glance.'

Nell felt the adrenalin surge again. 'You think he did something to the baby?'

Eve looked down at the cot. 'Wouldn't surprise me. Men like him don't like competition, even if it comes in the form of a baby.' She looked at Nell. 'Especially if it comes in the form of a baby,' she corrected.

Nell watched as Eve began to work, taking in the milky-white skin of the child, free from discoloration or bruising; noting the baby's hair still fluffy from her evening bath.

'What are your thoughts?' she asked.

Eve didn't reply. Her forehead furrowed as she gently examined the baby. Nell looked around the room for signs of neglect but found only a well-cleaned carpet, clothes neatly placed in a small white wardrobe, toys perfectly stacked in three clear plastic boxes. Sudden infant death. She was sure of it. Her heart slowed. The sickly smell of regurgitated milk and perfumed baby wipes was giving her a headache and the heat in the room was claustrophobic. The sooner they could close this one, the better.

'It's not a natural death.'

Nell turned. 'What?'

Eve's words jarred with the whole feel of the room.

'This baby was killed, Sergeant.' Noting Nell's scepticism, she added, 'Trust me, DS Jackson, this baby is dead because someone wanted it to be. And I don't mean that person to be God.'

Nell looked down at the baby, at the dried dribble of milk in the corner of her mouth, the sleep crusted around her eyes. She looked peaceful, not the recipient of a violent attack but a baby who had just forgotten to wake up. A mad moment, then? The baby crying for too long and too late, parents' frustrations spilling over into a single act of violence?

As if Eve could sense Nell's doubt, she said, 'Distended stomach, fluid from her ear, suggesting head trauma. Obviously, I'll find out more when I get her down the emergency room.'

Nell nodded. Babies didn't get taken to the mortuary, sensitivities rightly ensuring they were treated with more consideration than that, but even babies couldn't escape Eve's clinical eye. As the pathologist leaned down to put the blanket in an evidence bag, Nell felt the headache move above her left eye.

'The dad then?'

'No comment. Yet.'

'But deliberate?'

'Oh yes.'

Nell waited for more but Eve continued to slowly bag the contents of the cot.

Irritated, Nell turned to Paul. 'Let's go see the parents.'

He nodded, giving a quick glance at the cot before exiting the room, his relief obvious. Nell hesitated.

'Something worrying you, Sergeant?'

Nell looked over at the baby, just visible through the bars. She'd thought after eight years and the amount of shit she'd seen, with the very base of human nature coming at her day after day, she could take this in her stride. Turned out you never got used to this, however hard you tried. She looked over at Eve, who was studying her.

'Do you think it was in a fit of anger?'

Eve's look told her she knew what Nell was really asking. Nell didn't want a protracted abuse case. Not just due to the fact it would be a boatload of work for no positive outcome, but because she wanted the baby to have died quickly, loved for the brief time she'd spent on earth, not filled with fear and pain.

Eve was holding a stuffed bear, pink and almost brand new.

'All I'm saying is this child didn't die of her own accord. And anyway,' she placed the bear in the bag and sealed it, 'isn't motive your side of things? I'm just here to put the meat on the bones, as it were.'

They both knew Eve was there to do a lot more than that, but Nell wasn't in the mood to argue. Taking one more look at the baby, she made a move to go.

'Georgie,' Eve said.

Nell turned back.

'What?'

'The baby – her name is Georgie. I just thought I'd mention it.'

Nell watched Eve go back to work, an uneasy sense of guilt at her realisation that she hadn't thought to ask.

Shutting the door quietly, Nell walked down the narrow corridor, turning the name over in her mind. Georgie – a name you give a girl you wished was a boy? She walked past the kitchen and paused. Small and cream, it contained a tiny table, neatly laid for breakfast, at the far end under a window; freshly washed dishes on the draining board; a baby bottle filled with powdered milk just waiting for the water.

There was a future in this room, she thought, feeling the

headache spread to the right side of her head. Digging out a tired-looking sheet of pills from an inside pocket, she popped two and swallowed them dry. A future for all three of them – so what had happened to make Georgie's mum and dad take that future from her?

Two

Nell paused outside the door to the front room, one hand pressed against the cream-painted wood. She stared at the floor, letting her mind go blank, emptying it so the first impression of the parents would be more vivid. She wanted to see what Eve had seen; to find out from the get-go if her instincts mirrored those of the pathologist.

As Nell opened the door she could see Paul in the centre of the room, seated on a threadbare sofa. Opposite him sat Kelly-Anne Wilson and Connor O'Brian on two aged and mismatched chairs.

First thought – why weren't they sitting together? Nell had never seen bereaved parents do anything other than cling to each other, so tightly they almost appeared to be one rather than two.

Second – Connor was at least twenty years older than Kelly-Anne. Not a problem in itself, but the girl looked barely legal.

Nell took a seat next to Paul.

'I know this is really upsetting for you,' he was saying as the young woman silently cried, 'and I'm sorry to have to ask these questions at a time like this.'

A time like this. If Nell had a pound for every time she'd heard those words. She scanned the room: walls, like the hallway, stained with smoke and age; crumpled cans of lager on the table; an overflowing ashtray, which, despite being next to an open window, left the air heavy with the smell of stale cigarettes. There had been no thought given to the blind hanging loose from its fittings, she concluded, or the table ringed with cup marks, or the sofa Nell now sat on. In fact, the whole room was as devoid of care as the child's room had been full of it.

She turned back to the parents. Kelly-Anne's face was blotched red with tears and her hair was scraped up into a high ponytail typical of the teenage girls Nell saw on the estates of Oxford. She wore a light grey vest top that had probably once been white, with a pair of pink towelling shorts, and her bare feet were curled in on themselves, as if hiding. Christ, what was she, seventeen?

Connor, however, was a man of at least forty, probably older. His face was a mass of lines, spots and bristle. Nell noted the tattoo on his arm – faded blue, picture no longer clear – clocked the scabs littering his balding scalp: steroids, or something more? He was bulky, so maybe the former, but a faint smell of cannabis made her think the latter. And there was a barely suppressed anger about him, not just directed towards her and

Paul – for that was predictable; men like that wore their anger at police like a badge – but to his girlfriend sitting next to him, who shrank from it.

Nell began to see what Eve had seen and she didn't like it. Connor's height and width dominated the space around them, almost erasing Kelly-Anne's presence. It was clear that what mattered to him was the ongoing interaction with Paul, not the girlfriend sitting next to him, and certainly not the child in the bedroom.

'If you could just tell me again how you found Georgie,' Paul was saying. 'How you found her . . .' he paused, '. . . like that.'

Nell watched Kelly-Anne cower in on herself, tears flowing down her cheeks. When she spoke it was with the lilt of 'Oxford' – the raw end of it, not the silver-spoon variety.

'Georgie had been a bit cranky – but nothing we couldn't cope with,' she added hurriedly, eyes wide and fixed on Nell as if their shared gender would connect them. It didn't.

'I'd tried to give her a bottle but she wasn't having it, so Connor went out for Calpol, didn't you?' She looked to her boyfriend with lashes covered in thick mascara, clinging on despite the tears. Connor barely managed a nod in reply.

'You can give them Calpol you know,' Kelly-Anne said, turning back to Nell, her tone desperate.

Nell nodded. 'Yes, I know.'

Kelly-Anne seemed to relax a little, shoulders sagging. 'But we couldn't get much in her so I just lay her down in her cot and left her to cry it out a bit. You can do that too, you know? It's in the books and stuff.'

Nell nodded again. She didn't know and likely never would, but if it was in the books, who was she to judge? She wondered how they'd met. Kelly-Anne underage and down the pub on a Friday night; Connor seeing his chance as the shots took hold; a quick fumble a few hours later, then fast forward nine months and here they were with a screaming baby in a flat provided by the council? Or was it more than that?

Nell watched the hand movements of the pair, the way she pleaded with him to hold hers, the manner in which he batted her off. Connor was an angry man, that was clear enough. But angry enough to kill a baby? Probably.

'And what happened then?' Paul asked the pair. It was Kelly-Anne who replied; always Kelly-Anne, Nell noted.

'And then she stopped crying.' Kelly-Anne gave a small shrug. 'So we left her. I mean, that's what was supposed to happen, wasn't it? That's what the books say – you leave them to cry, then they learn how to put themselves to sleep, so we thought she had.'

Nell pictured the tiny body in the cot and wondered how anything that small could learn anything from being left alone in a room screaming – other than it wasn't loved – but she kept her mouth shut. The less she said, the more they would, and give them enough rope they might just hang themselves with it.

'So we left her for about an hour.' She looked to Connor with a pleading expression. 'And then you went to check on her, didn't you?'

When Connor raised his eyes, Nell saw no grief, just a challenge to her to prove what he was about to say was wrong.

'Yeah.' The strength in his body was not reflected in his voice and its pitch took Nell by surprise.

'Go on,' Paul said.

Connor shrugged.

'And the kid wouldn't wake up. I shook her and sort of pushed at her chest –' he imitated the movement with his hands, '– like I've seen on TV and that, but I couldn't get her to wake up.'

Connor sounded uninterested, the words rehearsed, but Nell could see from the twitch in his knee he was nervous. She leaned forward.

'So, you shook Georgie?'

Connor held her stare. 'No, I gave her a little shake to wake her up.'

'Is that usually how you wake your daughter, Mr O'Brian?'

Connor folded his arms, flexed his muscles. 'You know what I mean.'

'No, actually, I don't.'

Nell watched Kelly-Anne put her hand on Connor's arm and him shrug it away. The young woman turned to Nell, her face full of desperation.

'He's a good dad – he didn't do anything to Georgie, I promise.'

'Were you there with Mr O'Brian when he shook her?'

Before she could reply, Connor stood. His height seemed to suck the air from the room and Kelly-Anne shrank back in the face of it.

'I didn't bloody shake her.' He pointed down at Kelly-Anne,

red blotches on his face spreading down his neck. 'This is all your fault, you stupid cow. If you'd just woken her when I said.'

Paul stood and held out both hands to calm the situation. 'Mr O'Brian, no one is saying you shook your child to hurt her. Please sit back down.'

When he didn't move, Kelly-Anne reached up to him and tugged for him to comply. When he still didn't sit she looked imploringly at Nell.

'He shook her to wake her, not kill her.'

'Why did Mr O'Brian think you should have woken the baby earlier?'

Kelly-Anne opened her mouth to speak but Connor shut her down.

'We're not saying anything else.' He sat down next to Kelly-Anne and took her hand, squeezing it until she winced. 'Take us down the station if you've anything else you want to ask.'

Silence fell. Paul looked to Nell and gave a quick shrug, but she wasn't done.

'Kelly-Anne, did you hurt your baby?'

'Don't answer that,' Connor told her. Leaning across to the coffee table, he picked up a cigarette and lit it. After three short drags he gave it to a pale Kelly-Anne. Nell noted the shaking hand as she took it, the panicked look in her eyes, and waited.

'I know what you are all thinking,' Kelly-Anne finally said. 'Single mum on benefits with a con as a boyfriend.'

'Oh for fuck's sake, Kelly-Anne.'

But Kelly-Anne shrugged off his comment and folded her

arms tight across her chest, cigarette now dangerously close to the back of the chair.

'It's not like they wouldn't have checked,' she said, voice sulky. 'In jail twice, if you want to know.'

'How long did you spend in jail, Mr O'Brian?' Nell asked.

Kelly-Anne gave a bitter laugh and took a drag. 'Second time was long enough to miss the bloody birth.'

Connor relaxed back into his chair. 'Two months. Was just for a bit of weed, that's all.'

'Growing it,' Kelly-Anne added. 'Bloody growing the stuff he was. Stupid git.'

He threw her a warning look and the pair collapsed into silence. Had she got them wrong? Maybe it was Kelly-Anne who pulled the strings, in which case it was possible Connor was covering for her. But before she could push them further, Eve knocked on the door.

'Can I have a word?' Her gaze landed on Kelly-Anne before moving quickly to Connor, where it lingered, despite his cold stare back.

'Sure.' Nell nodded for Paul to join them, then pulled the door to. 'What you got?'

Eve removed her blue plastic gloves. She studied her hands as she did so, before looking down at Nell, piercing blue eyes a stark contrast to her pale skin. 'It's definitely not a sudden infant death. There are clear signs the child was shaken.'

'The boyfriend said he shook her trying to wake her – could that fit?' Nell asked, looking back at the closed door.

Eve gave a short, hard laugh. 'I'm sure he did say that. Trying to cover their tracks, no doubt. But no, the way the blood has collected suggests there was limited movement after death.'

'What, they didn't even pick her up?' Paul asked, his tone full of disgust.

'Doesn't look like it, no.'

'O'Brian also said he tried to resuscitate her with chest compressions – any sign that's true?' Nell asked.

'Well, there are a few broken ribs, as far as I can tell, but I don't think that was post-mortem. They most likely occurred before death. There are clear marks on her chest, which wouldn't be apparent had the father done what he said after the infant was dead.'

'So the shaking and broken ribs happened prior to death?' Nell asked, just to make sure.

'Yes, in my considered opinion that is correct.'

Nell looked at Paul, who ran his hand through his cropped hair and whistled.

'And if you want my considered opinion,' Eve said, throwing the gloves into a contamination bag, 'it was the mother who did it.'

Nell stared at her. 'What?'

'The mother, Sergeant. The bruising is light, not consistent with a man that size.' She nodded towards the closed door.

'That's quite an allegation there, Doc,' and Paul's expression told her what he thought of that.

Eve put down the bag and folded her arms.

'Don't be fooled by that little-girl-lost act, Constable.' The pointed reference to his lower rank didn't go unnoticed. 'Girls like that,' she continued, 'can be just as brutal as the men who brutalise them.'

'Girls like that?' Paul sounded disgusted. 'What, young, vulnerable girls with no money, family or support?'

Eve gave him an appraising look before speaking. 'As I said earlier, I'm not here to solve the case, just to give you clues to do so yourselves. If you wish to ignore them,' she gave a little shrug and picked up the bag, 'then so be it.'

She turned to go but Nell put her hand on the woman's arm. 'Are you sure enough for us to arrest her?'

'No. I won't be sure until I've done a full post-mortem. I'm just giving you a heads-up so you can be ahead of the game.'

'Thanks for the consideration,' Paul snapped back. Nell threw him a warning look.

'Well, thank you for your time, Eve,' she said. 'Let me have the results ASAP, OK?'

Eve nodded and when she'd left the hallway, Paul exploded.

'What is she on? How can she tell it was the girl, not the man, who did it?'

Nell shoved her hands in her pockets and leaned back against the wall. She wanted a cigarette, badly. 'It is her job to know these things.'

Paul snorted his disgust and pointed his thumb back towards the door. 'What we doing with these two, then?'

Nell shrugged. 'Leave them until Eve gives us the green light.'

'Seriously?'

'Seriously. Do you really want,' she checked her watch, 'to

23

book them into custody at 22:59? It'll be 1 a.m. by the time we get to bed and I for one don't want to hang out with a grumpy custody sergeant and a suite full of drunks when we have nothing concrete to go on. Besides, the press would have a field day if we dragged a grieving mother in with no evidence.'

Noting Paul's look, she said, 'So what are they going to do, Paul? It's not like they've got the money to skip over to Spain and go on the run.' Nell knew how she sounded, but the case was already getting her down and the pills hadn't kicked in so her head was pounding. It was a dead baby, sad, tragic even, but it wasn't the sort of case she'd wanted to work on when she joined the police. And it wasn't as if the couple were a risk to the public. A single mother on benefits and a part-time drug dealer – a not very good one at that – what good would it do to take them down the station? It was going to be a cut-and-dry case, with little to do but watch the mother go down for it.

'Well, I'd like it noted I disagree with this course of action. Something's not right here and I don't like the look of the dad.'

Nell turned to go back into the front room. 'Noted,' she said.

Three

Now

It is 2 a.m. and my husband is lying awake beside me. We are each pretending the other is asleep, and for the moment this suits me fine. I listen to the distant hum of late-night Oxford traffic, the faint call of one student to another, watch the gradual arc of a car's headlights pass over the bedroom ceiling.

I feel peaceful, a feeling so alien to me over the last few months that I allow myself to be smothered by it, curling into it in an attempt to forget.

I feel his hand reach mine and take a hold. He squeezes, and I squeeze back, the spell broken.

'I'm sorry,' he says. My heart pinches. He has nothing to be sorry for. He has only ever been my supporter, my champion, my soulmate.

I take my hand from his and turn on to my side, hands under my cheek as if in prayer. 'You have nothing to be sorry for.'

He is staring at the ceiling, dark now after the brief car light. I stare at his profile: the solid nose, heavy brow, bristled jaw, and I mentally trace my fingers from the top of his head to his chin.

'Do you understand why I did it?' I study his face as I speak, trying to judge the response before it's spoken, but he gives me nothing – just continues to stare at the ceiling as if he can find the answer there.

'Eve has taken over my life—' I begin, but he raises a hand to stop me.

'No. You've let her do that.'

I'm so stunned for a moment I don't speak, then I push myself up by my elbow. 'And how's that?' My glare pulls his eyes to mine.

'You can choose whether she takes over your life.'

'My choice? All this was my choice?'

'Yes.' He is so definite it winds me. I fall back on the bed and roll on to my back, folding my arms against my chest.

It's his turn to roll towards me, an olive branch I don't want to take, but when he speaks his voice is gentle and I can't help but lean into it.

'Why did you write the letter?' His voice is calm, but behind it lie a thousand more questions, the answers to which I know he doesn't want to hear.

'To stop Eve,' I say. But I can feel his stare deep under my skin, breaking bones as it bores into me.

'And what do you intend to achieve? What do you want to happen after she gets the letter?'

The reply feels so self-evident I almost don't know where to begin. 'I expect her to listen, to help me put this all behind us, so I can move forward again and be who I used to be.'

Staring at the ceiling, he sighs.

'What?' I sound angrier than I am, so I lay my hand on his arm. 'Don't you want that too?'

'I don't think either of us knows who you are any more.'

It feels like a slap and I jerk my hand back. 'Well then that's another reason to get her to stop, tell her what she's done so she can't destroy another life like she's destroyed mine.'

He doesn't move. 'And what do you think the police will do?'

'What do you mean?'

'You've written a letter to a renowned pathologist accusing her of potentially misleading the police about a case she is working on.'

I huff, then feel like a child, so I cross my legs and make myself consider what he's said. The police are bound to be interested – if Eve tells them, that is. Maybe she won't. Maybe she won't want them looking into what she's done. But isn't that what I want? For them to know?

'What if you go to jail?'

I snap round to face him. 'Why would that happen? It's just a letter.'

'I can't be without you. Not after everything we've gone through.'

I scan his face, checking for signs of tears or anger, but he's doing what he always does – holding it together. For my sake. Always for me, never for him.

I lie next to him and wrap one leg around his. 'I won't go to jail.'

He turns to look at me. 'Sometimes I think that's what you want. That you want to be there as punishment for the guilt you feel.'

I hold his gaze. 'I won't go away. I promise.' My voice sounds as sure as I feel. I will never leave this man.

We stay like that for what seems like ages, until I feel sleep poke at the corners of my eyes, and my thoughts become hazy.

'I love you.'

He leans over and kisses me gently. 'I love you too,' he says, his nose close to mine. 'Just be careful, OK?'

'I will, I promise.'

'Because Eve's not going to go down without a fight.'

I feel myself starting to wake, so put my finger on his lips and close my eyes. 'I'm not going to fight her. I just want her to help me finish it.'

But as I lie and listen to his breath deepen, I know it isn't true. If Eve wants a fight, I'll be there, and I'll make sure her whole life crumbles before her while I watch and laugh.

Four

Crime analyst Carla Brown wiped the previous week's jobs off the board and wrote the three things she knew about last night's case: *Baby Georgie – dead, Kelly-Anne Wilson – mum, Connor O'Brian – dad.* She wondered, again, why Nell hadn't arrested one or both of them. Maybe the pathologist hadn't found anything conclusive at the scene, maybe Nell didn't want to clog up custody without good grounds, maybe she should stop second-guessing and wait for Nell to get in.

Picking up her still-warm coffee, Carla went outside for a cigarette.

The morning sky was a clear blue, the absence of cloud suggesting the heatwave wasn't going to break any time soon. Lining tobacco on the slim paper, Carla watched a two-seater plane come in to land at the airport across from Thames Valley North

HQ. She could do without the heat. White-blonde hair and pale skin meant the sun didn't do it for her, and zero air conditioning coupled with ineffectual office windows meant by midday the team had borderline heatstroke.

Exhaling smoke, Carla watched it drift aimlessly upwards. The side road was quiet, save for the chatter of birds congregating on the short stubby trees lining the middle, until DCI Max Bremer's black Merc pulled off the roundabout and headed towards the back gates. Carla stubbed her roll-up into a potted plant. Bremer was new enough to the team for her still to want to make a good impression, but she also hoped he'd be able to give her the heads-up on the previous night's job, let her get a start on it before Nell and Paul got in.

Getting out of the car, Bremer slammed the door and hung his jacket over his arm before retrieving his briefcase from the back seat.

'Anything from Nell?' he asked, looking back at her.

'No, I was hoping you'd have something.'

'Nothing as yet.' They walked towards the entrance, Bremer pushing open the tall glass doors for Carla to step through. Grey sofa to their right, reception desk to their left.

A woman stood with her back to them, thrusting a brown envelope at an uncertain-looking receptionist, who didn't take it. It took Carla a second to recognise her, although how she could mistake that cropped white hair and rigid posture for anyone other than Eve Graham was beyond her.

'Eve?'

The pathologist turned to face her. 'Carla.' Her gravelly voice echoed through the reception area. 'Long time no see. I hear from Gerry you're working with DS Jackson?'

Eve's husband, Gerry, had been Carla's first sergeant and for the subsequent eight years had been a constant source of support and advice. Carla and her fiancé, Baz, had often found themselves at the Grahams' dinner table, where Eve's insistence on Scotch for dessert always necessitated swapping their car for a taxi ride home. Carla had always found Eve distant, her hosting forced, laughter fake, and the intimidation she'd felt during those evenings was no less now they were meeting on Carla's home turf.

She nodded to the brown envelope Eve held. 'Can I help?'

'Oh. Yes, I suppose you can.' She handed it to Carla. 'It's a letter. I get them from time to time, but I discussed it with Gerry and he persuaded me to give it to you.' She gave a smile. 'Ever the overprotector is our Gerry.'

Carla looked at the blank envelope, its edge neatly opened. Why would Gerry bother about a letter if Eve didn't seem worried?

'I said it wasn't anything to concern ourselves with,' Eve went on, 'but it makes a reference to a case I'm working on, one with your DS Jackson, as it happens.'

Carla looked up, surprised. 'Last night's job?'

Eve nodded. 'Hand-delivered. No fingerprints. Typed.'

'What reference?'

Eve turned to Bremer, equal in height, she looked him in the eye. 'And you are?'

'DCI Max Bremer.' He didn't offer his hand and nor did Eve when she replied.

'Best you look at the letter for yourself, Detective Inspector.'

'Detective Chief Inspector.' His tone was cold. Carla tensed, but Eve's look told her she either hadn't noticed or didn't care.

Picking up her bag, Eve gave them a curt nod. 'Anyway. Must go. These bodies don't cut themselves up. Tell DS Jackson I'll let her know if I'm right about the baby by midday.'

And before Carla could ask what she meant, Eve pushed open the glass doors and headed out into the blinding brightness.

They took the lift. Carla hated the small space and the proximity to her boss, but it was preferable to taking the stairs in this heat. She looked at the envelope.

'What's the pathologist's story?' asked Bremer.

Carla looked up, surprised. 'What do you mean?'

'Well she's not exactly socially literate, is she?'

Carla laughed. 'I've heard Eve called many things but socially illiterate has to be the most apt.'

'Not well liked then?'

'Very well respected,' Carla replied. 'And I think that's what she values more.'

Bremer nodded. 'Fair point. It's not a popularity contest, after all. Although if it were, my money wouldn't be on Ms Graham winning it.'

She couldn't disagree. Eve wasn't everyone's cup of tea, and

Carla had been surprised when Eve had mentioned receiving other letters. Why hadn't Gerry ever mentioned it?

The lift doors pinged open and Bremer led the way to the office.

'Let me know if I need to worry about the letter,' he said over his shoulder, 'and shout me when Nell gets in,' before shutting the door to his office separating himself off with a plywood wall and a window that shuddered with the slightest movement.

Carla sat at her desk, one computer in front of her, one to the left and a police database a little further up, all pumping out heat that the stand-alone fan next to her couldn't even begin to tackle.

Pulling out the letter, she laid it on the desk, placing an old coffee cup on one edge of the pages to stop them from blowing away, pulled up her hair to allow a breeze to her neck and began to read.

Eve,

What is this, my third or fourth letter to you? By now you'll know what I'm asking before I even write it, but I'm going to keep on writing until you listen. Years ago you saw fit to take my life and dismantle it bit by bit. You hollowed me out and discarded the pieces like scraps of food not even fit for a dog.

I know you understand what it feels like to lose a baby. To be a mother without a child. Why punish others whose experience you share? You will do it again; a mother will be ruined because of you and I can't stand by and let that happen. Excuse yourself from the O'Brian case. Don't harm another young mother whose baby died. Try to imagine the pain and fear she feels; imagine the cold metallic panic on your tongue as your mouth goes dry when you realise someone is about to accuse you of killing the most important person to you. The power you wield is such that one word from you can destroy a woman like her.

A courtroom trusts you. I do not.

You have caused a woman to endure years of imprisonment for a crime she did not commit. Please don't inflict that same nightmare on Kelly-Anne Wilson.

M

Carla watched the pages flutter in the fan's wind. She wasn't sure what she had been expecting but it sure as hell wasn't that.

Her analyst mind kicked into gear, starting to isolate the key points: the author knew about the O'Brian case despite it being less than twenty-four hours old; the author was someone with a knowledge of Eve's personal life, if the reference to losing a child was to be believed; the author harboured feelings of revenge towards Eve, judging her responsible for a case of wrongful imprisonment.

All big allegations, but the only one that concerned Carla now was the reference to O'Brian. How could the author of the letter know about the death of baby Georgie when she, the analyst, and the DCI had yet to be briefed? No one knew about the baby's death except the 999 call handler and Bremer's team, and half of them didn't even know Eve had been assigned the case until this morning.

The office door banged open, making her jump.

'Jesus, man, you scared me half to death.'

Paul was carrying a cardboard holder with four takeout coffees. 'Sorry, had to kick it open.' He placed the holder on Carla's desk and pulled off his jacket. 'This weather is going to be the death of me. What is it, like 9 a.m.? And I'm sweating already.'

'Nice.' Carla took a coffee and two of the long white sugars perched precariously between the cups, knocking one on the edge of the table. Paul sank into his chair and wiped sweat from his forehead.

'Where's Nell?' she asked.

'Having a fag. God knows how she can in this heat, but there you go.' He peered at the computer screen dominating the centre of Carla's desk. 'What you working on?'

'Just something that's come up with the O'Brian case.'

'Shit. What?' Paul sat upright but Carla held up a hand.

'Nothing major. Just a bit of an odd link between your pathologist and Connor O'Brian.'

Paul relaxed back.

'Why? What did you think I was going to say?'

Paul pointed at the holder and she handed him a coffee. No sugar. He ripped off the lid and blew on the black liquid. 'Just we left O'Brian last night and it didn't feel right. Had a mad panic you were going to say he'd gone on a murderous rampage and we'd be hauled up for a disciplinary.' Paul took a sip and winced.

'What's the link to Eve?'

'Not sure yet. Did Eve say she knew Connor?'

Paul's look of surprise told Carla she hadn't.

'Did you see them together at all? See any interaction between them?'

'Not really.' Paul frowned at her. 'Come on, Brown, what you got?'

'You say "not really", so that means you did see them together?'

He laughed. 'I thought I was the police officer in this relationship. Eve just poked her head round the door when we were in with Connor and the girlfriend. But they didn't interact: no eye contact, no change in atmosphere when she appeared. She didn't like him, though. Made that clear.'

'Did she say why?'

'Just that he was controlling Kelly-Anne. But she doesn't think he killed the baby. She's got the girlfriend already banged up for that one.'

Carla emptied the second sugar into the coffee, stirring it with a pen. Interesting Eve didn't like him. But then she guessed Eve had seen enough shit in her time to be a good judge of character. Although it was also true to say the author of the letter didn't share that assumption.

'And there was no one else with you and Nell at the scene, other than Eve and the parents?'

'None. Well, except the uniform on the door and the two who'd been first to attend the scene.'

Carla discounted the two initial responders; they wouldn't have been aware Eve was assigned the case – only the uniform on the door would have known that.

'Did you get the uniform's name?'

Paul shook his head. 'No, but Cowley police station will know that. What's all this got to do with the O'Brian case?'

Carla handed Paul the letter, now in a clear plastic envelope, and watched while he read.

He looked up at her. 'Are they saying Eve's fitted someone up? On another job like the O'Brian's?'

'Looks like it.'

Paul let out a whistle. 'And they're saying she's going to do the same to Kelly-Anne? Well that makes sense. There's no way that woman killed her kid.'

Carla had already turned her back on him. Eve had said she'd get the results to Nell by midday so that gave her a few hours to do a bit of digging on Eve's past cases.

'You need me to do anything?' Paul asked.

'No thanks, I'm good.' Then she opened the intelligence database and started to search.

Five

Eve had been involved in three high-profile infant-death cases in the previous six years, all of which resulted in the conviction of the mother. Odd that they were all the mother when statistically speaking the father should have been involved in at least one, but then Carla wasn't an expert on sudden infant death.

She checked on the status of the three women: two remained in prison, one had been released six months previously. Well, she reasoned, that didn't preclude the other two from writing the letter, but Carla was pretty sure the prison authorities would have intercepted it at source, seeing as it contained a barely concealed threat against the person who had put them in jail.

So that left one. Carla clicked open the file of the remaining woman. She read it through, reread it just to make sure, then sat back.

'Shit.'

Paul looked up from his phone. 'Got something?'

'Come and look at this.' She pointed at the screen as Paul joined her.

'Eve's put away three women. Two are still in jail, but this one –' she looked up at him, '– this one was released recently.' She saw him frown. 'See what she was released for?'

'Jesus. Case was overturned?'

'Yep.' Carla scrolled through the document. 'Joanne Fowler, found not guilty on appeal after Eve's evidence was thrown out.'

'How long was she inside before the appeal?'

Carla checked. 'Two years.'

Paul sat on the edge of Carla's desk. 'Good reason for revenge, that.'

'Sure is.'

'Revenge?' Nell stood in the doorway, her hair pulled up into a bun, curls fighting to escape, her vest top already peppered with damp patches. She slung her bag onto the floor and walked over to them. 'Who wants revenge for what?'

'Joanne Fowler.' Carla handed her the letter. 'Potential suspect for this.'

As Nell read, Carla walked to the wipe board and wrote Connor's name on it, then Eve's, and drew a line between them. Writing Joanne's name alongside Eve's, she drew another line and stood back. 'If Joanne wrote the letter, what's her link with Connor?'

'Maybe it has nothing to do with Connor?' Paul said. 'Maybe it's all about Eve, and Connor is just the catalyst.'

Nell was studying him. 'Like a trigger? Joanne sees Eve is working on another sudden infant death case and it prompts this reaction?' She brandished the letter in the air.

'But that still doesn't cover how she *knew* Eve was working on the case,' Carla pointed out.

'I like the trigger idea,' Bremer said from his office door. 'But I agree with Carla – to be triggered she'd have to have known, and there's only one way for that to have happened.'

He walked to the wipe board and pointed at Joanne's name. 'Someone told her.'

Nell's phone rang. 'DS Jackson speaking.' Holding up a hand to excuse herself, she walked to the edge of the room.

'A leak then?' Paul said.

'Maybe, maybe not,' Bremer replied, 'but until we know I want radio silence on this one.' He looked to Carla and she knew what was coming.

'Not even to be discussed with Eve or her husband until we've ruled out a link to the O'Brian job, OK?'

Carla wanted to ask him if he'd have said that to a police officer, or whether the fact she was a civilian meant he felt the need to question her ability to keep her mouth shut, but she just nodded. Paul gave her a wink.

'Good.' Bremer looked over at Nell, who'd just hung up the phone. 'Anything?'

'Eve.' Nell walked back to the group and sat down on the chair next to Carla.

'She's sure it's Kelly-Anne who killed the baby, not Connor.'

'Do we believe her?' Paul asked.

'Why wouldn't we?'

Paul pointed to the letter. 'It's what they said would happen – Eve would blame the girlfriend. And she does have previous for getting it wrong.'

Before Nell could respond Bremer held up his hand. Speaking to Paul, he said, 'I get your point but I'll go with a pathologist over a poison pen letter until I'm proved wrong.'

'Eve is a good pathologist,' Carla added. 'Joanne, if she wrote the letter, obviously has an issue with her, and rightly so, but it can't stop us relying on Eve's word.' She looked at Bremer. 'Want me to do some digging on Kelly-Anne, see if she has form?'

Bremer shook his head. 'No, I want to see what Joanne knows about the case. Nell, Paul, you bring Kelly-Anne in.' He paused. 'And Connor.'

My God, so Bremer had his doubts too? Had everyone lost all reason based on a vicious letter? Irritated, Carla picked up her brown leather tobacco pouch. If they were going to rely on hearsay rather than facts she needed nicotine.

'And Carla,' Bremer continued, 'we'll go and see Joanne, see what light she can shed on the case.'

Nell stared at him, jacket half on, car keys in hand. 'What?'

Carla stared at him. Was he serious? She knew he hadn't minded causing a few stirs in his six months with them, but this was a whole other level.

'Do you have a problem with Carla meeting Joanne?' Bremer

held Nell's stare and the office atmosphere shifted. Nell put the keys on the desk.

'With all due respect, analysts don't go out on jobs, they stay here and do our research.'

Carla flinched inwardly. What Nell had said was true, in part, but it didn't stop the tone she'd delivered it in from stinging. Carla had been out on jobs – looking at crime scenes so she could better judge the evidence she was to analyse – but she hadn't sat in on an interview, merely watched an untold number via video link. But then Bremer was new to Thames Valley, arriving after ten years in the Met, and maybe they did things differently in London; maybe it was standard procedure to take an analyst along for the ride? But then this wasn't the Met and Carla wasn't in London.

'I think Nell's right. I'll just stay here and do some digging on Joanne, Kelly-Anne and Connor.'

Bremer swung his eyes to her. 'I want an analyst's eye on the Fowler woman, so what better way than to be there with me?' His eyes held a challenge Carla didn't feel she could match. If he wanted to buck the trend of all other DCIs she'd worked for, then so be it, but she was damn well going to have a cigarette first.

She picked up her bag, stuffed her tobacco pouch in it, and said, 'I'll meet you by the car, shall I?' Carla felt Nell's eyes on her as she walked towards the door, but what was she supposed to do, refuse? Her palms were sweaty before she'd even left the building, and as she pulled out a cigarette paper she realised her hands were shaking.

'Get it together, Brown,' she said into the empty stairwell and by the time she'd surfaced into the blistering heat, she'd half convinced herself it was all going to be fine. She licked the paper and rolled her cigarette in a single move. Squinting in the glare of the sun, she put her sunglasses on, lit up, and waited for Bremer.

The car ride to Joanne's home address was awkward. At least, for Carla anyway. As the green field by the airport – behind which was tucked an asylum detention centre – turned into a long, bare village sliced in half by a dual carriageway, Carla tried to ignore the silence and wondered what it was going to be like to meet the woman she'd researched.

Convicted at thirty-two and released six months ago, Joanne would be thirty-five now. The picture resting on Carla's knee was of a woman ravaged by grief and despair – her blonde hair dishevelled, her eye make-up smudged which caused her eyes to appear almost black – so she didn't dare think what the intervening years had done.

'You nervous?'

They were the first words Bremer had spoken and she turned to him in surprise.

'Yes, a little.'

He nodded, eyes still on the road, the slick hum of the Mercedes engine beneath them.

'Understood. And I'm sorry if it's put you at odds with Nell.' He glanced across at her. 'When I got here from the Met it took me by surprise how little analysts are involved in cases. Stuck in

43

little rooms away from the action.' He gave her a smile. 'You see to me, the analyst isn't there to do research for the officers, they are there to direct the officers. You find things out that direct where we go, what we see. It's important you're at the heart of the case, not on the periphery.'

Before Carla could reply, he carried on.

'So when we meet Joanne, just follow my lead. You're there to pick apart what she says, see what bits you can analyse. If you need to ask a question to help do that, feel free. If she agrees to speak to us it won't be a recorded interview so don't worry about ballsing up the case by not asking a question in the right way. It's just a chat, got it?'

'Got it.' Carla wasn't convinced she had but she sure as hell wasn't going to tell him now.

Bremer smiled again. 'Good. Right, address?'

Carla directed them through the myriad of roundabouts filtering cars to opposite ends of the city and led them towards Summertown, a suburb of Oxford where houses cost a minimum of a million and charity shops stocked the latest lines of discarded designer wear at a fraction of the cost.

The Fowlers lived in a cul-de-sac of tall town houses arranged around a neatly tended patch of grass that was ringed by a black iron fence and trees so tall they blocked out most of the light. Bremer pulled the car to the front of number 4. A set of smooth concrete steps led up to a light grey door framed on either side by two small round potted trees, a contrast against the pure white of the painted brick.

'Nice.' Bremer turned off the engine and nodded to two cars on the sloping drive. 'Looks like the husband's in.'

'You think they know we're coming?' Carla wasn't prepared for the husband too.

'I don't see how they'd know,' Bremer replied. Carla wasn't reassured by his tone, but then who would have told him?

As Bremer unclicked his seat belt, the front door opened and Joanne Fowler emerged, followed by her husband, Ian. Standing on the top step, she was wrapped in an oversize cardigan despite the midday heat, her husband's arm wrapped protectively around her. She looked just like the photo Carla had hastily shoved in the glove compartment, but smaller, like a tiny frightened mouse.

'Ready?' Bremer asked.

She wasn't. She felt her heart start to race and her hands get clammy. She took a breath.

'Ready,' she said, and climbed out of the car.

Six

Then

The day I meet Aoife is the day I'm taken into care, which means the best thing that's ever happened to me also coincides with the worst. I'm not sure which I would give up – finding her or losing my mum – but then I don't have a choice. I learned that the moment they put me in the back of a car and drove me away.

On the plus side, the room they put me in is bigger than nine at home. There's a bed in the far corner against the wall, but the one I'm sat on sticks out at a right angle. Both beds are waiting to be made and I panic when I realise I'm expected to make it on my own. I've never made a bed – mum always did it for me – so I try to reassure myself I can figure it out, but the panic keeps building and it makes me want to cry, because I miss my mum.

I start to unpack the little I was allowed to bring: a teddy, my Walkman and two cassettes, a little bottle of cheap perfume Mum got me last week and the earrings I took from her nightstand. She'll kill me when she sees they're gone, but she wears them every day and I wanted them to remind me of her.

I roll the large studs across my palm. They have dulled with age and the gold is starting to rub off. I smell them, breathing in the smell of Mum's perfume, but this makes me want to cry more so I put them in the drawer by my bed and tell myself I'll be able to give them back when I next see her. I try not to think about how long that will be.

Finished, I sit back down and look around the room. It's at the top of the house and the windows are small, covered by a layer of yellowed lace, and the wallpaper – faded pink and blue flowers on a cream background that may once have been white – is peeling in places, revealing a creeping black mould. I feel cold just looking at it. Pulling my cardigan around me, I decide to go downstairs, although it takes me a while to feel brave enough.

The landing outside my room is wide and long. My bedroom at home would probably fit in about half of it. The carpet is green with black and gold swirls that make me dizzy. The banister to my left is dark and solid, so I grip it and run my hand across the smoothness of the wood.

I can hear shouts from below – both children and adults – but it's not the general hubbub of family life, rather the pent-up energy and anger you get from a load of damaged kids being left with underpaid adults to care for them.

A girl rushes past me, pushing me aside in her dash for the stairs.

'Stupid,' she calls back to me. She can't be more than eight. I watch her unruly blonde hair streak out behind her as she skips down the stairs before hearing a shout from behind me.

'Come here, you little shit.' A woman, probably late twenties, runs out from the girl's room and follows her down the stairs. Glancing back, she gives me a look of frustration.

'Get downstairs, won't you? Dinner's up.'

I have never been less hungry, but the look in her eye propels me to the stairs and down them. When I reach the bottom she's disappeared and I'm left wondering where it is I'm supposed to go now. The panic I felt earlier returns and I want my mum. At fifteen I know that's not cool, but it's also not cool to be taken from her at four in the afternoon with not so much as a reason why.

Well. The reason why is also the reason my arm is in plaster, but that wasn't Mum's fault, and now I'm getting angry and want to go back to my room and scream into the pillow for her to come and get me. But before I can, the front door opens and a girl my age is dragged in.

'Get off me, get your bloody hands off me.' Her arms are everywhere and bright red hair covers her face like a blanket. Three staff members are trying to hold her but she squirms and wriggles like a newly caught fish.

I run up the stairs two at a time and crouch behind the banister. I hold my breath. I've never seen a girl fight with adults before, and certainly not one who looks like she might win. There is an energy in her so strong it seems to reach up and touch me: anger, hate, fear. All the things I feel but magnified five hundred times until they have a power of their own.

Two staff members have her on the floor now while the other tries to talk to her.

'Come on, it's going to be OK, just take some breaths, OK?'

The girl tosses her hair away from her face, revealing the palest skin I've ever seen, covered in a mass of freckles, and blue eyes that shine even as far up as me. I will her to win. I will her to fight harder, to win for us both, and when she spits at the woman crouched down next to her I push my hand over my mouth to stop from laughing. That'll teach her. That'll show them we're not animals to be caged.

Finally, they get the girl to stand, arms held tightly behind her back.

'Come on, Aoife. We'll go and see what's for dinner, shall we? Then get you settled in.' The woman is forcing a smile but the girl refuses to answer. They start to guide her towards a door at the far left of the hall but when they reach it Aoife turns and looks up at me.

I hold my breath. Scared, thrilled, in equal measure. Then she winks at me and I laugh.

We are going to be friends. We are going to be the very best of friends. And now I can stop feeling lonely.

Seven

As they climbed the steps, Bremer said, 'Hello, Joanne. I wonder if we could have a few minutes of your time?'

Joanne had an air of defeat, but her husband was full of barely contained anger.

'What can we do for you?' he asked, pulling Joanne closer to him.

'It might be easier if we came inside, Mr Fowler?'

Ian Fowler tensed, then looked down uneasily at Joanne. 'It's hard for us.'

He spoke to Carla, so she nodded, unsure of what could be said, or should be said, in situations like this.

'You have to understand we've come through so much, all as a result of lies told by the police, so we're both wary of any further involvement with you. Because we don't trust you,' he said simply.

Carla wanted to get back in the car and leave the pair alone, but Bremer continued, apparently unconcerned. 'We only have one question, Mr Fowler, then we'll be on our way.'

Ian gave a laugh. 'They said that the last time and it took us almost three years to get my wife home again.'

'I can assure you that won't happen this time.'

'Can you?'

'Yes,' he said. But Carla knew full well he couldn't.

The front room stretched the length of the house. Floor-to-ceiling windows at the far end let in bright sunshine; shadows from the trees danced on the light wooden floor. Despite its size it felt cosy, wood logs sitting neatly stacked up by the side of a wood burner that was glowing deep orange. Its heat seemed to go unnoticed by Joanne, who curled up on the sofa covering herself with a blanket. There was no offer of tea, no small talk. Ian got straight to the point.

'What do you want with us now?'

Bremer had taken the seat furthest away from the fire, leaving Carla to take the one directly next to it. Heat scorched her cheek. Why on earth did she need a fire in the middle of a heatwave? But Joanne appeared untouched by the heavy warmth. Her thin frame was obvious, even beneath the layered clothing and thick throw. Her face was pale and gaunt, blonde hair limp, and Carla was struck by the woman's obvious vulnerability.

'We'd just like to speak to Joanne about a letter we received regarding pathologist Eve Graham.'

The pair instantly tensed. Joanne's hands found her husband's and they clung to one another.

'What has that got to do with Joanne?' Ian's tone was cold, eyes angry. He was slight, like his wife. His hair, long on top, was greying at the sides. He was wearing a fitted T-shirt – brown and fashionably faded – with deep blue jeans, ironed.

Joanne put her hand on her husband's thigh and left it there.

'It's OK, Ian, I don't mind.' Her voice was soft, gentle, and it immediately defused the tension in the room. She turned to Carla. Wide-set eyes the colour of conkers caught sunlight from the window, creating little specks of gold.

'What would you like to know?'

It took a moment for Bremer to reply and Carla wondered if he was as disarmed by Joanne as she was.

'Mrs Fowler—'

'Joanne, please,' she interrupted.

Bremer dipped his head in acknowledgement. 'Joanne, we received a letter today accusing Eve Graham of deliberately providing false evidence at trials involving babies who died.'

Joanne looked as if she was going to speak, but Bremer continued.

'Furthermore, the letter alleges a current case involving the death of a child will be derailed by Ms Graham. Do you have anything to say about the letter and the allegations in it?'

Joanne ran her fingers across her husband's thigh and took his hand again.

When she began to speak, her husband watched her carefully, eyes never leaving her face.

'I had a little baby called Beatrice.' She gave a slight smile, eyes on the floor, as she remembered her daughter. She looked up.

'She was our miracle. It was our last attempt, after three failed IVF cycles, and for every day of my pregnancy I was sure she wasn't going to make it.' Her eyes shone as she continued. 'She was such a delight.'

Carla watched Ian squeeze his wife's hand as she smiled.

'Just a complete bundle of loveliness and for every waking minute I was grateful for her being given to us. For being the ones who got to love her and help her grow into the amazing person she would have been . . .' Joanne faltered, and when it looked like she couldn't continue, her husband took over.

'Beatrice went to bed as usual, the night she died. I was the one to put her down. I sang the nursery rhymes and read the stories. I was the one who found our baby four hours later, unresponsive in her cot. I gave her CPR while Joanne rang 999. Yet when Graham turned up, her conclusion was that Joanne was to blame.' His eyes flashed between Carla and Bremer.

'Every night for four months Joanne put Beatrice to bed. The one night she doesn't, our baby dies. And yet she's convicted of killing her. Can you even begin to—' His voice cracked and the pair fell silent.

'Joanne, do you blame Ms Graham for your incarceration?'

'Her wrongful incarceration,' Ian corrected.

'Do you blame Ms Graham for that, Joanne?'

'Of course she bloody does.' Ian tightened his grip on Joanne's hand.

'I'd like Joanne to answer, if you don't mind, Mr Fowler.'

'Yes. I do.' Her voice was firm.

'Because of her mistake?'

Ian laughed, but Joanne took her hand from his and clasped hers in her lap, her pain obvious to see.

'It wasn't a mistake.' Her voice was small again, all strength gone. 'She targeted me and convicted me.' Her eyes rose to meet Bremer's. 'What she did was deliberate.'

Carla suddenly felt cold. Joanne spoke with such conviction it was hard to believe it wasn't true, but why would a respected pathologist frame a woman she'd never met before?

Bremer took a moment before replying. 'Is that why you wrote the letter?'

Joanne frowned. 'I didn't write a letter.'

'Do you know a man called Connor O'Brian?' Bremer asked. Joanne shook her head.

'The letter we received suggested Ms Graham was going to falsify evidence against another woman, in the same manner you allege she did to you after your . . .' He paused, and Carla sensed he knew to tread carefully, avoid too much police speak. 'After your baby died,' he finished.

'Yes, but that doesn't mean I wrote a letter. I don't want revenge. I just want her to acknowledge what she did.'

'Well that's what the author of the letter wants too. And we are concerned whoever wrote it wishes harm to Ms Graham.'

Ian grabbed Joanne's thigh. 'Well I hope that person succeeds.'

Bremer's phone rang. Checking the screen, he stood. 'I'm sorry, I have to get this.'

And seconds later Carla was alone with the couple.

They sat in silence. Carla felt panic rising. Should she speak? She caught Joanne's eye and the pain in the woman's face stunned her. But it also seemed to be begging for her to ask a question, so Carla asked the only one she had.

'Joanne, why are you so convinced that Eve acted deliberately?'

Joanne's shoulders fell as if with relief. But as she opened her mouth to speak, Ian put his hand on her arm.

'Don't. It's not worth it. Please, don't risk it.'

Carla watched Joanne wrestle with her husband's words before calmly looking back to Carla and giving a small smile. It lit up her face and Carla thought, *This is what she looked like before her baby died.*

'I know because she told me.'

Carla hadn't been expecting that. 'Eve told you she knew you didn't kill your baby?'

Joanne nodded.

'When?'

'When Beatrice died, I wanted to see her one more time. I made them let me into the room. Her room.' She paused, fighting grief. 'Eve was there, standing over the crib. I asked her to leave, told her I wanted time alone with my baby, but she just stared at me. When I asked again, she said, "Sometimes people have to take the blame for actions they didn't commit. I'm sorry, but that's just how things are." At the time I didn't really understand what she was saying because all I wanted to do was get to my baby. But after, when I saw she'd blamed me, I remembered what she'd said.'

Carla opened her mouth to respond, but Ian stopped her.

'Enough. This is all too much. We've done nothing wrong. Not then and not now. I'm not going to stand by and watch my wife go to jail for a second time. You need to ask your patholo-gist these questions, not my wife.'

Carla watched tears start to roll down Joanne's face. 'I'm so sorry, Joanne.' She knew she shouldn't say it, but in the face of the woman's pain she didn't care.

Joanne nodded, taking the tissue her husband offered and wiping her nose. 'Thank you.'

Bremer was at the door. 'Carla, we have to go.'

'But—' Carla half turned towards the couple, but Bremer cut her off.

'We have to go. I'm sorry, Mr and Mrs Fowler, but we'll have to speak another time. And can I ask that neither of you contact Ms Graham before we do?'

The pair stared at him, speechless, but as he gestured at Carla to join him she rose.

'I'm sorry,' she said again. 'I really am sorry.'

Eight

In daylight, the block of flats looked much the same as it had the previous evening, except now bored teenagers had been replaced by equally bored pre-schoolers, looked after by a handful of kids Nell was pretty sure should be at school.

One child, no more than six, spotted their car pull up and screamed, 'Police!'

Nell and Paul watched the group disperse, screaming and shouting excitedly at this addition to their day, tiny legs furiously pedalling after longer ones whose scooter power far exceeded that of their younger counterparts.

When they rounded the corner, Paul pointed to the second floor. 'What's the family liaison doing?'

Nell followed his finger and saw a uniformed police officer on her phone, looking harassed. Catching sight of them, the uniform lowered her phone and waved, beckoning them up.

'Jesus. Bets?' Nell turned to Paul, who was studying the balcony.

'Connor's done a runner and Kelly-Anne has admitted he killed their baby?'

'Seriously?' Why the hell was Paul letting one letter throw such doubt on Kelly-Anne's guilt?

'Why not?'

'Because Connor didn't do it?' Irritated, she strode towards the stairwell.

'Why are you so sure she's right?' Paul called after her.

Nell stopped, turned to face him. 'Because she's a bloody pathologist. It's her job to know who did what and when.'

Paul jogged over to join her, then led the way up the concrete steps.

'You're really sure this Kelly-Anne did it, aren't you?'

Was she? Maybe. There was a control issue with Connor, that much was obvious, and Kelly-Anne could have silenced the baby at his request. Once Nell thought it, the more possible it sounded. In which case she'd get them both banged up for murder.

Nell noted the urgency of the uniformed officer's wave as they approached.

'Anyway, it doesn't matter what I think, what matters are the facts, so let's just see what's wrong, shall we?'

The officer's cheeks were flushed with heat and she had a panicked look in her eyes. Shit. One of them had done a runner, she knew it.

'Problem?' Nell asked.

'It's the father. He went out for cigarettes and hasn't returned.'

Paul threw Nell a look and it wasn't hard to know what it said – they should have nicked the pair last night.

'How long ago?' she asked.

'About forty-five minutes.'

Nell checked her watch – you could get a long way in forty-five minutes. 'Does Kelly-Anne know where he could be? How far is the shop?'

'About four minutes away. I've been down there and they don't recall seeing him. It's pretty small and I bet he's a regular, so I'm guessing he hasn't been in.'

'And Kelly-Anne? What's she said?' The heat was making Nell's jacket stick to her, emphasising that this was a ball-ache she could well do without.

'She's distraught, says he's left her. She's spotted he's taken the overnight bag he uses when he walks out after the baby's crying gets too much.'

'So he's got form for going AWOL?' Paul asked.

'Seems so.'

'Does she know where he goes?'

'She didn't say.'

'Well, let's go ask her again, shall we?' Nell said.

Kelly-Anne's mascara was halfway down her face. As Nell took a seat opposite, the girl wiped half of it away with her hand. Leaning forward, Nell thought she looked smaller than she had last night; her young age more apparent. She felt herself soften slightly, tried to remind herself Kelly-Anne had lost a baby last night and even if she had killed Georgie, it didn't mean she hadn't loved her.

'Kelly-Anne, do you know where Connor is?' She made her tone soft, or as soft as she could get it.

'I don't think so.' The young woman looked away, only briefly, but enough to tell Nell she was lying.

'You said there's a missing overnight bag? The one Connor used for when Georgie got a bit much?'

'It's not about Georgie,' Kelly-Anne said, her hands shredding the tissue on her lap. 'It's about me. He takes off when I've done something to piss him off.'

'Like what sort of stuff?'

Kelly-Anne gave an exasperated sigh. 'I dunno, depends on his mood. Could be I've not cleaned the kitchen enough, or I'm wearing a dress he don't like.'

'Does he often leave?'

'About twice a week, I suppose.'

'And you were left alone with Georgie? That must have been hard.'

Kelly-Anne looked up and Nell could see she sensed a trap.

'It was hard, but it didn't make me hurt her, if that's what you're getting at.'

'That's not what I meant at all,' although of course it was.

Nell changed tack. 'How about Connor? Didn't he ever struggle with Georgie?'

Kelly-Anne looked hesitant. 'He . . .'

Nell watched her struggle for the right words.

'He could get angry if Georgie didn't shut up. But babies don't, do they?' Her tone was pleading for Nell to understand. 'So it wasn't my fault. Not really.'

'Of course not. Babies cry, it's what they do.'

Kelly-Anne looked relieved. 'Yes. And I tried my best. I always tried my best for them both.' Her eyes filled with tears. 'But now they've both left me.'

'Kelly-Anne,' Nell said, shifting to unstick the fake leather sofa from her jeans, 'why didn't you tell us Connor was in jail for assaulting his girlfriend?'

Kelly-Anne looked surprised, then quickly angry. 'Because she's a lying cow. She just wanted to get him in trouble because he preferred me to her. She's been a nightmare ever since we got together and she's been worse since I had the baby.'

'The report says he harmed her child. Is that true?'

'No! She made that up so she wouldn't lose custody of the kid.'

'But the father knew Connor was hurting his child?' Nell could tell from Kelly-Anne's expression she was pushing it, so when Kelly-Anne didn't reply, she said, 'Kelly-Anne, did Connor hurt Georgie?'

The young woman seemed to shrink in on herself. Wrapping her arms tightly across her chest, she began to cry again, tears falling silently onto her lap. Nell pushed away the first feelings of guilt. This was her job. However bad Kelly-Anne felt, it was Nell's job to get to the truth. Even if it did make her feel like a shit.

'He didn't mean to.' Kelly-Anne spoke quietly and the air in the room seemed to still. 'He was back from the pub and Georgie was crying. I'd tried to stop her before Connor got in, 'cos I know it does his head in, but I couldn't, so I put her in her cot and shut the door and went to make Connor's dinner.' She stopped speaking then, and as if realising for the first time she was crying, wiped at her face with the palms of both hands.

'And then what happened?'

'He didn't like the dinner I was making, so he started to walk around the front room, shouting about this and that. What a bad mum I was, a crap girlfriend, said he'd rather be with her.'

'With the girlfriend he was with before you? The one who lied about him hitting her?' She chose her words carefully, keen not to trigger a defensive reaction now Kelly-Anne had started to speak.

Kelly-Anne nodded and Nell looked to Paul, who quietly left the room.

Turning back to Kelly-Anne, Nell asked, 'And what then?'

'Georgie was really yelling by then, and I mean really yelling. He told me to shut "it" up, so I went into her room and—' She stopped, and the expression on her face told Nell she was back there, seeing her baby in the cot.

'She was all hot and red and damp from crying,' she continued, 'so I picked her up to give her a cuddle. I walked round the room with her, whispering for her to stop before Connor came in, but she didn't.' Kelly-Anne looked to Nell, her eyes wide. 'I did my best to stop her crying, but Connor couldn't take it any more – it wasn't his fault, it was mine.' Her tone pleaded with Nell to understand.

'So Connor entered the room?'

Kelly-Anne nodded again. 'He took her off me.'

'The baby?'

'He said he'd stop her crying and I tried to get Georgie back, but he told me to go back to the kitchen and make him something he could eat.'

'So, you left him alone with Georgie?'

'Yeah. I went into the kitchen and started to make some dinner again and then Georgie just stopped crying.' She gave a small shrug. 'Just stopped, she did.'

'Did you go back into the room or remain in the kitchen, after she stopped crying?'

'I went back to thank Connor for helping me, you know, help-ing me with the baby.'

Nell nodded.

'And Georgie was back in her cot, asleep.'

'You saw she was asleep?'

'Yeah, she was lying there, all quiet, so of course she was asleep.'

'But you didn't touch her?'

Kelly-Anne shook her head. 'No. Connor came over to me and pushed me out the room – but only to make sure I didn't wake her again,' she added.

'And where was Connor when you walked in?'

'By the cot. He had his hands on Georgie, patting her.'

'Patting her?'

'Yeah, you know, to make her sleep.'

Nell wondered how hard you had to pat a baby in order to crush its ribs. 'Was he patting her with the palm of his hand?'

Kelly-Anne shifted in her chair, pulled at a strand of hair that had come loose from her tight bun. 'What? I don't know, I can't remember.'

'Was his hand like this?' Nell raised a palm. 'Or was it like this?' She made it into a fist.

Kelly-Anne opened her mouth to speak, then stopped.

'His fist was patting the baby, wasn't it? And he wasn't doing it to make sure she went to sleep, he was making sure Georgie never got to bother him again, wasn't he?'

Kelly-Anne didn't speak, so Nell went in for the kill.

'Did Connor O'Brian kill your baby?'

Kelly-Anne stared mutely at her.

'And you saw him do it, but covered up for him – that's right, isn't it? You saw Connor hit Georgie with his fist and you couldn't stop him, so rather than lose them both you chose to stick with him and lie for him, didn't you?' Nell felt her heart race and took a couple of deep breaths to steady it. She didn't want the red mist coming down now, not when she was near the finishing post.

She stood. 'Kelly-Anne, I'd like you to come to the station with me. Give a formal statement. Will you do that?' She didn't want to have to arrest the woman if she didn't have to, but if Kelly-Anne wouldn't come quietly she damn well would.

When Kelly-Anne didn't move, Nell leaned down and gently took her arm.

'I didn't let him kill her,' she finally said. 'Honest I didn't.'

Nell didn't believe her and the defeat in Kelly-Anne's tone told Nell she didn't either. As Nell walked her to the door, she saw Paul, phone in hand, on the balcony that spanned the length of the block.

He was going to be insufferable when he found out Kelly-Anne's account didn't match Eve's. But then that was the least of her worries. She needed to find Connor, see if his account matched Kelly-Anne's, because someone was lying and despite Kelly-Anne's convincing performance, Nell still wasn't ready to believe it was Eve.

Nine

Bremer slammed the car door shut and looked at Carla.

'I don't have time to worry what it is you're sorry for, but never say sorry. Not even if a judge from the last Court of Appeal tells you to, got it?' He started the engine and moved the car towards the junction of the cul-de-sac.

'Got it,' she said. But she didn't regret it and she'd do it again if the same situation arose.

'Connor's gone AWOL.'

Carla turned to Bremer, who kept his eyes on the traffic as he pulled across the main road, away from Oxford, towards HQ.

'The call I got was from Nell. They've taken Kelly-Anne in but we need you to find possible addresses for him.'

It was suddenly obvious why Bremer was so tense. And Nell must be kicking herself for not bringing them in the night before.

'I'll get on it as soon as we are back. How long's he been missing?'

'About an hour and a half.'

'Shit.'

'Precisely.' Bremer joined the dual carriageway and pressed on the accelerator. 'He could have got anywhere in that time.'

Connor didn't strike Carla as the adventurous sort, more a creature of habit, but when someone's back was against the wall you never could tell where they'd go.

'Did she say why?'

'Why he did a bunk? Seems Eve was wrong. Kelly-Anne saw him kill the baby.'

Carla stared out of the window. She itched to be back at her desk. If Bremer hadn't dragged her out of the office she probably would have found Connor by now. Instead she had to wait another ten minutes for HQ to come into view and before Bremer had even switched off the engine Carla had unbuckled her seat belt and had her hand on the door.

Paul and Nell were seated at opposite ends of the office, as if the heat made sitting too close unbearable.

'What's happened to the air con?' Bremer pulled off his jacket and laid it carefully over the back of a chair.

'Broken.' Nell fanned herself with her notebook as if to emphasise the point. She looked irritated, but then so would Carla if she'd just lost the main suspect in a murder inquiry.

Bremer approached the wipe board, pen poised. 'Right – Connor. How long's he been gone for?'

67

'Almost two hours,' Nell replied.

Carla started up her computer, half listening to the rest of the team behind her.

'Kelly-Anne's not saying much,' Nell said, 'but I get the impression he stays local when he does a bunk.'

'Yeah, but this is the first time he's done it off the back of a kid being killed,' Paul pointed out.

Carla wanted to point out this was getting them nowhere, wanted to tell them to leave her alone to find addresses they could go and knock up, but she didn't need to.

'That's Carla's job. She'll find him,' Bremer said. 'In the meantime, why don't you go and—'

Carla interrupted him. Two hits on the intelligence database and she'd already got a lead.

'Try the betting shop in Rose Hill. He goes there frequently and they may know more.'

She didn't bother to take her eyes off the screen. As leads went it was weak so she needed more, but it was only when the pair had left the office that she settled into her stride.

Carla checked to see if O'Brian's flat had any registered vehicles – none, good, that narrowed down his transport options, legal ones at least. Then she wrote down all known telephone numbers for him based on his criminal record papers and all intel logged about him. Three in total. She'd need to get the Telephone Unit to check their activity but she wanted to get the basics out the way first.

She went back to his criminal record. O'Brian had been put

away for assault on a previous girlfriend, Gloria Benote, and then later for possession with intent to supply. Carla wrote down Gloria's address – not far from O'Brian's flat, she noted – then Gloria's telephone number before phoning Council Tax to check the number and address were still current. They were. So far so good, but would a victim of assault harbour her assailant? Carla had seen enough domestic abuse victims to know the answer was yes, very likely.

She looked down at her notes. There was something familiar about one of the numbers. She wrote it out again, then again, before underlining it. Carla rarely forgot a number from a case, so there must have been one she'd worked on where Gloria's number had featured heavily, but which one? Frustrated, she ran through cases in her mind, each logged, checking numbers, car number plates, addresses, for a clue as to which it was.

And then there it was. It hadn't been her case at all, but it had been the first time she'd ever taken the dock, and she remembered now the look of fear on the victim's face as she recounted the number of times the defendant had called her; the number of text messages Connor O'Brian had left in the run-up to his assault on her—

'Carla?' Bremer was standing next to her. 'You look a million miles away.'

'I was involved in the original O'Brian assault case.'

Bremer stared at her. 'What?'

'I know. I feel awful I didn't remember her. Awful I didn't remember his girlfriend, Gloria Benote.'

Gloria's face came at her, tight, drawn, eyes pleading with Carla to stop saying the words that would help put her boyfriend away.

'Go on.'

'It was the number I recognised. That's why I didn't connect the two.' She felt shame rise to her cheeks – how could she not recall a victim but remember their telephone number? When had that happened? 'I was called in to do telephone analysis on this domestic violence case. They needed phone evidence as he'd harassed the hell out of her using his mobile.'

Carla remembered the rows of numbers – the highlighted ones indicating O'Brian had called Gloria – and how she'd been shocked at just how many there were.

'But that was all it was to me. Numbers. And now he's killed a child.'

Bremer didn't speak for a second or two, but when he did he spoke quietly and deliberately. 'If we held every case in our head we'd go insane. If we didn't let go of victims, or perpetrators, after each case was closed, then how could we function? I'd give us each two years, and that's being generous. We deal with as much shit in a week as most people deal with in their whole lives. You save lives with numbers, so if that means you remember them above the victim, then I for one am glad of that.'

Carla didn't know how to reply. Bremer put a hand on hers.

'You've got the number. Now find out if it means we can catch him. OK?'

And in those few words he managed to refocus her. She had the number. 'OK. I'll need half an hour.'

Bremer smiled. 'Good. See you back here in thirty.'

Carla picked up the phone.

'Telephone Unit.'

'Carla Brown. I've got a murder and need some telephones checking.'

'Go ahead.'

Carla read out the phone numbers she'd got for Connor and Gloria. 'Oh, and check out his girlfriend's while you're there.' She gave Kelly-Anne's number on the off chance Connor had contacted her and the woman knew more than she was letting on. 'Incoming and outgoing calls, please.'

'Got it. What about the victim's phone – want me to run that too?'

'Too young.'

'Shit.'

'Yeah, three months old.'

'Jesus.'

They paused to acknowledge the magnitude of the crime, but in truth they'd both been there before.

And there Gloria was again. Seated in the corridor, hands clasped between her knees, her son playing with a fire engine at her feet. Shit. She'd forgotten the woman had a son: small, brown-haired, always alert, looking to his mum for direction. What had he been then, two?

'Is it a threat to life?'

Carla sighed. 'He's a danger to his current and ex-girlfriend,' she said. 'But I wouldn't go as far as a threat to life.'

'Got it. I'll do it as soon as I can, but—'

'Yeah, I know, it's lower on the list. Just as soon as you can,' she added.

She hung up and turned to find Bremer at his door, watching her.

'It all points to Gloria,' she said, 'where else would he go?'

He nodded. 'I'll tell them to go easy on her. Thank you.' He pulled his mobile phone from his back pocket. 'Now go home. Back in early doors.'

As he walked off, Carla checked the clock on the wall. Shit. She was already an hour late for her fiancé, Baz. It was a wonder the man hadn't left her by now. But as she grabbed her bag her desk phone rang. She paused. Shit. Shit shit shit.

'Carla speaking.'

'Telephone Unit. Got a partial result.'

'That was quick.'

'I had O2 on the phone while I was speaking with you and asked them to run O'Brian's numbers over.'

'Can you send them across? Anything interesting?'

'Yes and no.'

'Go on.'

'Well the only call he's made in the last twenty-four hours is the one he made to 999.'

'What, nothing at all since then?' She hadn't expected miracles but had hoped for the start of a lead. A number he'd called to indicate where he'd gone. But no calls at all? Where the hell was he then?

'You said yes and no. Is the yes a little more helpful?'

'It is, as a matter of fact. There's a number O'Brian called just before 999—'

'How much before?' Carla interrupted.

'Two minutes, thirty-nine seconds. And that number called O'Brian three times in the last twelve hours.'

'But he didn't pick up?'

'No, all unanswered.'

'Can you trace the number for me? As a matter of urgency?'

'Well that's the thing. I don't have to.'

'What?'

'It's a number from the list you gave me.'

Carla rested her head in the palm of her hand, because of course she knew the answer.

'Who?'

'Gloria Benote. I'll send it all over now.'

Carla snapped her head up. 'No.' She glanced at Bremer's closed door. If she got the call data now she'd have to tell him Gloria was definitely involved and that would mean her hauled in to a cell overnight and her kid carted off by social services. If she waited until morning that would give Nell and Paul time to check out Gloria's flat, and if O'Brian wasn't there then they could just ask Gloria about the calls in the morning.

'Carla?'

She realised she'd been biting her lip. 'Sorry. Can you send it over in the morning? I've got what I need and can pass that to the team to action tonight, yeah? If you send me the whole lot I'll never get out of here.'

'Sure thing. I'll send off the others to Vodafone now.'

Hanging up, she sat for a moment. The morning would be fine; one sheet of call data wasn't going to change the whole case. And still trying to convince herself of that, she picked up her bag and left.

Ten
Now

I'm wondering if I should regret sending the letter to Eve. I've had no reply and it's obvious the police are rattled. I can hear my husband reprimanding me.

'But that's what you wanted, wasn't it? To get the police involved?'

Except, of course, he wouldn't because he doesn't know that was my intention; he doesn't know I referenced Connor O'Brian or that Eve is working the case. As far as he's concerned I only want to get Eve to acknowledge what she did and stop her doing it again. But I need help to do that and who better than the police? They'll look closely at Eve now I've piqued their interest, so all I need do is sit back and wait.

But I'm still uneasy. I feel I've started something yet have already lost control. I pour myself a glass of wine and stare out of the kitchen window at the fading light. A moth hits the window, again and again, relentlessly trying to get through the glass. I take a sip and wait for it to give up, but when it doesn't I turn my back to it. I've had my fill of watching people try to escape the future they've been given, so I'll be damned if I'm going to waste my time watching an insect do the same.

As I take a seat at the kitchen table my husband looks round the door.

'You OK?'

He's frowning so I smile as brightly as I can.

'Good.' I raise my glass to prove the point and he laughs. It's good to see him smile after all I continue to put him through.

'Popping to Sainsbury's – need anything?'

Relief floods me – a couple of hours on my own is just what I need – but I try to look hesitant, play along so he doesn't change his mind and stay.

'No thanks,' then add, 'A bottle of red.'

He looks at the glass in my hand. 'You sure?'

I smile. 'I'm sure.'

'OK, well, I won't be long. Text if you think of anything we need.' He hears the knock-knock of the moth on the window and points. 'Why don't you let it in? Put it out of its misery.'

I just smile. He walks over and kisses me on my forehead, rubbing my back.

'Take your time,' I say as he goes to leave. 'No rush.'

When he's gone, I drink steadily, letting the light fade around me. The moth has stopped its incessant banging, leaving me alone in the silence. I wait. Feel a blanket of calm settle round me.

'Aoife.'

Her name fills the room, spinning into the edges and the cracks, like a spider's web.

'Aoife?'

The web stirs, a ripple running through it.

'Am I doing the right thing?' I ask. Silence is the only answer.

I wish I was by the sea, watching the possibilities roll towards and away from me, before the tide washed up death and horror; I wish I could go back to that night and stop the decisions we made from the choices we were given. I wish those choices had been different and our lives could have become the possibilities contained within them.

'But isn't that what everyone wishes?' I say into the dark. 'We were no different.'

I feel the silence judge me. Hanging there like a pointed stare.

Anger blows the web away.

'I did my best with what we had. I've always done my best for us.' My heart is thudding against my chest, but when I feel it creep to my throat I say, 'Fine.'

Righteous molten anger takes over.

'Have it your way.'

I pour what's left of the wine and down it.

'If a letter won't bring an end to it,' I stand, 'I'll stop her myself.'

Eleven

Arriving at the rooftop bar, Carla pushed her way through the crowd of city workers, students and tourists before placing her gin and tonic on a tall circular table. Hot, flustered and irritated, she kissed her fiancé Baz on the lips.

'Sorry I'm late,' she said, taking a seat on one of the three bar stools. 'Work.'

'Fighting the good fight.' He smiled, tipping his half-empty glass towards her, clearly two pints down and well on the way to a third.

'How was your day?'

'Two leaks and a minor flood,' he replied.

'Fighting the good fight,' she grinned, watching him laugh.

Carla turned to look out at the view across the Oxford colleges, with their spires and arches, feeling the stress of the day falling away. God it was beautiful, like you'd landed in another world – if you ignored the McDonald's round the corner whose doorway served as a makeshift homeless hostel.

She took another sip of her drink and was just about to start rolling a cigarette when she spotted Gerry, Eve's husband, in the corner of the roof terrace. He was seated alone but two half-full glasses sat on the table in front of him and he was tapping his finger on the surface of the table as if waiting impatiently for someone to return.

'Isn't that Gerry?' Baz said, following her stare. 'What's he doing here – not exactly his scene, is it?'

'Maybe he and Eve are branching out, spicing it up a bit.' She grinned at Baz's horrified expression.

'But imagine having sex with the ice queen. Terrifying.' He looked back across the terrace. 'Hey, Gerry, mate,' he waved his pint in the air, 'over here.'

Gerry looked over in surprise but waved back when he recognised Carla. Leaving both drinks on the table, he pushed his way through the crowd, taking the empty stool Baz had pushed towards him.

He looked tired, the stubble on his chin unusual, and Carla thought he'd put on even more weight, so that his stomach strained against the shirt he was wearing.

'You OK?' she asked, suddenly concerned.

'Yeah, long shift, that's all.' He gave a wry smile and rubbed his hand across his chin.

'You here with the missus?' Baz nodded in the direction of the drinks. Gerry glanced back and then to the door leading to the toilets.

'No, just with a friend.'

Carla looked at the drinks: one pint of beer, one small white wine. 'Anyone we know?' she asked, turning back to the table.

'Nah, just an old mate from training school.'

Carla had never in her eight years with the police seen an officer drink wine – beer with a whisky chaser maybe, but never wine. Not even Nell.

She caught Gerry's eye. He shifted on his seat.

'So, how's work?' he asked. 'Eve said she met your new DCI. She didn't seem impressed, if I'm honest.'

Carla grinned. 'Is Eve ever impressed with anyone?'

Gerry tipped his head towards her. 'Good point, well made.'

'He had me out on a job today,' she said, adding, 'which riled Nell.'

Baz stared at her. 'What do you mean, he took you out on a job?'

'To go out to speak to people.' She put a hand on his arm, amused by his concern. 'It's fine, totally normal, and very safe.' She pictured Joanne and couldn't imagine a less threatening woman.

Baz looked unconvinced. 'Well, be careful. You wouldn't do that when you're pregnant, would you?'

Carla was oddly offended that he was more concerned about their as yet unconceived child than about her. And anyway, pregnant officers went out on jobs, so what made her so different? Clearly sensing discord, Gerry interrupted.

'It's not that unusual. Some new officers like to take analysts out with them. Wouldn't ever be to a dangerous situation, though, health and safety would have a fit.' He looked towards the door again, finger tapping on his leg. 'Besides, Bremer is probably just flexing his muscles and showing who's boss, that's all.' He turned back to Baz and smiled, but stopped when he saw it wasn't returned. 'Anyway,' he stood, stretching his back as he did, 'best get back to my drink. Nothing worse than lukewarm beer.' He offered an apologetic smile to Carla and she gave him a quick shake of the head to tell him it was OK.

As he walked off she wished he'd stayed long enough to ask about the letter Eve had received, but then probably better not to while Baz was around. She looked over at her fiancé and took his hand.

'I'll be fine. Nothing is going to happen to me.'

He squeezed it and put his other hand on her thigh. 'OK. But don't let this Bremer bloke wheel you around like a trophy.'

Carla burst out laughing. 'A what?'

'Come on. Gorgeous civvy? Thames Valley's answer to Marilyn Monroe? No wonder he wants you on his arm.'

She stopped laughing. 'I think he wanted me there for my professional opinion.'

Baz shrugged and she couldn't believe he was so annoyed.

'All I'm saying is, don't let him take the piss.'

Carla took his chin with one hand and turned him to face her. Leaning over, she gave him a long hard kiss and by the time she pulled back, she could see he'd relaxed.

'I promise never to be a pin-up for anyone but you.'

Baz ran his hand further up her thigh, his eyes holding hers. 'Let's get out of here, shall we? That baby isn't going to make itself.'

Carla kept the smile on her face despite the lurch in her stomach. She downed her drink and picked up her bag. 'Come on then. I'm dying for a fag anyway.'

Baz followed her across the terrace. 'You should write romance novels, you know that?'

Carla paused at the door and looked back to Gerry's table. Empty, both drinks gone. Damn it. Now she'd never know who he'd been meeting.

'You think he's having it off with someone?'

Did she?

'Man must have balls of steel if he's going to cheat on the ice queen, though,' he added.

She gave a little laugh. 'Yeah, he probably isn't. He loves her.'

Baz put his arm round her and pulled her in for a hug. 'You're such an old romantic – that's why I love you.' He leaned down and gave her a kiss. 'Don't stress it. Gerry's as loyal as they come. He'll just have been meeting an old mate like he said.'

Carla didn't think so. Gerry had been meeting someone he didn't want her to see. But who? And why?

Twelve
Then

It turns out Aoife and I are sharing a room. I sit on my bed and scratch under the edge of the cast on my arm while I watch her unpack. She's tied her hair back now and I can see she has a black eye and a cracked lip. Her skin is almost translucent; veins, like blue roads on a map, make their way across her arms, neck and face. Her teeth are white, but one is chipped, giving her a jaunty look.

When she's unpacked what little she brought with her, she flops onto the bed and crosses her legs, facing me.

'What you in here for?' Then she sees my plaster cast and rolls her eyes. 'Nuff said.' She looks at me, blue eyes serious. 'No one's signed it. Wait.' She jumps up, all legs and arms, and grabs a pen from my desk. *Aoife was here*. Then she draws the top half of a face looking over a wall, his hands gripping the edges.

'That's better.' She tosses the pen on the floor and flops back onto my bed, legs from the knees down dangling over the edge.

I stare at her, then my arm. Her words are a flurry of lines and they take up the entire length of my arm. Looking at it I feel an emotion I'm not sure of. I test the edges, poke the sides: pride?

Aoife sits back up. 'Do you speak?'

I open my mouth, then shut it. I feel a burst of something like bubbles in my chest that push their way out into a laugh and once I start I find I can't stop. There is nothing to laugh about, seeing as I've been wrenched from my home with barely ten minutes' notice, but here I am, unable to breathe, clutching my chest so much I worry I'll wee.

Tears stream from Aoife's eyes as we roll on the bed, each releasing whatever it is that caused us to be here. When we come up for air our faces are close; I can feel her breath on my cheek.

'Shit, isn't it,' she says. She smells of peppermint.

'Do you miss your mum too?' I ask.

She considers this for a moment. 'You see this?' She points to her cracked tooth. 'Boyfriend number four. And this –' she lifts her sleeve to reveal a small mark the size of a cigarette butt, '– her third.'

I don't ask what number caused the black eye.

'I miss what I imagine a mum to be,' she says. 'But mine? Not so much.'

I think about my mum, all round and smiley. How she packs me lunches for school and makes sure I have the salt and vinegar crisps. How she always asks how my day was, regardless of her own, so that even when I visited her in hospital in a daze – accompanied by an overzealous social worker – her first words were 'How was school?' as I tried not to notice the blood at the edges of her mouth or the eye that couldn't open.

'I miss mine,' I hear myself say. 'But she prefers my dad.'

Aoife nods.

We lie for a while, listening to the cries and the shouts from below and above, before Aoife rolls over to face me, both hand palms tucked together under one cheek. 'School tomorrow,' she says.

I stare at her. There's the slightest edge of fear in her eyes and it makes my heart start to pound. She squeezes my arm and I squeeze hers back. It anchors me.

'Together, yeah?' she says.

I stare at her: freckles, red curls, big, searching eyes. 'Yeah,' I reply.

Thirteen

When Nell's mobile rang it took seconds for it to drag her from a dream she instantly couldn't remember.

'We've got a body.'

Nell could barely focus on Bremer's voice.

'A body?' She cradled the mobile under her chin and reached for the glass of water beside her bed.

'Yes, and from the description, it sounds like Connor O'Brian.'

The man's body lay face down on the floor, the back of his head caved in. Nell pulled on her blue plastic gloves as Paul nodded downwards.

'The pathologist has had a look at the face and it's definitely O'Brian.'

Nell didn't need a pathologist to tell her that, but she nodded just the same. 'Who's the pathologist?'

'Eve Graham.'

'Twice in one week, lucky us.' Nell refused to think about Kelly-Anne's confession and the doubt that threw on Eve; what she needed to do was go through the scene, and do it methodically.

Nell knelt on the floor, noting the congealed blood matted into what was left of O'Brian's skull. 'Did Eve give us any idea of time of death or method used?'

'She gave her usual "I'm not committing to anything until I've got him on the slab", but she did say she thinks it was within the last eight hours and death was due to blunt trauma to the head.'

Nell looked over at him. Paul held up his hands.

'They've got to call it, even if it is bloody obvious.'

'Where is she now?'

'In the kitchen, or what passes for a kitchen anyway, checking out a couple of blood patches.'

Nell looked around the room. The flat was situated above a betting shop in Rose Hill, the one Carla had flagged up and which Nell and Paul had visited the evening before. Had he been dead then? Lying here in his own blood while they talked crap to the shop owner?

She noted the tidy bedside table, a tube of moisturiser, a half-read book. 'Who owns it? The flat?'

'No you don't,' Paul stopped her. 'You know the drill. You call the killer's gender from the same information as I have. Just what's in this room.'

It was a game they played. One of the little things that made the harder parts of the job more bearable.

Nell looked at the rose-coloured wallpaper – a little ripped at the edges – the chest of drawers on which stood a mirror and a brush, a book placed at an angle on the bedside table, and it occurred to her it looked just like a stage set.

'I'm calling a woman.'

'That's a bold statement, Jackson.' Paul's tone told her what he thought of her conclusion but she just shrugged.

'The room is bare, but what's here suggests a female occupant.' She looked at the hairbrush that'd be ripe with DNA to prove her right. 'And attacking from behind suggests the need for surprise – to give the killer a chance.'

Paul looked unconvinced. 'Yeah, but a man could just as well have needed surprise. Not all men have these.' He flexed his tattooed biceps, thick from hours in the gym each night.

'But why would a man be up here with him?' She pointed to the bed, sheets ruffled. 'I think whoever did it was here with him, then something happened to make her kill him. Maybe he got violent, she felt threatened, got what was nearest to her and hit him with it.'

'But what? There's nothing obviously missing, so what did "she" kill him with?'

He had a point. There was no obvious murder weapon, unless Eve had bagged it already. But if she hadn't, if there wasn't a murder weapon used in the heat of the moment, that would only indicate one thing.

Nell looked to Paul. 'You think someone brought the murder weapon here deliberately?'

'Maybe.'

'Which would mean it was premeditated.'

'Yup. And hours after his kid is killed? Too much of a coincidence?'

'Kelly-Anne?'

'She hasn't been at the station long. She had ample time before to sneak out and meet him. Maybe they argued. She accused him of killing their child, they fought, she killed him.'

'But that sounds premeditated. If the murder weapon was brought to the scene, she would have had to consciously choose an appropriate item, carry it on her, then be calm enough to take it away again after she'd killed her partner.' And from what Nell had seen of Kelly-Anne, this seemed unlikely.

A short cough from the doorway made Nell turn in surprise.

'Sorry, Sergeant, did I scare you?' Eve was dressed in an all-blue plastic suit, her white hair tucked neatly inside the hood, and she wore the barest hint of a smile as she walked over to O'Brian's body.

'I won't shake hands.' She stopped by the remains of his head. 'Cross-contamination and all that.' Her blue eyes studied Nell for a moment before turning to look down at the body. 'I see you're familiar with the back of Mr O'Brian's head? Or lack of it, I should say.'

'Any idea of the murder weapon?'

'Not yet, but then it will no doubt be pretty standard – a hammer, fire poker. Criminals these days lack originality.'

Nell doubted they ever had it, and certainly none she'd ever come across. 'So, something metal you think?'

Eve crouched down by the body. 'I didn't say that, Sergeant.'

Paul opened his mouth but Nell gave him a quick shake of the head. Eve's list of murder weapons suggested metal, but Nell wasn't going to argue and she certainly didn't need Paul leaping to her defence.

Eve lifted O'Brian's T-shirt. 'Have you seen this?'

Nell crouched down beside her, taking in O'Brian's exposed flesh, the hair on his back just below two bloodied letters inscribed on his chest.

' "A W"?'

Eve didn't reply, instead she traced a finger around the edges of the wound. It seemed oddly intimate and Nell averted her eyes.

'What would "A W" stand for?' Nell looked up at Paul, who thought for a moment then shrugged.

'Nothing I can think of.'

'No, nor me.' She looked to Eve. 'Any ideas?'

Eve kept her eyes on O'Brian. 'No. But someone wanted to leave you a message, that's for sure.'

'Well, I wish they could have been a bit clearer,' Paul said. 'What the hell is "A W" going to tell us?'

Eve smiled up at him. 'Well, that's for you to find out, isn't it?'

'Must be pretty important if the killer wrote it on O'Brian's skin.' A thought came to Nell. 'Did they do it prior to death?'

'I'd say post. I'd have expected more bleeding if it was prior.'

Well, that was something, she supposed, but Nell still couldn't see Kelly-Anne doing something like that, even if he was already dead. It just clashed with her portrayal of the downtrodden girl-friend. Unless a portrayal was all it was.

'Do you think, having seen Kelly-Anne and O'Brian together, even briefly,' she added as Eve gave her a warning look, 'that she would be capable of doing this?'

Eve let out a short laugh. 'That girl wouldn't tie her shoelaces if he didn't tell her to.' She pushed herself up to standing. Nell joined her, knees protesting.

'The thing about girls like that is they've been brainwashed so much they can't countenance any action without prior approval. O'Brian will have worn her down until every little thing she did required his permission. And not because she was some poor little victim – although of course she was – but because his love for her was the world. And however misguided that idea of love was, however wrong, she'd had no one else to tell her love could be any other way.' Eve looked down at O'Brian. 'Children without love goad their abuser into hitting them so they can at least feel a human touch.' She looked to Nell. 'It's what we need. And we get it however we can.'

Nell looked at what was left of O'Brian's head. That was some need for human contact, beating a man's brains out.

She felt Paul behind her, unsettled, keen to get on.

'You done with us?' she asked Eve.

'I'll let you know when I've done the report.'

'Thanks.' She paused. 'Odd it's the father of the dead baby, don't you think?'

'Why?'

'Well, they must be linked.'

'Must they?' Eve's face was unreadable.

'If they aren't, that's one hell of a coincidence.'

Eve smiled. 'Coincidences do happen, Sergeant.'

Nell contemplated her for a moment. Yes, they did. But she'd never come across such a case, and she doubted this was going to be the one to break the mould.

Fourteen
Then

Our school uniforms are a mix and match of whatever the staff could find in the cupboard. Aoife is looking scornfully in the bedroom mirror while I pull my skirt down in a desperate attempt for it to be half decent.

'I don't know why you're worried,' she says over her shoulder, red hair tied up in a bun. She's put on a bit of blusher and it lifts her whole face, making the blue of her eyes stand out even more. 'Better a tart than a nun.'

She turns back to the mirror, turning over the waistband of her skirt until she seems satisfied, then grabs the hand-me-down school bag and rolls her eyes. 'I mean, honestly, they might as well brand us with "Kids from the stinky care home" with all this lot.'

I feel the nerves that'd woken with me start to clamour for

attention. I want to be going to my old school. I want to have new pens, rulers and rubbers.

Aoife throws a jacket at me. 'What you thinking?'

'Nothing.' I don't want to admit I'm frightened of going to school, but she must be able to see it because she pauses, then flings herself on the bed, tickling me until I think I'm going to wee.

'Stop!' I say, breathless. We are lying back on the bed and she grins over at me.

'It's going to be fine.' She takes my hand and squeezes it. 'I won't let anything happen to you.'

I feel tears in the corners of my eyes and when I blink a few run down the edges of my cheeks. 'Promise?'

'Promise,' she says and brushes them away.

School is awful and Aoife finds me at lunchtime hiding in the toilets.

'Ah, what's up?' She's leaning against the door and I'm so relieved to see her I almost cry. She looks at the sandwiches in my lap, their edges curling, and grimaces.

'I wouldn't even try eating them, you'll probably choke.' She grabs them off me and turns to put them in the bin just as the door slams open and three girls walk in.

They stand in a line, arms folded. 'Another little reject,' the tallest one in the middle says to Aoife. I cringe by the door, trying to think of a way round them, but they're blocking our exit so I hover behind Aoife and try not to look as scared as I feel.

'Don't see why we're lumbered with you just because your mums didn't want you.' She peers around Aoife. 'What you hiding from? Are you scared?' She says this in a leering tone and I freeze.

'I had to throw away the pens you dropped,' she continues. 'Had to pick them up with my sweater.' She turns to the other girls. 'God knows what we would catch off them.'

They all laugh and I see Aoife roll both hands into fists, straightening her shoulders, lifting her chin a little higher. The girls see it too and stop laughing.

'What you going to do? Fight us?' The middle one grins at the others but I can tell they are unsure now. They shuffle either side of her; one takes a long piece of hair and twirls it round her index finger. I don't take my eyes off her as Aoife speaks.

'If I have to, yeah.'

The room stills, the only sounds from a leaking tap and a cistern refilling behind us. The middle girl steps forward. 'Come on then.'

Aoife moves forward too, and it makes me think of two pawns opening a game of chess. Then before I can work out who hit who first, arms and legs come at me. My hair is pulled, my lip is split by the heel of a shoe, and as I grab my chest to stop the kicks all I can hear is the ear-splitting scream of Aoife as she fights them off me.

It's over as quickly as it began. The girls leave, swearing they'll get us properly the next time, and I lie curled in a ball on the floor.

'Come on, sit up.' Aoife has toilet roll in her hand and as I gingerly obey she gently dabs the edge of my mouth. When she's done, she sits back on the floor and lets out a breath. I see her tights are ripped and her hair has come loose from its bun. Red curls hang around her face, as wild as if the wind had come in and blown them that way.

'Come on, girl, let's get the hell out of here.' She stands and holds out a hand to me.

'Leave school?'

She rolls her eyes but not in an unkind way. 'You want to stick around for more of this?' She holds out the toilet roll stained with my blood.

I shake my head.

'Thought not,' she says, and grabs my arm.

We make our way to the sea and as soon as I smell the salt I feel my body relaxing. Wind whips around us, little grains of sand stabbing our faces like needles. Aoife swirls round and laughs, her hair streaming out behind her, face lifted towards the cloudy sky. Her eyes are shut but the expression on her face is still one of freedom.

The waves crash behind us, each one keener to reach the shore than the last, while gulls swoop and try to make themselves heard above the wind. We are alone on the pebbles, or so I think until I glance up towards the promenade and see a man standing, watching us.

He is as solid as the sea: black jacket, black hair around a face I can't make out, and the way he watches us makes the hair on my arms stand up.

'What?' Aoife stops dancing and follows my stare. We stand for a moment, the three of us, watching, before he turns and walks back to the run-down café behind him. I read the battered sign – *Alf's Café* – written in red, a large plastic ice-cream cone swaying underneath.

Aoife looks at me and grins. 'Fancy a Mr Whippy?'

I look back at Alf's Café, its windows dark, upturned chairs on tables outside.

She grabs my arm. 'Come on,' she says. 'Let's go and get this Alf to give us two on the house.'

My stomach rumbles so I follow, skipping over pebbles as we scramble to the top.

The man is standing by the door as we reach the wall. He watches as we climb the steps, sand making us slip, and holds the door open for us.

'Hello, girls.' His voice is low and hard. 'Come inside.'

Fifteen

Terry, owner of the betting shop below O'Brian's dead body, was sitting ashen-faced in the corner of the room. His hair was curly and lank, his faded black jeans smeared with grime, and he wore a greying band T-shirt. The television remained blank, betting slips untouched by the morning crowd.

He was holding a cup of tea and a cigarette burned almost down to the filter. As Nell and Paul approached, he pulled out another, lighting it from the first, before stubbing the first one out in an old coffee cup already overflowing with fag ends.

'I don't suppose you're going to do me for smoking in my own shop, not with –' Terry gestured to the ceiling with his cigarette, '– that up there.' He took a long drag and it was only as Nell took the seat next to him that she saw he was shaking.

'It must have been quite a shock, finding him like that.'

Another drag. 'Yeah, you could say that.'

She picked up the packet of cigarettes and tapped one into her hand. 'May I?'

Terry paused, then leaned over and flicked open his Zippo. 'Sure.'

Nell took a drag and waited for the nicotine to hit. 'What made you go up and check the flat?'

'I'm the caretaker and the woman renting rang and asked me to look at her window catch. Broken, she said.'

'It isn't?'

'Didn't get a chance to look. Got a bit distracted by the dead body in the middle of the floor.' He attempted a laugh but only managed a fit of coughing. Nell blew smoke towards the ceiling and waited until he'd finished.

'And the name of the woman who rents the flat?'

Terry frowned. 'Shit. Can't remember.' When he looked up, he seemed lost. 'I only spoke to her yesterday as well.'

'Do you have the name written down anywhere?' Nell gestured to what seemed to pass for a desk.

'Oh, yeah. Course.' He stood, and Nell noted the beer belly and sweat marks under his armpits. Her stomach churned.

'You've met her then?' she called after him as he went to the desk.

Terry shook his head as he dug under paper and discarded cups and plates. 'No. Heard her on the phone and seen her on CCTV.' He suddenly held up a piece of paper. 'That's it. Benote,' he said. 'Her name is Gloria Benote.'

Nell glanced at Paul, then asked, 'You sure?'

'Yeah, says so right here.' He waved the paper to make his point.

'Did she have anyone staying with her? A child maybe?'

He shook his head. 'No, it wasn't that kind of flat, if you get my meaning.'

Nell's look told him she didn't. Stubbing out the cigarette on the nearest plate, he shrugged. 'It's a bit more of a use-by-the-hour sort of a job.'

'Gloria's a prostitute?'

How the hell had Carla missed that? Unless Gloria had never been picked up, in which case there'd be no trace of her on the system. But Nell doubted Gloria would have avoided all police contact; Oxford was small enough for cops to know most sex workers by name, so something would have been logged, even if it was just an intel report. Maybe Carla just hadn't looked?

Terry fell into another fit of coughing and sat down behind the desk. 'As far as I could tell,' he said when he'd cleared his throat. 'Didn't ask, of course, not the gentlemanly thing to do.' He winked at Paul, whose face remained the same, making Terry shuffle awkwardly in his seat. 'Anyway, not my business, is it?'

'Not your business if someone is breaking the law over your shop?' It was fine not to want to be involved, but Nell knew betting shops got enough visits from police without adding a resident prostitute into the mix. So why not shop her? Unless Gloria was giving sexual favours in return for his silence, which was possible; given the state of him, she imagined he'd be hard-pressed to get it any other way.

When he didn't answer she asked, 'And when did you last see her?'

He paused. 'Maybe about ten yesterday morning.'

'Is that normal?'

'Normal?'

'Is it the time you usually see her?'

Terry thought. 'No. She usually comes round about eight in the evening. So I suppose it was a bit unusual.'

Nell nodded. 'And O'Brian?'

Terry stared at her. 'I didn't really get a good look at the bloke, seeing as most of his head was sprayed all over the carpet.'

He had a point.

'OK, so have you noticed anyone hanging around? Anyone who doesn't look like a punter?'

Terry considered this for a second. 'Well, there was this bloke who popped up every now and again. He'd come in for a bet, then would disappear about the time the woman turned up. Always had the same overnight bag. That's what made me notice him. You don't usually carry an overnight bag for an hour's knock-up, do you?'

Nell had no idea what men took with them when they went to a prostitute and she couldn't say she wanted to. But Kelly-Anne had mentioned O'Brian's overnight bag and his regular absences, so that fitted. O'Brian had been using Gloria as his escape route and she'd obviously welcomed him.

So why kill him? Revenge? Frustrated, Nell pointed to the television screens. 'I assume you have CCTV and it's working?'

Terry nodded, heaved himself out of his chair and walked slowly behind the counter. 'Inside and out. Want both?'

Paul nodded, following him across the room as Nell took out her phone and headed outside.

Lighting a cigarette in the alley beside the betting shop, she dialled the office. 'Carla? Nell. Gloria rents the flat O'Brian was found in. Can you run a check on her, a proper one? Known addresses, vehicles, the usual. See if you can find her for us.'

Carla was silent for a moment and Nell's irritation grew. What was it with Carla and this Gloria? They all had one victim who stuck with them; why the hell did Carla's have to be on her case?

'A *proper* one?'

'Sorry?' Nell blew smoke towards the bright blue sky, feeling the sweat under her armpits start to spread to her ribcage.

'You said a *proper* one, as if I haven't done a proper job on Gloria before. If you're suggesting I'm deliberately protecting her, I'd rather you just said.'

Nell rolled her eyes. 'Sorry, no, I'm rushing. I just meant a thorough one.'

'So I haven't been thorough?'

For God's sake. Nell stamped on her half-smoked cigarette and turned to go back inside.

'Can you just check it out, please?'

'Is she a suspect then?' Carla clearly wasn't going to let it go.

'You don't think she's viable?'

'I just can't imagine her having the balls to do it. She was . . .'

Carla searched for the right words, '. . . addicted to him. Why would she kill him?'

'Jesus, I don't know – jealousy, love? Pick any of the emotions women say makes them kill.'

She heard Carla sigh.

'OK, I'll do some digging then.'

Her tone let Nell know she thought it was a blind alley, but what the hell else did they have to go on? O'Brian had been murdered in a flat Gloria rented. Did Carla expect her to gloss over that because Gloria had once been his victim? If anything, it made it all the more likely.

'Thanks. And can you send me over a screenshot of Gloria. We're about to go over the CCTV and I want to know who I'm looking for.'

'Sure, will do.'

Nell hung up. The pain in her right eye had got worse and all she wanted was Carla to do her job – plus a paracetamol and a bottle of Coke.

As she made her way to where Paul and Terry sat, engrossed in CCTV footage, her phone pinged. Opening the text message, she saw a picture of a young blonde – no more than twenty-one – looking at the camera as if it were about to attack her. *Victim shot*, Carla had typed, then underneath, *just after O'Brian broke her arm*.

Ignoring the passive-aggressive tone, Nell scrolled down, seeing pictures of the injuries Carla had pointedly added to the message, noting the slim build, the skinny arms. Could she have lifted a heavy object and brought it down so hard it made

O'Brian's brain explode out the other side? The final picture was one of Gloria and her son, both smiling at the camera, Gloria's arms wrapped tightly around the little boy, hugging him close.

'Jesus,' Nell muttered, shoving it back in her pocket. She knew why Carla had sent that one – make the victim a real person and it increased your desire to help them. But Gloria wasn't a victim, she was a suspect, at least to Nell anyway.

'Got anything?' she asked as she joined the two men.

'Yeah – see.' Paul pointed to the screen. 'Got her coming and going over the last month, mostly at the start of the week. Don't think she sleeps here, mind. Seems to arrive, followed by a steady stream of men, before leaving at about midnight most nights. Last time seen, yesterday, 23:54 hours.'

'What time does she usually arrive?'

'About 20:00 hours.'

Nell nodded and dragged a chair over. 'Show me.'

Terry showed her two weeks' worth of footage, then rewound the previous night's tape until a tall woman appeared. Pausing, she looked right and left before running across the road and approaching the flat door, taking a quick look behind her before she disappeared inside.

'Can you rewind that again?' Nell leaned closer to the screen, noting the dark brown hair and thick legs. Nell watched the woman again as she crossed the road. 'Have you got a close-up of her face?'

Terry loaded another cassette and up sprung Gloria's face, looking at the flat door as she keyed in the entrance code.

'What's the date of that image?'

'One week ago.'

'And last night?'

'I can't get a close-up for that.'

Nell pointed to the close-up of Gloria a week earlier. 'How long has that woman been renting this place?'

'Dunno. About six months. Not long.'

Nell could see from Paul's expression he needed an explanation. She gave the woman's face one more look, then nodded for Paul to follow her.

'What is it?' Paul asked as they walked to the far side of the shop.

'That woman, the one in last night's CCTV, isn't Gloria Benote. The build and colouring are all off.'

'I don't understand. There are two women?'

'Looks like it, yes.'

Paul glanced back at Terry. 'So Gloria was renting with someone else?' He turned back to Nell. 'Like a mini brothel set-up?'

'I don't think so, no. The only woman going into that flat has been Gloria. Except last night it wasn't Gloria, it was someone else.'

'Do you think Gloria knows who that was?'

Nell looked up at the blackened window behind which O'Brian's body lay. Why would Gloria hide O'Brian and then let someone in to kill him? Why not just do it herself? And if she had given access to the flat to another woman, then who the hell had a better motive to kill him than Gloria?

'We're going to have to bring Gloria in.'

'That'll be two to interview then, we've still got Kelly-Anne waiting for us.'

Kelly-Anne. Shit, she'd forgotten about her.

'Do you think Kelly-Anne might have been the one Gloria let in?' she asked.

Paul took out his car keys and put on sunglasses. 'Maybe they decided to work together. Punish him once and for all.'

Nell wasn't convinced Kelly-Anne had it in her, but then she'd never met Gloria, so Paul could well be right.

'OK. Let's get back to the station and get Gloria in. One of them is going to cave and I'll bet you a hundred quid it's Kelly-Anne.'

Sixteen

Carla had woken to a cup of tea by the bed and a note from Baz telling her he loved her. She'd pulled open her bedroom drawer, taken out the contraceptive pills hidden there and swallowed one down, trying to ignore the guilt she felt every morning and the lies she told Baz every time he mentioned babies.

The bus ride into work had been consumed by thoughts of Gerry and his mysterious meeting and by the time she was at her desk she felt tired and irritated, so Nell's thinly veiled suggestion she wasn't doing her job well stung. Particularly as Carla was worried she was right.

On the day Carla gave evidence, Gloria had been standing in the court hallway with the family liaison officer and Carla had been struck by the woman's youthful appearance, and how much this jarred with the child nestled on her hip. It was day two of

O'Brian's trial and Gloria was pleading with the family liaison officer to let her see him.

'I just want to see him, just for five minutes – I need to say I'm sorry.'

Carla had stared at the bruise running down Gloria's cheek and thought she wasn't the one who should be apologising. The family liaison officer clearly agreed.

'But Gloria, you do understand it's not you who's to blame, don't you? That what he did to you was wrong?'

Gloria looked frustrated. Adjusting the dummy in the toddler's mouth, she said, 'You don't understand. I made him cross and he couldn't help himself.'

'You didn't make him cross, Gloria, you made him a dinner he didn't like.' The family liaison officer's tone was flat and Carla wondered how many times she'd heard the same thing: women so beaten – emotionally and physically – they could no longer see a reality outside the one their partners had created for them.

Gloria had never been persuaded to blame O'Brian and when the judge sentenced him to jail, she'd wept in the gallery as he was taken down. Carla thought of that image as she opened up the intelligence database, hoping she wouldn't find anything to tell her O'Brian had got his hooks back into Gloria and forced her into prostitution. Because Gloria loved her child, would never do anything to endanger him, the only person who could challenge that commitment was O'Brian.

The search came back clear – not a trace of Gloria on any police system. Carla leaned back in her chair, relieved. It didn't mean she hadn't been selling sex, but at least she hadn't been caught. Yet. Carla tapped her pen on the table. She'd get hold of the landlord, confirm the tenant's name, and work from there. Maybe it wasn't Gloria at all and a check of who was paying the rent could tell her that.

A quick call to the Oxford City Council Tax department and she had the landlord's number. Dialling, she tried to think of what could have made Gloria attack O'Brian. It didn't fit with anything she knew about the woman. It wasn't just her adoration of him, her general nervousness suggested she wasn't the type to commit cold-blooded murder – unless it had been an accident? But Nell had been pretty sure it wasn't.

'Yes?' The voice was deep, heavily accented and obviously annoyed at having been disturbed. 'What do you want?'

'Hello, this is Thames Valley Police. I wanted to check on a tenant you have living at 34 Rose Way?'

'Where they found the body?' He sounded so matter-of-fact Carla was taken aback. He filled in the gap created by her hesitation.

'I told the officer I'd be in tomorrow. It will have to wait until then. I have matters I need to attend to.'

'Of course, sir, yes, that's for your statement to my uniformed colleagues. But we have an urgent enquiry that I was hoping you could help me with now.'

She heard him sigh heavily down the phone. 'Well then, what is it?'

'I just wanted to confirm the tenant's name at the property.'

'I said this. Gloria Benote.'

'Yes, thank you. Do you recall who paid the rent? The name on the bank account details, for example?'

'Isn't what I've told you enough?'

'No, sir. Your tenant may have registered in Ms Benote's name, but the payment details would confirm this – or not,' she added.

Another sigh. 'Hold on.'

Carla heard metal drawers being opened, paper being rustled, before he came back on the line.

'Gloria Benote. Banks with Lloyds.'

Shit. 'OK, thank you, sir, that's very helpful.'

'And is that it?'

Carla had a thought. 'Was Ms Benote renting any other property off you?'

'Yes, she was.' He sounded surprised, suddenly interested.

'Can you let me have that address please?' She took the pen lid off with her teeth and wrote down the details as he gave them. 'Thank you, you've been really helpful.'

He hung up without a goodbye, but Carla barely noticed. The second property must be where Gloria lived with her kid while she used the flat for work. A bit like renting office space.

Bremer appeared at the door with two takeout coffees. He handed one to Carla and sat down next to her. 'Have you spoken to Nell?'

'Yeah, looks like Gloria was hiding O'Brian.'

Bremer stirred his latte with a wooden stick. 'Nell wants to bring her in. Have we got an address?'

'Just got it from the landlord.'

'Right. Good work.' He paused. 'You know Eve's the patholo-gist for the O'Brian murder?'

Carla didn't. 'Is that a problem?'

Bremer leaned back in his chair. 'Not sure. But it doesn't feel ideal.'

'Because of the letter?'

He nodded. 'I'm just wary of her being on the same case she's been accused of tampering with. And I know,' he continued, before she could speak, 'it's just a letter and there is nothing to link her to the case.' He looked at Carla.

'Nothing at all,' she confirmed.

'But I still think we're treading a thin line.' He took a sip of coffee and stirred it again. 'You know her husband, right?'

'Yeah, he was my first sergeant.' She knew the next question so answered before it could be asked: 'Straight down the line, not a dodgy bone in his body.'

'Good.'

'You want me to speak to him, don't you?' Carla wasn't sure how she felt about that. It seemed a little underhand to use their friendship to get information on the case, but on the other hand, Eve had brought the letter to their attention, so it wasn't a conflict of interest, not really.

'It might be good to see what Gerry knows,' Bremer replied, watching her reaction.

She smiled and picked up her notepad.

'Sure. He's on duty today so I'll go and find him.'

Bremer looked pleased. 'Good.' Picking up his half-drunk coffee, he stood. 'And then, when Nell gets in we'll see where we are with O'Brian. We're going to have to bring Gloria in, but I want to think of the best way to do it. Strikes me she's going to be easily spooked.'

And Carla thought that was a pretty fair assumption to make.

Gerry was in the canteen. He rose when he saw Carla, enveloping her in a bear hug, before sitting down across from her.

'Sorry I didn't say goodbye last night,' he said when they'd taken their seats.

'No worries. I did look for you, but you'd gone.'

'Yeah, it was only a quick catch-up . . .'

'With your old mate,' Carla finished for him.

He smiled and they let the lie sit there for a moment before he said, 'Can I get you a coffee?'

'No thanks.'

He looked questioningly at her. 'What's on your mind? Is it the letter?'

Carla picked a grain of sugar from the table with her finger. 'Eve said you told her to bring it to us?'

He sighed, leaned back in his chair and folded his arms over his stomach. 'I did. She didn't want to, being Eve, but the reference to the case she was working on worried me. I mean, how would the letter writer know?' His brow creased in thought. 'It just struck me as more sinister than the rest, like someone was watching her closely, stalking her almost.'

'But Eve doesn't feel threatened?'

'Eve just thinks it's part of the job. She's convinced it's just some nutjob letting off a bit of steam.'

'But you don't think that?'

Gerry rubbed the back of his neck. 'I did, until this last letter. Now I'm not so sure.'

It suddenly occurred to Carla that Gerry was referring to letters, plural. 'So Eve has had others?'

Gerry's hand stopped moving. He studied her for a moment before leaning forward, hands together on the table, pointing towards Carla. 'There have been five before this.'

'Five. Jesus, Gerry, why didn't you tell me?'

He held up his hands. 'It wasn't my business to. They were sent to Eve; it was for her to decide if they warranted police action. I have them all in my office for when she feels able to show them to you all, but until then they are staying there.' His voice told Carla this wasn't up for discussion, but she pushed him anyway.

'Why keep them in your office then, if you don't want them seen?'

'Because Eve wanted them out of the house, but I didn't want to throw them away, so it seemed the obvious place.'

'So there was something in them that made you worried? For you to keep them, I mean?'

Gerry smiled. 'You'll make a detective yet, Brown.' He sighed before continuing. 'They contain personal information, stuff we both don't really want gossiped about. They weren't threatening, but I considered it would be best to keep them in case they became so.'

'Which they have.'

'Yes.'

'I need to see the letters, Gerry.'

He shook his head. 'No way. Not until Eve's ready.'

Carla sat back, exasperated. 'Gerry, this is serious. Whoever is writing them may be involved in Connor O'Brian's murder. I need to see the others – all of them.'

'Carla, I can't without Eve's say-so.'

'She agreed to one – she must have known the others would come out.'

Gerry looked sceptical.

'You got her to show us the latest one, so you may as well give us the rest.'

She kept her eyes on him, but he still hesitated.

'You're not going to make me get a court order, are you?' She laughed, Gerry didn't, because they both knew she could.

'I'll get them for you,' he said, pushing back his chair to stand. 'But let me tell Eve first, OK?'

'Of course,' she smiled, 'and thanks, Gerry.'

Seventeen

Then

Alf's Café is a mix of old and new. The tables and chairs are totally 1970s, but the photos on the wall are present-day and I wonder if he's taken them himself: black and white, the odd moody colour shot, all depicting shadows from people lying in the sun.

As I examine each picture I wonder why he doesn't want actual people in them, but adults are strange and get odd fixations, so this is probably one of his. Shame, though. Surely people are more important than their shadows?

'Ice-cream waffle?' Alf's voice fills the café. I stop looking at the photographs and check to see what Aoife says. She's sitting on the counter, legs swinging.

'Sure,' making it sound like it's not the biggest treat we've had since we got here. 'With sprinkles?'

Alf grins. His teeth fall all over each other and I'm not sure where one starts and another stops, but his eyes are bright like a cat's, so I can't help but smile.

'Sprinkles it is,' he says.

We eat warm waffles dripping with ice cream as Alf quizzes us about our families.

'So, you have a dad?'

Aoife shrugs.

'And what about your mum?'

Aoife points to my plastered arm, her mouth full, and while I'm annoyed about the inaccuracy – it was after all my dad who broke it – I can sort of see her point. Where is my mum?

Alf is watching our exchange. He's standing behind the gallery kitchen divide, hands behind, like he's about to pull himself up onto the work surface. But of course he won't: too much effort, too much weight, even I can see that.

When we're finished eating Aoife says we should go, but rain is pounding the windows so hard it's almost impossible to believe they won't crack.

'You want a lift?'

'It's OK, we'll be fine.'

I know why she doesn't want him driving us. It's because he'll see where we live and then we'll just be another pair of care-home girls – rejects, unlovable, unwanted – and she wants to hold on to us just being us for a little bit longer. And I want to as well. I feel like I've been floating around on the edges, like it wouldn't matter if I just upped and died, because who would notice? Who would care? But here in this café, I feel seen. I'm stapled to the floor, I belong, and I don't know if it's being here with Aoife, or the way Alf listens to us chat – as if what we say really matters – or just sugar from all the waffles, but it's how I feel and I like it.

Alf reaches for his car keys and I see a flash of panic from Aoife, but suddenly I know Alf won't mind where we're from, I just know it. I tug at her sleeve. 'Come on, it's fine.'

She looks doubtful, but then Alf says, 'Big house on the end of Roseway Drive, yeah?'

Aoife looks up and I grin. See, I knew it! He already knows where we live and while a little bit of me feels like we must have a stamp on our heads or something, the rest of me just feels relieved. He knows where we're from and he doesn't care.

'What do you think of him?' Aoife asks.

'Fat,' I say, and we fall backwards onto her bed, laughing. When we stop Aoife turns to face me, hand on her cheek.

'What did your dad do to you to make you come here?' she asks. 'Can't just be a broken arm – they don't put you here for that.'

I feel the waffle in my stomach churn. When I don't reply Aoife sighs and lies back down.

'My dad did it too. I think most dads do. Men are just made that way, I suppose.'

I try not to think of mine, of his smell, the stubble on his face.

'Did your mum know?'

I turn to stare at her. 'No.'

Aoife looks unconvinced, so I repeat myself.

'No.'

She gives a small shrug. 'Most do, they just don't want to admit it. I mean, unless your dad was really clever, but I doubt it.' She yawns. 'Mine didn't bother hiding it and Mum couldn't have cared less. Got him off her back.'

I want to cry so I push my fingernails into the palms of my hands. It's strange to think of other people walking around with the same feeling of cement in their stomach, the same dread as the footsteps get closer, pretending to be asleep but still feeling the hand on your shoulder to wake you. I feel a little bit lighter knowing Aoife understands. 'Do you miss your mum?'

'God, no. She's worse than him. At least with my dad I got to know what was coming. Mum was all nicey-nicey one minute, then the next, *bam*.' She punched her hand into the pillow.

'She hit you?' At least my mum hadn't done that. The worst she'd done was let him do it.

'Yeah. But I didn't mind that so much as the silence. The pretending I wasn't even there. However much I said "Mum", she'd ignore me until I was so desperate to be seen I'd throw a tantrum and then she'd hit me.' She was staring at the ceiling. 'My own fault then, really.'

I don't know if it was or not. There are so many rules adults give you, rules that seem to switch daily, it's impossible to keep up with them all, however hard you try. And just when you think you've got the hang of one, it goes and changes, and you're back to square one.

'What do you want to be when you're an adult?' I ask. She thinks for a while and I get sleepy waiting.

'Dunno. A scientist.'

I almost laugh. 'You need to go to school for that.'

'I'll pull it off. I can do anything.' She speaks with such certainty it doesn't occur to me to think she won't.

'Like one in a white coat and lab glasses?' I ask.

'Maybe. Or a renowned physician who travels the world lecturing people on how clever they are.'

'Why a scientist?' I've never met anyone who wanted to be that before; it seems as impossible as being an astronaut or the prime minister.

'I went to hospital once, after boyfriend number two broke my leg, and when I asked why they were taking my blood and what they were going to do with it, they pushed me to the lab so I could see. It was amazing. This big room with bottles and machines and a woman was there in a white coat and a clear face mask. She took my tube of blood and showed me how they can find out every little thing about you just from one drop, like our whole lives are there in that little speck, telling her if I like baked beans or if I'm going to die when I eat a peanut.'

She's speaking so fast I can barely keep up, her expression caught up in the memory of it.

'You can find out all this stuff about people from one tiny bit of them, then solve all their problems, like you're a god or some-thing.' She grins at me. 'Or a superhero. I want to be a scientist superhero!' She raises her fist and I laugh.

'What do you want to be?' she asks.

I want to be a mum; I want to love my kid more than anything else on earth. And I want to love other people's kids, kids who don't have enough love themselves so haven't any to spare. But I don't tell Aoife this, it seems silly when she has such grand things lined up for her life.

'Not sure yet. Probably a teacher or something.'

Aoife nods, then yawns. 'I'm tired.' She moves her head slightly, so she can see me. 'Shall we go and see Alf again tomor-row? Get more waffles?'

I grin. 'For sure.'

'He's nice, isn't he?'

'Yes.'

We sit for a while, swapping stories about our mums until I feel almost better about mine.

'Do you believe in God?' Aoife suddenly asks. She points to the Bible by my bed and I notice her nails are encrusted with dirt. I shake my head.

'We all get them. When we arrive. You'll have one in your drawer.' I nod to the side of the room where she sleeps and the little brown wooden box by her bed. She doesn't follow my eyes and instead throws my Bible to the floor.

'God doesn't exist. He's just made up by adults who want to control us.'

I'm surprised by how angry she sounds. 'Control us?'

She squints at me as if I'm half mad. 'Of course, dumbo. They pretend God made all these rules that we must follow and use them to punish us when we don't. So they get to be in the right when they're beating on you, because they are doing it to make God love you.' She leans in closer and I smell sweetness on her breath. 'But it's a lie.' Her Irish accent is thicker now, and I struggle to make out her words.

'You know why my mum had me?'

It's not really a question, so I wait for the answer.

'She had me because God said it was bad if she got rid of me. But God lets her boyfriends put me in hospital? Let her lock me out of the house all night because they don't want me around? What sort of God is that?' She stops speaking and lies still, her breathing hard and fast. I take her hand and we stay like that until her breathing slows. After a while she picks up her torch and a book. Pushing pillows behind her, she half sits and opens at the first page.

I lie with my head on her stomach and listen to her tell me stories before sleep pulls me down. As I drift away I make her promise to read every night. She strokes my hair.

'Sure thing, dumbo.'

'I don't mind you calling me "dumbo",' I whisper.

And when I wake in the morning, Aoife strewn across me like a rag doll, I realise it's the very first night in my life I haven't wet the bed.

Eighteen

Gerry walked back into the canteen carrying a brown envelope. Taking his seat, he pushed it across the table to Carla.

'We've had six letters in total. Started six months ago and there doesn't seem to be a pattern as to when they're delivered.'

'Posted?' Carla pulled out a pile of paper.

'No, arrived by hand.' He pointed to the first letter in the pile. 'That was the last one Eve got, until the new one. Four weeks ago.'

'Are they threatening?'

'More . . .' he searched for the right word, '. . . a warning. No explicit threat or I'd have made her go to the police,' he added. 'Go on. Read one. Let me know what you think.'

Carla picked out a typewritten page, noted the same typeface, the same font size as the letter in the office.

When I Lost You

Dear Eve,

*I want you to know I understand and that your husband has
reminded me of the reasons why you've behaved as you have.
These are clear, but, of course, I can't excuse what you've done.*

*I wanted to tell you the death you struggle with will never
go away. But you can't continue to use it to attack others.
Your grief must find its own course, find whatever way it
needs to expunge the anger it creates, but I won't be the
recipient of your anger, no more than I should be anyway.*

Carla stopped reading. 'They say they met you?'

'I know. I've gone over and over it and I can't think who it
could be. I've never spoken about Eve with anyone.'

Why were his eyes averted? Why was he tapping the plastic
spoon on the table?

'So I wondered if they'd got the wrong person, but the tone
suggests they know Eve. At least on some level.' He looked at
her. 'Could it be a stalker? That sort of thing?'

Carla knew he didn't believe it – or expect her to. The refer-
ences were too specific. Whoever was writing these knew Eve,
knew her life, and knew it well, even without taking into account
the O'Brian reference in the most recent letter.

'They mention Eve's "situation",' she said. 'Any idea what
that refers to?'

Gerry shook his head. 'No. There is no situation, not that I
know of anyway.'

'And Eve is OK?'

Gerry leaned back, folded his arms. 'In what way?'

'Well, anything happened recently to make her on edge? Or something that could have triggered the letter writing?'

'Nothing. Our lives are as they always are: work, dinner, bed.'

Carla nodded. 'OK.' But she had a growing sense of unease. Gerry seemed defensive, but she couldn't see why. Unless she wasn't asking the questions he expected her to ask. But then what were the ones he wanted?

'And the death the writer refers to, Eve's grief, do you know what that might be?'

He flinched.

'Gerry?'

He sighed and put his hands on his thighs. 'It's partly why Eve didn't want the police involved. It's a very private and upsetting thing.'

She waited for him to continue, but when he didn't she said, 'It may help me to know? It may help us find out who is writing these letters.'

'I doubt it.' He took hold of the half-empty coffee cup and moved it a little to the right, then tapped his finger on the rim. 'We had a baby. It died.'

'Oh Gerry, I'm so sorry.'

He shrugged, eyes on the table. 'Eve miscarried. Four times.'

'My God, Gerry.' She felt winded. What words could she muster that would do justice to a pain like that?

'We stopped trying after the last one. Couldn't stand the hurt.'

'I'm sorry.' The words felt so insignificant it was almost as if she hadn't said them at all.

'It's OK. It was a long time ago and we've both made peace with it. Well, I think I have; Eve sometimes still struggles. It doesn't help, of course, that we haven't told people. She has no one to confide in and I think she feels she's exhausted the subject with me. Which she hasn't. I'll talk about it with her whenever she wants,' he added. 'But as time passed she just buried it away in her heart and sealed it up.'

Carla felt a wave of guilt: guilt for never imagining Eve as a mother; guilt she could probably have a baby but was actively trying not to; guilt she was lying to Baz about it; and guilt she was making Gerry talk about it now.

'Hey.' He reached across the table and touched her hand. 'You look like you're going to cry. It's OK, really. I'm fine. We are both fine.'

She nodded. Then thought of something. 'You said you hadn't told anyone.'

'Yeah, it felt too raw, and by the time it didn't – if that's possible – the opportunity had passed.'

'But then how does the letter writer know?'

Gerry frowned. 'What?'

'Well, they say they know about Eve's grief, which suggests they know about the babies. Could she have told anyone?'

He considered this for a moment. 'I don't see who she would have told that wouldn't have also mentioned it to me.'

'What about you? Anyone you casually mentioned it to, even in passing?'

Gerry gave her a measured look. 'It's not exactly something you casually mention, Carla. And no, I've told no one.'

Carla remained silent. She thought about the letter writer saying they'd spoken with Gerry; the half-empty wine glass at his table last night.

'I haven't met anyone, Carla.'

He sounded definite and she knew she should believe him. Yet, she didn't.

'What about the doctors?' he said. 'They would have known about the deaths.'

'OK, can you get me a list of their names?' She didn't hold out much hope they would be relevant, but she should probably cover all angles. 'What about Joanne Fowler?' she asked.

'Fowler?'

'Yeah. She has an axe to grind with Eve, so maybe she found out about the babies and is using that against her.' But then that would mean Gerry had spoken with Joanne and surely he'd tell her that?

'It's nothing to do with Joanne Fowler.' He sounded so sure it took a second for Carla to reply.

'But she was released around the same time the letters started and she has a reason to hate Eve. She must be in the frame?'

Gerry considered this for a moment. 'I don't think so. How would she know about the babies?'

'Well, the letter doesn't actually reference a baby, so maybe they're just fishing? People suffer grief all the time. Maybe Joanne was putting her grief onto Eve. I don't know.' She stopped, frustrated.

Gerry pointed to a letter. 'This one mentions a baby.'

Dear Eve,

I know you lost a baby too but I also know that isn't the only pain you carry and that pain goes much deeper. You're trying to make it right but I beg you to stop. Stop increasing others' pain to alleviate your own. Please.

Because until you do, I won't stop. I won't let you continue. If you don't reconsider, I will have no choice but to stop you myself. You don't want that, Eve. You want control of your life, so take it, control the things you can change and let go of those you can't.

This is my final plea to you.

Mary.

Stunned, Carla looked to Gerry. 'Mary?'

Gerry held up his hands. 'I've gone through everyone we've ever known. Neither of us knows anyone called Mary.'

'Is Eve sure?'

'She says so.'

'And do you believe her?'

'Of course I believe her, she's my wife.' His raised voice drew glances from the two uniforms sitting behind them. Gerry leaned forward, hands together on the table.

'Eve doesn't know who's doing this, Carla. Trust me on that.'

Carla studied his face. He had to know – how could he not? The signs were all there. Eve knew the identity of the letter writer. But maybe she hadn't told Gerry and he genuinely believed it was some random stalker.

Gerry pushed back his chair. 'I've got to go. I've given you the letters. That's all I wanted to do.'

Carla stood. 'Will you let me know if you get any more?'

'Of course.' He looked uncomfortable.

'You did the right thing, showing me,' she said.

He half smiled. 'Did I?'

'I promise I'll find out who is sending them.'

He gave a short laugh. 'Yeah, that's what I'm afraid of.'

And before she could ask him why, he gave a brief wave, picked up his cold coffee, and left.

Nineteen

Nell could see Bremer in his office, but there was no sign of Carla. Irritated, she took two more pills, swigging them down with a cold coffee from her desk.

'What the hell's the point of having an analyst if she's never here?'

Paul glanced up from his phone. 'Even civvies are allowed to eat.' Seeing Nell's questioning look, he added, 'I saw her in the canteen as we went past. Talking to that big sergeant from downstairs.'

'That doesn't narrow it down much.'

'Eve's husband.'

'Oh. What's she doing with him?'

'I asked her to speak with him.' Bremer was leaning against the frame of his office door. 'Is that all right with you, Sergeant?'

Paul looked away from Nell, lowering his eyes to his phone. She was on her own then.

'Of course. There's just a few things I'd like her to check out for me.'

'Well, you know where her computer is.' He smiled brightly and she wished the pills would kick in quicker. What was it with him and Carla? Was she his pet project or something?

'Sure, I'll take a look.'

Bremer smiled again. 'Good. She'll be back any minute now. I asked her to speak to Sergeant Graham about his wife and the letter we received.'

Paul looked up. 'Has there been a development relating to the O'Brian reference in it?'

Bremer walked over and sat on the edge of Carla's desk. 'No. But when I found out she was the pathologist on his murder I wanted to make sure our backs are covered.'

'You think Eve is involved?' Nell's tone was meant to suggest that she didn't.

'No. But the letter writer clearly knows a lot about our Eve and our work, so I think it's an angle we ought to pursue.' He smiled at her. 'Even if we do only send a civvy to do the job.'

There it was again, that smile, the one that didn't bother hiding the obvious point behind his words. What was his problem? Was it because she wasn't going to succumb to his charm – because he certainly had that – and Carla might?

'Mary.'

Carla was standing by the door, her face even paler than usual. 'The woman writing the letters is called Mary.'

Bremer stood. 'You've got a name?'

'Yes.' She threw her notebook on the desk and explained what she'd learned from Gerry as she passed the letters around the team. When they'd all finished reading, Bremer turned to Nell.

'We know of any Mary linked to the O'Brian case?'

'Not yet, no.'

'Do you want me to look into it? Or focus on O'Brian?' Carla asked.

Bremer kept his eyes on Nell. 'Thoughts? You've just come back from the scene. Do you think looking into a potential link is worth it yet, or do we just focus on what we know so far?'

'I'd like to focus on the scene first. Leave this development until we've got more of a hold on the case.'

Bremer nodded. He sat down and folded his arms. 'Tell us what you've got.'

Nell relayed all they had learned from Terry and the CCTV: the figure they'd seen arriving at the flat just before Connor was killed, and the fact she bore no resemblance to the picture Nell had seen of Gloria.

'Have you got the CCTV footage?' Bremer asked.

'Yes.' She pulled the evidence bag out of her jacket pocket. 'It's not good quality, but it's good enough.'

Bremer turned to Carla. 'You know this Gloria, don't you?'

'Yes, but I haven't seen her in a few years.'

'But you'd recognise her if you saw her?'

'Yes, I think I would.'

'Right, I want you to confirm the woman on the tape isn't her. And when you've done that, you and I are going to pay Gloria a visit. Find out why she's been paying the rent on a flat she's supposedly not using.'

Nell stared at him. He was kidding, right? What was Carla going to do in an interview?

'I'd like Paul and me to speak to Gloria, if that's OK?'

'No. I want you both on Kelly-Anne. You've had contact with her and I like consistency. She'll just be thrown by new faces. Besides, as you rightly pointed out earlier, Carla is a civilian, so she'd not be any good in an interview.'

His words were pointed. Well, fine, if that's how he wanted to play it. Bloody Met cops coming to Thames Valley and thinking they know best.

Bremer was staring at her. 'I'm also aware, after a bit of research, Gloria has a tendency to clam up in the face of authority, so a friendly female face might do a bit to assuage that.' He cocked his head to one side. 'Do you have a problem with that?'

Nell clenched her jaw and shook her head. 'No, sir.' Clearly her face wasn't female or friendly enough.

Bremer stood. 'And don't be fooled by Kelly-Anne's grieving-mother routine – she knows something and I want you to find out if there's a connection between her and Gloria.'

'Yes, sir.' Nell could hear the irritation in her voice, but Bremer just flashed her a smile before looking down at Carla.

'Get your coat,' he said.

Nell's boots squeaked on the polished floor as they walked to the interview room. She didn't want to sit in a stuffy room interviewing a distraught mother; she wanted to be out there finding Connor's murderer. But that seemed to have become Carla's job.

'I mean, have you ever heard of a civilian going out with a DCI to interview anyone?' she said. 'Let alone a potential murderer.'

'Well, strictly speaking Gloria isn't a suspect.'

Nell threw Paul a look. 'Everyone is a suspect at this stage, you know that, Mackintosh.'

'Does it really bother you she went out with him?'

'Yes, doesn't it you?' She couldn't believe Paul didn't get where she was coming from. An analyst visiting a suspect, witness, whatever – surely it broke some law, something that would get the case thrown out of court when they did catch the killer?

'And what will the CPS say? They'll have a field day.'

They came to a stop outside the room where Kelly-Anne Wilson was sitting, waiting for them. Paul's hand was on the door handle, but he hesitated.

'Got something to say, Mackintosh?'

He pulled his hand away and leaned back against the wall. 'Is your problem with Carla to do with that?' He pointed at the scars that ran along Nell's arm like tracks for a train.

Nell pulled her sleeve down.

'Because it wasn't her,' he continued. 'She isn't responsible.'

'Obviously I know that.' She rubbed at her arm, trying not to see the man's face.

'Well, just so you know, it might be the reason why you feel resentful about Carla.'

'Jesus. When did you become the force counsellor?'

Paul grinned and pushed himself away from the wall. 'I'm a man of many talents is all.'

'Yeah, right.' She nodded to the door, pressing on her scars to stop the itch. 'Let's just do this, OK?'

'Sure thing, boss.' And with that he opened the door and they walked in to face Kelly-Anne.

Twenty
Then

Our after-school visits to Alf become a regular thing. The café is almost always empty and I sometimes wonder how he makes his money, but not often; mostly I'm just eating waffles and ice cream and listening to Aoife chat at him about her day.

'So, this boy comes up to me today,' she says with her mouth full, 'and is all like, "Fancy a snog?" and I'm like, "Ew, back off, dude, your spots make me gag."' She swallows before laughing until she almost falls off her chair. I'm grinning at her, but then I notice Alf and he's not smiling. Not at all.

'You were wearing that short skirt?' he asks, pointing to her uniform.

She looks up at him, laugh still hanging there. 'Yeah, so?'

'Maybe that's why he said it.'

Aoife remains silent.

'Maybe,' he says, 'you should be careful not to give boys a signal with what you wear.' He smiles. 'Not everyone is as understanding as me.'

The words aren't threatening but his tone makes me tense. I see Aoife stop swinging her legs and bite her lip.

When he moves to the kitchen – pans clashing, dishes slamming against the metal sink – my mind goes on full alert, searching his body language, facial expressions, for clues, reading the coded pointers that tell you more about a person than their words ever could.

'Are you saying I'm deliberately leading boys on?' Her tone is belligerent, but I can hear the undercurrent: caution mixed with fear. She's reading the codes too.

Alf stops what he's doing and puts his hands on the counter. He has sweat patches on his white T-shirt, rolls of fat straining against it, and his thinning black ponytail looks held back by grease.

'Course not. Don't be so sensitive. You've just got to watch out what signals you go off giving. Men, and boys, are like foxes after a chicken when it comes to girls.'

We all relax a little, but Alf isn't finished.

'And I don't want people talking about you coming here. You know what the locals can be like, so if you make them think you're loose that's going to look bad on me. And then you won't be able to come here any more.' He tries to look sad but it comes across as more of a threat and I put my fork down. I want to go home. Proper home, not care-home home.

'And what would a nice Catholic girl like you do if you got pregnant?' he continues. 'You'd be stuck with a screaming kid before you hit sixteen. A single mum on benefits. That what you want?'

I look to Aoife. She is sizing Alf up, judging how best to get him to stop. Crossing her legs so her skirt gets even shorter, she smiles. 'Alf. Boys my age wouldn't get a look-in. I prefer my men to be more experienced.'

I hold my breath as Alf considers her. The room feels hot from the oven and damp from the rain outside. I want to leave so much I have to dig my nails into my leg just to stop myself.

Alf claps his hands. 'Anyway,' he says. 'What are you girls up to tonight?'

'Nothing much. Any ideas?' Aoife cocks her head to one side, resting her chin on her palm. She's placating him in the only way she knows how but I see the look he returns and my stomach churns with the familiar fear. *Leave it, leave it, Aoife, he's stopped now.* But when they continue to stare at each other, I stand.

'I need the loo.'

Neither of them looks at me so I leave, pushing past the beaded room divide to reach the toilets that stink of damp and wee. I wet my face in the sink, trying to get rid of the feeling that presses against my chest. The girl who stares back at me in the mirror looks tiny and pale, her lips cracked at the edges, hair matted, dark circles ringing her eyes.

'I just want my mum,' I say to her and her face looks sad in return. I stand for a moment, hands on the sink, staring at the girl in the glass.

'You're just trapped like me, aren't you? Stuck in there like I'm stuck out here.'

She nods and so do I. I hear Aoife laugh and it makes me jump.

'Bye then,' I say to the girl. But I don't want to leave her.

'Bye then,' she says back, watching me as I walk to the door.

I go back to the table where Aoife is sitting close to Alf. His hand is on her thigh and she is laughing. It's not her real laugh but I don't think Alf knows that. It's the laugh she will have done for every dodgy boyfriend her mum brought back to the flat – her survival laugh – and it makes me want to grab her and run.

'Aoife?' I move to the door. She turns to me, as does Alf, his expression amused.

'We should go now. Homework.'

Alf laughs. 'You pair don't strike me as homework types.'

I can see a flicker of relief in Aoife's eyes. She turns back to Alf, leans over and kisses him on the cheek, and I'm not sure if it's a consolation prize or a promise.

'See you tomorrow,' she says, grabbing her bag from beneath the table. Alf looks irritated but flashes us his crooked teeth.

'Sure thing, girls. See you tomorrow.'

As we walk back across the pebbled beach, the wind blowing our hair together so it becomes intertwined, red and brown indistinguishable in the dark, I ask her, 'Are you Catholic?'

She laughs and the wind carries it away. 'No. I don't like God, remember? But he thinks I am because I'm Irish. And he is half right, I suppose. I was born a Catholic 'cos of my mum.'

I don't really understand how you can be born religious but I don't say that.

'She came over from Ireland to have an abortion, though, so I suppose she wasn't all that Catholic either. Didn't manage it, mind. Spent the money on drugs and six months later I arrived.'

I want to say 'I'm sure she doesn't hate you,' but what do I know? Maybe she does, but it still makes my heart squeeze tight at the thought of her not having a mum like mine.

'Come on,' she grabs my hand, 'race you,' and with that she's off into the dark, waves crashing onto stones, wind spraying the sea onto our faces as we stumble and fall across the beach to our home.

Twenty-one

Kelly-Anne Wilson sat huddled in her chair: head down, arms wrapped around herself as if she wanted to disappear, which Nell thought she probably did. Discarded tissues lay on the table along with an untouched cup of tea. Someone had obviously told her about Connor.

Paul nodded at the tea.

'Would you like a fresh one?'

Kelly-Anne looked at the cup as if seeing it for the first time, then shook her head. 'No thanks, I'm not thirsty.' As Paul and Nell took the seats opposite, she unfolded her arms and rested them – hands clasped – on the table.

'Thank you for coming back in and I'm sorry we didn't get to take a statement from you yesterday, we were a little,' Nell paused, 'busy.'

'You found him. That's why I was told to go home and come back. That's why you were "busy", wasn't it?'

Nell shifted under Kelly-Anne's stare. They should have been the one to tell her, not some random uniform turning up on her doorstep. But nothing she could do about that now. Mistakes happen.

'Yes, I'm afraid we did, Kelly-Anne. This morning we found Connor in a flat.'

Tears ran down her cheeks. 'How did he die?'

'I'm afraid we don't know that yet.'

'But . . .'

Nell knew what she was asking. 'We're treating his death as murder.'

Kelly-Anne froze. 'Why murder? Why do you think that?'

Nell pictured Connor's head smashed in, the letters 'A W' carved into his chest. She chose her words carefully.

'We believe Connor was struck on the back of the head with an object, which caused massive bleeding. It is probable the strike caused his death.'

Kelly-Anne watched Nell speak. Her eyes – free now from all make-up – looked painfully young and shone with an intensity that made Nell want to look away. Either Kelly-Anne was a great actor or there was no way this woman killed Connor. Hard to fake pain like that.

'Do you know who did it?' Kelly-Anne asked.

When Nell didn't reply immediately, Kelly-Anne put her hand to her mouth. 'My God, you think it's me, don't you? But I didn't –

I couldn't. I love him, so why would I?' Before Nell could speak, Kelly-Anne continued, words forming before thoughts.

'Because you think he killed the baby and I wanted revenge? But he didn't, he didn't kill my baby.'

Nell took a breath. 'But someone killed your baby, Kelly-Anne. So if it wasn't Connor . . .' She let the words settle, watched realisation dawn.

'I didn't kill Georgie.' She said it with such certainty Nell was in no doubt she meant it. And in truth, Nell had never believed she had, regardless of Eve's conclusion. That thought unsettled her for a second.

'Kelly-Anne, do you know why Connor was at flat 2, 34 Rose Way?' She watched the woman's jaw clench, her shoulders rise.

'It would be really helpful if you could have a think, let us know if Connor went there regularly.' Paul's voice was silky smooth and Kelly-Anne immediately relaxed at the sound of it.

'I never saw him go there. But people told me he did.' She looked ashamed. 'But I sort of just ignored it, you know?'

Paul nodded. 'Yeah, I get it.'

She gave a small smile. 'Like, if I said I knew, it would make it real and I didn't want it to be.'

Paul nodded. 'I get that too. Been there, done that.' He rolled his eyes, only slightly, just enough to let her know he was on her side. Man, he was good.

'So, what had people told you?'

'That he was seen going to the betting shop and then going up to the flat after.' She paused. 'They said it was his ex-girlfriend's flat.' She looked Paul in the eye. 'They said she was a prostitute.'

Paul took his time to reply. 'How did you feel about that?'

Kelly-Anne thought. 'Angry. Like, why go to a prostitute when you have me.' It wasn't said with arrogance, nor was it posed as a question, because she obviously had no desire to hear the answer.

'Have you ever met Gloria?'

Kelly-Anne tensed. 'Once. She came to our flat screaming about money he owed her. But I didn't speak to her. I just watched from the balcony while Connor talked to her.'

'And how did that end?'

'She went away. And that was that.'

'You didn't think of confronting her when you heard Connor had been visiting her flat?'

Kelly-Anne wrapped her arms around herself again. 'What would be the point?'

'Well,' Paul's tone was reasonable, 'to ask her to back off from your boyfriend?'

'No. I never talked to her. Connor said not to, so I wouldn't have.'

Nell thought that was probably right. Kelly-Anne seemed the type to do whatever Connor told her.

'Do the initials "A W" mean anything to you?' Nell asked.

'No, why?'

'It's just something we found at the flat where Connor died. We think it might be important. So, can you have another think?'

'I don't need to. I don't know anyone with those initials.'

'Not even from the pub?' Paul pressed. 'Not someone who told you about Connor going to the flat?'

Kelly-Anne shook her head, hugging herself more tightly. 'No.'

They were losing her, Nell could tell. She gave it one last shot. 'Do you know anyone called Mary?'

Kelly-Anne eyed her carefully. 'No. Why?'

Nell felt a spark of adrenalin at her wariness. 'We think a woman called Mary may be linked to Connor's death.'

'How?'

'We don't know. That's why we'd like to find her.'

Kelly-Anne paled.

'Do you know someone called Mary?' Nell repeated.

'No. I don't know anyone called Mary.'

But the way she stressed the 'know' made Nell want to keep pushing.

'Have you heard of anyone called Mary? Anyone spoken about her in your group of friends?'

'No.' She was staring at the table now, her tone almost sullen. Like a teenager, which, of course, she was.

'Kelly-Anne.' Nell waited until she looked up before continuing. 'If you know something and aren't telling us, that's perverting the course of justice. If we find out, and we will, that charge carries almost as high a sentence as murder.' She let the words sink in, watched Kelly-Anne struggle to decide – tell the cop what you know and potentially land someone else in it, or keep quiet and throw herself head first into a pile of shit. Nell knew which she'd choose – shit over a murderer any day – but then the workings of the criminal mind still managed to surprise her.

'I got a note.' Kelly-Anne looked at the floor and spoke so quietly Nell wasn't sure she'd heard right.

'A note?'

Kelly-Anne nodded.

'Who from?'

'I don't know her,' she started to say animatedly, 'it was just a note put through the door after Georgie died. I didn't see who posted it and you can't say I did, because I don't know her.' She looked at Nell almost triumphantly.

'Who was it from?' Nell repeated.

'I don't know.'

'Then why did you mention it when I asked about a woman called Mary?'

Kelly-Anne blinked, opened her mouth to speak, then shut it again.

'Well?'

Kelly-Anne sighed. 'It was signed with an "M". I don't know if that means Mary, but it made me think of the note when you said the name.'

Nell sat back in her chair. Well, that wasn't going to be a coincidence, was it? So it was probably safe to conclude that a woman called Mary had written to Eve and Kelly-Anne. That linked Connor's case to the letter writer, which she supposed was something, but Mary had been writing to Eve long before his case came along, so even though there was a link, what did it mean?

Frustrated, she listened as Paul took over.

'What did the note say?' he asked.

'She said that the woman with the white hair in our flat wasn't to be trusted and she'd say I killed Georgie when I didn't.'

Nell was starting to worry that was a pretty accurate statement of the facts.

'Anything else?'

Kelly-Anne frowned. 'I can't remember. I was dead upset when I got it.' She sounded apologetic. 'I was thinking about Georgie and all, and I didn't understand why someone would send it, so I just put it in a drawer.'

'So you kept it?'

'Yeah, it's in the flat,'

Nell leaned forward. 'We'll need to get that.'

Kelly-Anne nodded. 'But it's proof, yeah, that I didn't kill Georgie?'

Nell didn't think she'd ever heard less proof in her life, but she let it go. 'Thank you, Kelly-Anne, you've been really helpful.' She pushed her chair back.

'So I can go home now?'

The hope in Kelly-Anne's eyes almost made Nell wince. She never could decide which was worse – dealing with people so clever they ran rings round you, or with people so stupid they ran rings round themselves.

'Not yet.' She tried to sound gentle. 'We'll need to ask you a few more questions when we've seen the note.' And ignoring

Kelly-Anne's disappointment, she nodded to Paul it was time to leave.

'Poor kid,' Paul muttered as they walked back to the office.

'That "kid" watched as her boyfriend killed their baby.'

'We don't know that yet.'

'No, we know it, we just haven't got proof. Yet.'

'Still got to feel a bit sorry for her.'

'No, I really don't have to at all.'

Back in the office, Nell went over to the wipe board. 'Right,' she said, then wrote *Mary*, *Eve* and *Joanne* on the board under the names of Kelly-Anne and O'Brian.

'We've got Joanne accused of writing letters to Eve.' She drew a line between their names. 'And Mary has written to Eve.' She drew another line. 'Are two people writing to Eve, and if so, what links them?' She stood back to look at the board. 'Is the answer on here or haven't we found it yet?'

'You haven't put Gloria on there.'

Nell unclicked the pen lid. 'OK, but even so . . .' she wrote the name next to Joanne's, '. . . Gloria is only linked to Connor, not Eve, as far as we know,' she added over her shoulder.

Paul was staring at the board, looking as frustrated as she felt.

'Ever get the feeling this case is becoming less about Connor and more about Eve?' he asked.

She did. Turning back to the board, she searched it for answers. Maybe Carla and Bremer would come back with something from

Gloria, but something told her they wouldn't. No, it was here, she just had to see it.

'What about Joanne?'

She turned to Paul. 'What do you mean?'

'Well, if she's writing to Eve – she could have written to Kelly-Anne. The case is similar to the one that saw her chucked in prison.' Clocking her doubt he held up his hands. 'I know, it doesn't help us find out how this M fits in, but one tenuous link, is still a link.'

He had a point. It did link Joanne to both Kelly-Anne and Eve. Wouldn't stand up in court, mind, but they'd only just started and as it looked like it was the only lead they had, it must be worth a go.

'OK. We'll wait for Bremer to get back, see what they've got, then tell them our theory.'

'*Our* theory?' Paul looked amused.

'OK, *your* theory. I'm fine with that. If you're right I'll still get the glory, but if you're wrong I'll just sit and shake my head knowingly from the sidelines.'

'Such a supportive sergeant.'

'Always, Paul, always.'

Twenty-two
Then

'MARY!'

I am late to the café so Aoife greets me with a massive hug when I walk through the door. I smell wine on her breath and look over at Alf, who is smiling at us. A bottle sits on the table, between two glasses.

I'm unsure what to do, knowing I don't want to be here but unable to think of a way to leave. He's looking at Aoife like he wants to strip her of her red dress, and the look he gives me is more of the same.

'Come and join us,' he says, his arm over the back of Aoife's chair. She smiles at me, her eyes glassy, and I wonder how much she's had.

I hesitate. He frowns.

'What's wrong? Cat got your tongue?'

I move to the table, programmed to please. He pats a chair next to him and pours me a glass of wine before lighting a cigarette and leaning back, watching me drink. It tastes sour – dry – coating my tongue, stinging my throat.

I try to catch Aoife's eyes, to let her know we need to get out of here, but her head is leaning to one side, lids half closed. I start to panic. How will I get her home if she can't stand? We're on our last warning at the care home as it is.

Alf taps my glass. 'Drink up.'

I swallow one mouthful, then another and another until the room begins to sway away from me, or I from it. Alf is speaking to Aoife, but all I can think about is his hand on my bare leg, slowly moving upwards, the roughness of his hands grating my skin.

That night smells of onions and cigarettes, blood and semen, warm rubber discarded on a café floor. I don't say no. I lie there and hope the pain will pass, curled in on myself and waiting for it to end, knowing any move I make will only make it worse.

It doesn't take long to get used to the way things are. That's not to say we like it. We accept that our role in life amounts to this, having never been gifted the aspiration to make it otherwise. Besides, the treats improve – cake becomes drugs; hot chocolate, whisky – and thanks to the clothes Alf buys us, neither of us has ever been better dressed.

And I think we're grateful. We play the game to keep him happy, because what else is there? Back to a life of hand-me-downs and rumbling stomachs, of pitying glances from our fellow pupils at best, sneering looks at worst?

But tonight Aoife isn't playing ball. She's been odd all day, spending longer than normal in the bathroom and baulking at food she'd normally devour.

I'm on the sofa. We've long since moved on from the café to his flat, and the room is the usual blur of cigarette smoke and alcohol. My head is spinning and I grab at the frayed brown corduroy with the hope of steadying myself. Aoife is alone in the corner of the room. Even through the blur I can see her willing Alf to give her a break; her sudden realisation that all the new clothes in the world can't make up for how she's feeling right now.

'I said, come here, Aoife.' Alf is angry and it's the third time he's demanded it. I worry for a moment I'll have to do the work for both of us, but I can tell he's bored of me by now; he's turned his attention back to her. Through the smoke I can see she's frightened, and I know why: the red dress pulls around her middle, the tiniest bulge protruding over the edge of a black lace belt, threatening to reveal her secret.

I try to pull at Alf, to stop him moving towards her, but miss and fall in a heap on the floor. The threadbare carpet scratches at my skin and I shiver, suddenly aware of my nakedness. I curl up into myself as Alf reaches Aoife and shut my eyes, refusing to acknowledge her begging words.

Play the game, Aoife, I want to say, *just play the goddamn game.*

But it doesn't work, playing the game, does it? How stupid we both are: so convinced we're the captains of our own ship, we haven't seen the rocks in the dark. We haven't even bothered to look for them.

A week later Aoife joins me in bed. She pulls the covers up to her chin, her big eyes and red hair the only thing I can see.

'I haven't had my period.'

I have a vague understanding this isn't good.

'So I need to do a test.'

I nod. 'OK. That's what we'll do,' though I'm not sure of where to get one or how to get the money. 'Then—' I stop. Then what?

Aoife stares at me. The bedroom floor is surrounded by discarded clothes and cassettes, their boxes long since lost, but all I notice is that her eyes are desperate pools of hope.

'And what then?' she prompts.

I don't know, but I sense it's up to me to find out. Our relationship seems to have shifted and now I'm the one with the power. A guilty little bit of me likes it.

'We could tell the home staff?' I quickly take it back when Aoife looks ready to cry.

'Or a social worker.' I let that sit in the air before we laugh. Telling a social worker would be as bad as confiding in Alf; both options would see us kicked onto the street the second we turned sixteen, without a penny to our names and a baby in tow.

'We'll do a test and see after that.' My tone far exceeds the confidence I feel.

'How will we get the money?'

I look around the room, deciding what's best to sell, before realising there is a far better option.

'Alf. He's not going to notice a couple of quid going missing from the till. Then if we need more, if the test shows we do,' I add, 'we'll take a bit more.'

Aoife looks scared, but nods anyway, because what other option do we have? That thing's going to grow in her whatever we do, so better to run the risk of Alf's anger now instead of when it comes kicking and screaming into the world.

That night we fall asleep together, just as we did the night Aoife arrived. While she sleeps I lay my hand on her stomach and think of what our lives might become. We could run away together, I think. I'd get a job while Aoife stayed with the baby and we'd have a tiny flat far away from any sea: I picture faded pink wallpaper, against which sits a cot, a white mobile swaying gently above it. Yet when I look, the baby isn't soft and pink but red and cross, bringing with her the wrath of Alf, and as she screams I know we won't ever be free of him, however far we go.

I remove my hand and slide it under my neck. She stirs, eyes flickering, confused.

'Hold me, please?' She turns and I wrap my arm across her stomach, imagining a baby curled up inside her.

I realise I'm jealous. That baby is guaranteed Aoife's forever love, regardless of what it does or how it behaves. I've always assumed that was my role, that Aoife came to fill the gap left by my mum, but now she is going to love something more than she loves me. And in that instant, a crack appears in our bond, a tiny fissure that worms its way through my chest and into my heart, where it settles to grow in time with Aoife's baby.

Twenty-three

Opening the door, Gloria welcomed Carla and Bremer with a look of doubt. The years hadn't been kind to her. Thick foundation exaggerated the wrinkles around her eyes and mouth, and her skin, once young and plump, was now dry and blotchy.

'Come through.' Gloria gestured towards the room at the end of the narrow hallway. As Bremer walked on in front, she glanced at Carla, who gave her what she hoped was a reassuring smile.

As they sat in the cramped front room – filled with toys, and knick-knacks that Carla assumed belonged to Gloria's mum – Gloria asked her, 'Do I know you?'

Carla froze. Could she mention the previous court case? Was that allowed or would she be breaking some law she didn't know existed?

When it was obvious she wasn't going to reply, Bremer said,

'This is Carla Brown, an analyst with Thames Valley Police. I believe she provided evidence against Connor O'Brian at his trial. You may recognise her from that.'

Recognition dawned on Gloria's face. It quickly changed to concern. 'So why's she here now?'

Carla relaxed a little, relieved Gloria's memory was as vague about their meeting as Carla herself had been, though she wished her presence wasn't making Gloria twist her hands nervously in her lap.

'I asked her.' Bremer smiled. 'I thought it might be good to have a friendly face.'

'You not friendly then?'

Touché, Carla thought, but Bremer just smiled and continued.

'Gloria, we have reason to believe you rent a flat in Cowley Marsh, is that right?'

Gloria blinked, stole a look at Carla, then said, 'Yes, what of it?'

'Has Connor O'Brian visited the flat?'

Gloria opened her mouth, then shut it again.

'We don't care what you use the flat for, we just want to know about Connor.'

'No. I haven't seen him since the trial, years ago.' She shifted awkwardly on the fuchsia-coloured sofa and even Carla could see she was lying.

'Gloria,' Bremer leaned forward, his voice soft, 'Connor O'Brian was found dead at your flat this morning.' He let his words settle and they watched as Gloria's expression went from disbelief to horror, before shutting down defensively.

'I didn't kill him, if that's why you're here.'

'We don't think you did. We've seen CCTV of the woman we want to question. We just need you to tell us who she is.'

Gloria looked desperately at Carla, then back to Bremer. 'I don't know anything about it. I live here, I just dump stuff there, like a storage room,' she stalled, clearly not wanting to reveal the reason she rented it; not wanting to mention clients and paying by the hour.

Bremer looked at Carla, then stood. 'I'll go and make us tea.' One more glance at her from the door, a pointed look to tell her to take over, and he was gone. With his absence, the atmosphere lifted. Gloria visibly relaxed, and although clearly still upset, she was obviously beginning to think.

'Why was Connor in my flat?'

Carla couldn't tell if it was a genuine question or an attempt to cover her back, so she said, 'Gloria, at the moment, we don't think you killed him. But the more you lie to us, the more we may start to question that assumption.'

Gloria stared at her, eyes pleading, but Carla held the look and didn't back down.

'Ugh.' Gloria sank back in her chair. 'I'm fucked, aren't I?'

'Did you let Connor into your flat?'

'Yes.' She wiped a tear from the side of her right eye. 'Connor would come over when he'd had a fight with her.' Gloria's expression clouded. 'So I just assumed he'd had another one and let him in.'

'Have you met his girlfriend?'

Gloria snorted. 'God, no. Connor would have killed us both. Or we would have killed each other,' she added.

'Did they often argue?'

'How often did he come over, you mean?' Gloria shrugged. 'Once every few weeks.'

'And the last time he called, what did he say?'

'Just that he'd had another fight and needed a place to bunk down. I didn't stay with him, I never did, just gave him the keys and left.'

Carla doubted that. 'And he didn't say anything else about his fight with his girlfriend?'

'No. Like what?'

'I don't know. I just wanted to see if he had. Gloria . . .' Carla knew she shouldn't ask, but she had to know, '. . . why did you let Connor stay, after what he did to you?'

Gloria looked surprised. 'Because I love him.'

Such simple words.

'Even after everything he did to you and your family?'

Gloria floundered for a moment. 'I love him and I hate him, if that makes sense.'

It did.

'Did you kill him, Gloria?'

'No,' she said sharply.

'Then who was the woman that went into the flat?'

Gloria looked pleadingly at her, begging her not to make her say.

'Gloria. We need to know.'

Gloria burst into tears and it was seconds before she could

speak again. 'You don't know what it's like, trying to raise a kid on your own.' She wiped her nose on her sleeve. 'Mum helps, but she's got to work too, and I couldn't get a job, so some weeks we just couldn't eat.'

Carla dug a tissue from her bag and handed it to her. 'Go on.'

'Well, that's when I started . . . you know,' she averted her eyes, 'went on the game. And I don't regret it.' Her eyes caught Carla's, this time with a flash of defiance. 'But it was still hard. It takes a while to build up a client list and I was still struggling and Billy needed new school shoes and Mum couldn't fill the electric card, so . . .'

'So?'

Gloria exhaled, sank back into the sofa. 'So, I said OK. I mean, wouldn't you? Someone offers you £500 for one night in a flat that costs you £300 a month? How could I say no to that?' The tears began again but Gloria continued to speak. 'I didn't know she was going to kill him. How could I have known that? And I'd *never* have taken the money if I knew she would do that. I loved him,' she repeated, before falling silent.

Carla saw Bremer appear at the door. He gave her the thumbs-up, but she couldn't share his sense of victory. And as he walked over to Gloria, handing her a cup of tea, all Carla could feel was guilt.

'What was the woman's name?' Bremer sat back down in the armchair. 'The one who gave you the money?'

'I don't know, she didn't say.'

'How do you know it was a she?'

Gloria hesitated. 'I don't know, I suppose I just assumed, what with why I was using the flat . . .' She floundered, clearly not wanting to implicate herself further, keen to keep 'running a brothel' off her charge sheet.

'Did they pay you in cash or by cheque?' Bremer asked.

Carla knew the answer; a cheque was traceable, cash was not.

'Cash – it's over there in the drawer.' Gloria nodded towards a wonky-looking dresser.

'It's OK, we don't need the money.'

Carla felt a rush of gratitude towards Bremer. Gloria was going to be in for a rough time of it and that money was going to help tide the small family over, especially after her clients got wind of police sniffing round.

'How did they contact you? By phone?' Carla asked, knowing the answer would be no; phones, like cheques, were traceable.

'No, they left me a note.'

'Where?'

'It was just put through the letter box. I found it when I got home from picking up Billy.'

'Do you still have it?' Bremer asked. Gloria shook her head.

'How did you reply to them?'

'I didn't. It just said if you want £500 then leave the key in the phone box.'

'The phone box?'

'Opposite the flat. They said they only needed it for one night. Said they'd leave the money in the phone box when they left.'

'Did they say why they wanted to use the flat for one night only?'

Another shake of the head.

'And you didn't ask?'

'No.'

'So why was Connor there?'

'What do you mean?'

'Well, if the flat was to be used by someone else, why let Connor stay?'

'I got the note after he'd gone in, so I called him to tell him to get out.' She looked at Carla. 'Why didn't he leave? Why did he stay, even though I said she'd be going over?'

Carla had no answer, but it was a good point: why had Connor remained in the flat even when he knew someone was arriving? Had the woman made contact with him? She made a note to chase Connor's phone bill as soon as they were back in the office.

Bremer leaned forward. 'Gloria, would you mind coming down to the station to view a CCTV tape, just to see if you recognise a woman on it?'

'The station? Why the station?'

Bremer spoke calmly. 'Because that's where the CCTV tape is and it would help if you took a look at it for us. If the woman knew Connor was at the flat, it's likely she had been following him, in which case you might have seen her without realising it.'

Gloria turned to Carla. 'But Billy will be home soon and I've not got anyone to have him because Mum's on nights.'

Bremer looked like he was going to insist and Carla felt another stab of guilt. God, there was a reason she'd taken a desk job, and this was it.

'OK, Gloria. Nine a.m. at the station OK for you?'

Gloria looked as though she could cry with relief. 'Yes, thank you.'

Walking them to the door, she asked, 'How did he die?' Her back was to them and Carla shook her head at Bremer.

'We aren't sure yet,' he said.

Gloria spun round.

'Then how do you know he was murdered?'

'He had an injury to his head. The injury suggests it wasn't an accident.'

Carla could see Bremer was choosing his words carefully, but it did little to soften them.

'I killed him, didn't I?' she said to Carla. 'Even if I didn't do it myself, I may as well have.'

'No, Gloria, you didn't kill him.'

'But I must know the person who did, or how would they know to contact me? I can't think of anyone who would kill a person.'

Carla thought she probably did, but let it go. 'Have you noticed anyone hanging around recently, anyone you haven't recognised?'

'No.' Gloria looked desperate. 'No one.'

'Do you know anyone called Mary?'

'No!' Her voice was rising and Carla believed her. Bremer gave her a look that said they needed to get going.

'See you tomorrow, Gloria.' She really hoped Gloria would

recognise the woman in the CCTV, because the other explanation was far worse, yet it was one she kept coming back to – who would have known about the death of Connor's baby, and then had access to the resources to connect Connor to Gloria's flat, other than a police officer? And if it was an officer, Carla didn't even want to start thinking of who it could be.

Twenty-four

They met in the office for a debrief. Nell picked up the desk fan and directed it at the base of her neck. Every item of clothing stuck to her and she didn't dare to reveal her armpits because there wasn't a deodorant invented that could fight this heat.

'I want to let Kelly-Anne go.'

Nell lowered the fan and stared at Bremer. 'Why? We haven't done a second interview yet. Eve said she killed the baby and I think she saw him do it, so either way she's involved. And we haven't had enough phone data back yet to see if she's also involved in Connor's death.'

Bremer turned to Carla. 'How long for the phone intel?'

'It was a category-two request, so should be back tomorrow.'

'Couldn't you have run it as category one?' Nell snapped, brushing off the warning look from Paul.

'How? There was no threat to life. Connor was already dead.'

Nell knew Carla was right.

'Can't we hold her until tomorrow then?' Nell had given Kelly-Anne the benefit of the doubt once before and Connor had turned up dead. She didn't want to make that mistake again.

'It's no longer open for discussion, Nell.'

'I respectfully disagree with this decision, sir.'

'Noted. I'm going to let the custody sergeant know she's free to go, then how about a wind-down in the pub? I think we all deserve it, don't you?'

Nell couldn't think of anything worse, but when Paul gave an enthusiastic response she knew she'd look sulky if she refused.

'I can't, I'm afraid,' Carla said. 'I've got a date night with Baz.'

'Family first.' Bremer smiled. 'Meet the rest of you at the Jericho Tavern in half an hour.'

Nell was in the alley by the pub and wishing she was elsewhere when Bremer appeared.

'May I?' He gestured to the cigarette in her hand.

'You smoke?'

'I'm one of those irritating social smokers.'

She handed him the pack and the lighter, then watched as the flame lit up his face.

'It must have been tough.' He blew smoke into the still night air, refusing to catch her eye.

Tough? She studied his face for clues, but when he finally

looked down at her she knew instantly what he meant. She also knew she'd give anything for him not to continue, but he did.

'The stabbing.'

And there it was. Darren's face in front of her. Six foot two. Tiger tattoo on the arm holding the knife.

She'd become separated from her team so it was just the two of them in the men's toilets of a shitty little pub. She'd already had her baton up, but then he'd lunged, digging into her skin – searing pain, surprise, shouting, staring down at blood pouring like rain, falling—

Nell took a long drag of her cigarette. Why was he bringing this up now, didn't they have enough to think about?

But of course she knew why. She cursed Paul for interfering.

'Did you blame yourself for not wearing a vest,' Bremer asked, 'or the intel unit for not knowing you needed one?'

Did. Past tense. She almost laughed; nothing about that event was past tense.

'I should have worn a vest.'

'But?'

Nell stubbed out the cigarette with her boot. 'But intel didn't say I needed one.'

Bremer nodded. Took a drag. 'The analyst missed it.'

There it was.

'Yeah. I read the report before we kicked the door in. Nothing about a knife.'

She thought about the incisions he'd made in her body, always there, seen but not seen. Hard lumps of scar tissue that would never go away, though they might dull with age, hopefully like the memories.

'From what I read, they did check, but missed it.' Bremer was watching her carefully, as if judging her reaction to each word. 'They did an officer safety check, ran the address through all the databases to see if any warning signs came up, but they got nothing. Then they double-checked on description and name, linking it with drugs and the name of the pub, but again, nothing.'

Nell lit up another cigarette. She felt oddly calm even though she could see Darren's face as she fell to the ground: sneering, ugly, hate-filled. She remembered the heat around the incision, panic, hands cradling her as radios crackled.

She took another breath filled with smoke. 'So how come they missed it? Because it was there – the court case told us that.'

'It was the tattoo,' Bremer replied. 'They didn't check it. The analyst should have run it through the database, which he did the next morning, and there was the intel report that described the perp exactly. No name on the report, but the tattoo was a giveaway, so he would have linked the two. And it warned he was known to carry a weapon. A knife.' He let the words hang there, judging rightly she needed a moment to digest them.

Nell remembered when she'd finally woken up enough to understand why her body was wrapped in bandages, why the dull throb still made its way through the morphine, along with shock and fear.

'I'm sorry. I shouldn't have brought it up,' Bremer said.

Nell shook her head, 'No, I'm OK.' She paused. 'Do you

think it affects my ability to do my job? Because if that's why you mentioned it, it doesn't. Months of therapy saw to that.'

'I have no doubt that you are an exemplary officer. I just sensed an issue between you and Carla and I wondered if it had to do with past events. I need to make sure the team runs smoothly, so I'd prefer any issues to be out in the open.'

Nell felt strangely let down that his concern wasn't for her but for the team as a whole.

'And I wanted to make sure you were OK,' he added, reading her expression.

'Carla wasn't the analyst that missed it.'

Bremer didn't reply. Shit. She was going to kill Paul for being right.

'OK, I get your point. Maybe I was *subconsciously* –' she stressed the word, '– linking Carla with *past events*.' She made tiny quotation marks in the air. 'I'll keep a check on it.'

Bremer looked satisfied. 'I place a lot of emphasis on intelligence-led policing and I'm more than happy to fully include civilians in the team. I don't want that to be a problem.'

It felt like a question so Nell shook her head. 'It isn't. Carla's a good analyst.'

'She is. And you're a good detective.'

'Then why override me when I said we should keep Kelly-Anne in?'

Bremer's expression didn't change. 'Because I think Eve has a few secrets we don't know about and I think they relate to Connor's murder.' He looked down at her. 'Maybe Kelly-Anne did help kill her baby. If so, she'll go down for that. But she's not a threat to anyone else and I don't think she was a threat to Connor. Do you?'

Nell had to concede his point. 'But then which of the other suspects are a better bet?'

'Well, I'm sure things will become clearer as we progress.' And he smiled his irritating smile, although now Nell didn't seem to find it quite as irritating as she had before.

Twenty-five
Then

I'm running down the beach. It's dark, but for some reason I don't slip. I want to turn to Aoife and call back, but Alf is standing on the wall and I know he wants me to come to him.

'Mary,' she calls again and this time I stop. I look at Alf, then back to Aoife. She's so far away I can hardly see her, but in her arms I notice a blanket clutched to her chest, and the kitten-like mew from the child wrapped within it carries itself to me on the wind.

'Mary!' Alf's voice is next to me and I jump. 'She'll ruin it for us. She'll always put the baby first and when she does, you'll be left all alone. There's no turning back, Mary.' His breath hits my cheek. 'It's Aoife or me.'

I wake with a start. I have no air in my lungs and I start to panic, hunched over, clawing at the blanket on my bed as I try to pull in a breath.

'Hey, Mary, what's the matter?' Aoife looks over from her bed, my desperate noises having woken her, and she's up and over to mine when she sees I'm in trouble.

'Come on now, just calm down.' She's stroking my back and I try to focus on the rhythmic movement. It helps. I feel slivers of air run down my throat before I take a huge breath and then two more. I collapse back on the bed, panting.

'Jesus, I thought you were dying.'

'So did I.' I try a laugh but it doesn't come. Aoife lies down next to me.

'Bad dream?'

'Yeah.'

'Want to tell me?'

I shake my head. The residue of the dream hangs between us. I look at her stomach, growing bigger by the week. 'It's all going to change, isn't it? When it's born.'

She follows my eyes and puts a hand on her stomach, something she's been doing more and more. 'Well, there will be a baby, that's definitely a change.' She laughs, but when she sees my face she stops.

'I meant between us. Things will change between us.'

Aoife shakes her head, red curls emphasising her point. 'No. Nothing will change. This baby is as much yours as mine. We got into this together and we'll get out of it the same way.'

She gets up to dress and I watch her scoop clothes off the floor and I try to ignore the feeling that's recently started tap-tap-tapping in my head. I bury my face in the pillow and mumble the words just to get them out. 'I wish it hadn't happened. I wish we'd made it go away.'

But it turns out, Aoife is more Catholic than either of us thought.

In the evening we go to Alf's flat. We get ready together with the same excitement we would for a party, hair and nails done, creases on our best dresses smoothed out. Because for all the bits we don't like, we can't help but like the way our time with him makes us feel; it takes us from a world where we are a problem to be solved to one where we are princesses and told we are something special. Time stands still when we are with Alf. We have no past, no rejection, and no one expects our future to be full of failure. We are just two girls living a life we've chosen rather than the one given to us.

But tonight, as soon as we open the door, we know something feels different. Alf is on the sofa where he always is, but there is a man to his right and one at the table. We pause by the door.

'Come in, girls,' Alf calls. 'My friends have popped over.' He grins at the men. 'Hope you don't mind.'

He's in full-on Alf mode and we get swept up in his enthusiasm. We sit and watch as he jokes with his friends, take every drink offered to us, and feel the room fill with laughter and fun.

Then Alf looks at Aoife and things seem to still. His smile remains but it's changed in a way you can never point to, but you just know what lies behind it isn't good any more. He gestures to her to go to him and she obeys. He pulls her down on his lap and she laughs as he pushes her down and kisses her.

'You're so beautiful,' I hear him whisper. 'The perfect fit for me.'

The men are watching this, their eyes fixed on Aoife; they don't smile or laugh, just watch, and the way they are looking at her makes my stomach feel like it's full of bees.

Alf looks up and catches the eye of the man on the sofa, then he looks to me. I sit dead still. I don't want him to say what he's going to.

'Come and sit down over here, Mary.'

I walk across, wishing my dress was longer and my lipstick less red. The man on the sofa next to Alf smiles and suddenly I'm so relieved to see he has nice eyes just like Alf, warm and friendly. I sit next to him and smile back.

'Wow, that's a pretty smile you have there.'

I smile a bit more and he laughs.

'A right proper little Cheshire cat.'

I relax back into the sofa and look up at him. He strokes my hair and I almost close my eyes, and then I finally do when he carries on for what feels like hours.

Alf nudges me. 'Hey there, sleepyhead. Drink this, it'll perk you up.'

I sit up and take a mouthful. Knowing the acrid smell will make me gag, I concentrate on not breathing. I take another and another and within five minutes the world starts to slide away from me: I am happy and a giggle comes out of nowhere.

I struggle to focus on Alf, but I see him nod to the man next to me and I swing my head round to him. He smiles, I return it.

'Come on, you sweet, sweet thing.' He stands and helps me off the sofa. I feel his arm round my waist and I laugh because it tickles. He moves me towards Alf's bedroom and I try to turn round to see Aoife, but the man stops me.

'Come on now, you don't want to disappoint Alf, do you?'

And of course, I don't. I'd never want to do that. So I just smile again and follow him inside.

Twenty-six

The bus dropped Carla in the centre of Witney and after a short walk she pushed at their front door. Something barred her way and it was only after squeezing through the tiny gap that she saw what was causing it: Baz's overnight bag.

'Baz?' She threw her keys on the hall table. What was his bag doing there? Was he on a late call-out? But since when did that mean he took his bag?

She called again, forcefully this time, as she looked in the tiny kitchen before carrying on to the front room.

He was sitting on the sofa. The room was lit only by the street lights outside and she felt panic compress her chest. He'd found them. She was sure of it.

'Baz?'

He didn't turn, and Carla's heart began to pound high up in her chest.

When finally Baz turned to look at her, the pain and confusion in his face made her stomach lurch. And then she saw them, lying on the coffee table, a white packet bright in the gloom: her contraceptive pills.

The breath left her, as if he'd hit her, and maybe it would have been easier if he had. Words wouldn't come. She was floundering, drowning in all the words she wanted to say but which wouldn't form.

'I found these.' His voice was steady, calm, but the hand picking up the pills was shaking. 'What are they?'

Her anxiety turned into panic, thoughts running in all directions, none linear enough to make sense. How had he found them? Why had he been going through her bedroom drawer? Could she say that, turn it round to make it about him – how he had betrayed her trust?

Shame brought the thoughts to a halt. He had been betrayed, not her.

Carla searched Baz's face for a clue as to what he was thinking, something to hang on to, a beginning. All she found was confusion and hurt.

Suddenly she remembered the case by the door and felt a punch of nausea. Why had he packed a bag? Was he leaving her?

When words finally formed, they tumbled out of her.

'I'm so sorry. I wanted to tell you, I really did, but the longer I took the harder it became. And I didn't want to upset you by telling you I'm just not ready for a baby – not yet, I mean.' She stopped. There, it was out, and despite the pain of seeing Baz so crushed, she couldn't help but feel relief.

'So it *is* the pill then, the contraceptive pill?'

'I do want a baby, I just don't want one yet. My job is going really well, I'm on a new team that's starting to come together, and . . .' She paused again, unsure how to go on, but then panic hit and she retched. Bending over close to the floor, she tried to regain her breath, to keep the vomit from coming, while Baz silently watched her.

When she finally looked up he threw the pills on the table next to three empty beer bottles. How long ago had he found them? How long had he been sitting here alone, wondering what he'd done to deserve such a betrayal?

'But we've been trying, Carla, trying for a baby.'

His confusion made her chest constrict again.

'We've been trying to make a baby and each month it hasn't happened I've worried it's me, that I'm not going to be able to give you the child you want, and yet all this time, *all this time*,' he emphasised, 'you knew that wasn't true – none of it was true. And what does it *mean*?' His voice rose. 'That you never want a baby? Or is it just that you don't want a baby with me?'

'How could you think that? How could I not want a baby with you? You're kind and loving and patient and funny . . .' She reached over to him, but he pulled back; the rejection felt like a slap.

'Of course I want a baby with you,' she continued, desperate to persuade him, to convince him it wasn't him, it was her. 'And I was coming home to tell you, to tell you about the pills, to explain I just don't want one *now*.'

'How do I know? How do I know anything you say is true any more? You could be shagging half of Thames Valley for all I know.'

'Baz!' How could he accuse her of that? She felt the conversation spiralling out of control and tried to pull it back. 'Baz. Come on. Don't you think you're overreacting a bit? I'm just not ready yet, that's all.'

'That's *all* ? You lie to me for months and "that's all"? And I'm "overreacting"?' he shouted.

They stared at each other. A stand-off. Then he stood. 'I'm going to Mum's.'

She panicked: what would his mum say? Would she make him understand? Tell him he was being ridiculous and to go back home? Or would she hate Carla like Baz now did?

She followed him down the hall, emotions burning away all pride. 'Please don't go. Stay and we'll get wine and a takeout and talk things through. *Please*, Baz.' The panic surged as he reached for his bag. She couldn't let him leave. Whatever happened, she had to stop him leaving. She reached to take hold of his arm. 'Please, surely we can get over a small packet of pills?'

His back was to her but he paused. She grabbed the opportunity. 'I love you, Baz. We'll have hundreds of kids one day. You, me, kids . . . them running across the beach while your mum and you chase them and I hide under a sunshade.' She tried to conjure up all the dreams they'd made, the future memories they'd already created. If she could just piece together the right words, he wouldn't leave. 'Please stay – we can talk about it, work it out. I'll stop taking the pill.' But even as she spoke, she knew it was the one word she shouldn't have said.

Shaking off her grip, Baz reached for the latch, and before she could get any more words out he'd walked out of the flat and slammed the door shut between them.

Twenty-seven

Nell hadn't slept well. Bremer's mention of her attack had given her subconscious free rein, and a morning call from him telling her to bring Joanne in for writing a few dodgy letters had done nothing to improve her mood. By the time they reached the interview room, her scars were itching, her head was pounding and as the room had no windows or air conditioning, she was sweating before she'd even finished the caution.

Joanne sat with her hands clasped between her legs, the shock of being brought to the station still evident.

'I just don't understand why I'm here. I told your DCI I didn't write any letters.'

'Where were you the night before last, Ms Fowler?'

'I was with my husband all night. Why?'

'And he'll confirm this?'

'Of course!'

'And what did you have for dinner?' Nell asked.

'Dinner? I can't remember. Probably pasta. It's all I can really cook.' She gave Paul a Princess Diana flutter of the lashes, which he returned with a smile. Nell looked at him in disgust. Jesus, men were so gullible, even six-foot, built-like-a-brick-shithouse cop ones.

'So you had this pasta, the one thing you can cook, and then went to bed after watching two television programmes?'

Joanne nodded.

'Who fell asleep first?'

'I don't know. Me, I think.'

'And did you wake before morning?'

'I always wake during the night. I go downstairs and have a drink of water, then go back to bed. It's sort of a routine.'

'Does your husband notice when you wake and go down-stairs?'

'No, never. He sleeps like the dead.' She froze, but whether that was due to the poor turn of phrase or because she'd given the game away, Nell couldn't tell.

'I didn't creep out and murder anyone, if that's what you're getting at.' She was irritated now and that was good; irritated people weren't in control; irritated people made mistakes.

'Did you know a Mr O'Brian?'

'No.'

'You didn't come across him when you left a note for Kelly-Anne?'

Joanne looked confused. 'What note? I didn't write a note.' She looked at Paul. 'And I didn't write any letters.'

'The note said,' Nell went on, causing Joanne to look back across at her, 'that Ms Graham was going to say Kelly-Anne killed her baby and she wasn't to believe it. Its tone,' she continued, despite Joanne opening her mouth to speak, 'was identical to the tone of the letters Ms Graham received from you.'

Joanne sighed again and leaned back in her chair. 'I've said it enough times now – I didn't write those letters.'

'But you know there are letters, plural? When DCI Bremer spoke with you we only had knowledge of one.'

'I know because you just told me.'

'Who is Mary?'

Joanne stared at her. 'What?'

'The letters were signed by "Mary" and the note by "M". So who is Mary?'

Joanne's expression turned from confusion to fear in a matter of seconds.

'I don't know anybody called Mary.' Her voice wobbled as she spoke and she clutched her cardigan tightly around herself.

My God – was Mary a pseudonym? Nell glanced to Paul and could see he saw it too. She decided to go in hard.

'Ms Fowler, why are you sending letters to bereaved parents and using a pseudonym to do so? Isn't that a bit insensitive, in light of your own bereavement?'

Joanne looked as though she could launch across the table and grab Nell by the throat, which was exactly the reaction she'd wanted.

'The fact I know how it feels to have a baby die is exactly the reason I wouldn't write such a note. I am not here to bring additional pain to another mother.'

'What are you here for then? To get revenge on Ms Graham?'

'I'm here because you dragged me in here. I can assure you I've seen a lifetime's worth of interview rooms, and I don't welcome the fact I'm now back in one because of your stupid assumption I'm someone called Mary.'

'*Are* you Mary?'

Joanne looked confused. 'What?'

'You said I think you *are* Mary. But I merely said I thought you were using the name Mary to distance yourself from the threats made against Ms Graham. The two are very different.'

Joanne contemplated her for a moment before replying. 'My name is, and has always been, Joanne.'

'And your surname before you were married?'

'Rathbone.'

'And where did you grow up?'

'Portsmouth.'

Nell nodded. 'Nice. By the sea.'

Joanne shrugged. 'It was OK.'

'Were you close to your parents?'

'What has this got to do with anything?'

'Just answer the question, please.'

'Not really. I was adopted because they thought they couldn't have kids, but when they had two of their own they forgot about me.'

It was a frank admission and took Nell by surprise.

'I'm sorry about that.'

'I doubt you are, Sergeant.'

'Can you tell me your parents' names and those of your siblings?'

'None of them are called Mary, if that's what you're looking for.'

Nell smiled. 'Just the names please,' then noted them as Joanne spoke.

'Thank you. Do you happen to know what name you were given at birth?'

Joanne stared at her, horrified, and even Paul shifted a little uncomfortably in his seat.

'Well?'

'I haven't seen my birth certificate.'

Nell doubted that was true. 'What about your husband?'

'What about him?'

'Does he share your obsession with Ms Graham?'

'He blames her as much as I do, if not more, if that's what you mean.'

'He was very supportive of you during that time. Must have been hard on him.'

Joanne nodded. 'He had to cope with losing our baby and losing me. It was a difficult time.'

'So in a way he probably resents Ms Graham even more than you do?'

Joanne remained silent.

'What does he do?'

'He's a car salesman.'

'Has he ever sold a car to O'Brian?' Nell joked.

Joanne glared at her.

'He must feel guilty you had to go through that when he didn't.'

'Maybe, I don't know. He never doubted me for a moment. He knew I would never kill our child, not after we tried so hard to have one.' Tears threatened to fall. Nell let them ferment for a moment.

'I'd feel guilty if it was me. I think the hate would grow and grow until maybe I lost it one day and bashed someone's head in.'

Joanne opened her mouth to speak, then shut it. Folding her arms across her chest, she stared accusingly at Nell, who didn't care. There was something not right, but try as she might, Nell just couldn't picture Joanne having it in her to kill O'Brian. Too delicate. So there was only one other person who hated Eve as much as Joanne did and that was her husband. Had he done it to frame Eve? Down the line, were they going to find some evidence he had planted to make them think it was Eve? Good revenge that – make her go to prison for a crime she didn't commit, just like his wife.

'Did you ever wonder whether it was your husband who killed your child?' Nell knew she was going a bit far – Paul's look told her as much – but she had a train of thought now and it wasn't going to stop. 'If it wasn't you, could it have been him? Did you ever consider that possibility? And maybe the guilt of that is what's really eating him up?'

'No, because neither of us killed our baby. She went to sleep and never woke up, and Eve Graham lied to make me guilty.'

Nell wanted to ask *why?* Why the hell would a respected and career-driven woman like Eve frame a grieving mother for murder? But she knew she'd lost Joanne now. All further questions would be met with a stony silence. Nell had been in enough interviews to know when she'd fucked up and in her considered opinion, she'd done so royally in this one.

'Thank you, Mrs Fowler. Interview is terminated, you are free to go.' And ignoring the looks of surprise from Paul and Joanne, Nell got up and left the room.

Twenty-eight
Now

All I seem able to think about now is Alf. I try to picture him sitting in his cell for what he did to me and Aoife. Or maybe he's out now and living his life again, undeterred by what he turned us into. Maybe – and the thought makes me turn ice-cold – he's walking past my door and I don't even know it, or watching me from the corner of the street.

Would I recognise him? The face he used to have is burned into my dreams, soaking me in sweat as I wake screaming, but the one he has now may be different, thinner perhaps after years eating prison food, or fatter from the lack of exercise. I think back to the last time I saw him, standing in the dock as the judge sent him down, the words ringing through the courtroom, and I remember feeling nothing but guilt for being the cause of it.

'This has been,' the judge said, 'the most depraved case of

child cruelty and exploitation I have ever come across. You subjected these girls to months of abuse, but worse, you manipulated them to think you cared for them when in fact you were using them as one would a toy. You preyed on the most vulnerable children you could find and then shared them around like bags of sweets without one thought for their happiness, only for your own depraved gratification.'

I had wanted to scream, 'No, he did care!' because right then the idea he didn't, after everything that had happened to Aoife, was too much to bear. I thought I'd lost her and I couldn't stand to lose him too.

It took me years to finally accept what sort of man Alf was. To accept I had allowed him to treat me like that because no one had thought to tell me I was worth more, and longer still to feel I was. So it angers me to have him back in my life, my days filled with thoughts of him, and even Aoife can't stop the waves of hate when they hit.

I stand and pick up my coat. Men like Alf deserve to die. Just as men like Connor deserve to die, and if the law can't protect women like me and Aoife I'm happy to take on that role. But first I need to deal with Eve. The letters haven't worked, she hasn't even had the decency to respond, so I don't care any more; I don't care what her husband told me or how much he begged me to bide my time. I'm going to write Eve one more letter, and this time I'm going to hand deliver it myself.

Twenty-nine

Carla had been at her desk for three hours. She'd finally given up on sleep and decided she would distract herself with work. But looking at her empty notepad, she might as well have stayed in bed.

She typed Eve's name into the intel database and noted every job she'd worked on in the last ten years in which a dead baby was involved: five in total, including the O'Brian case.

Carla opened each case file and scanned the text: infant found dead, parents accused, mother convicted. All serving prison terms of varying lengths, from two to seven years, depending on the severity of the child's injuries.

Was it statistically likely that all five deaths would've been unnatural and that in each instance it was the mother who was found guilty? She'd have to check Eve's ratio of female convictions against stats from other pathologists to be sure, but still, wouldn't at least one of the five couples have experienced the sad yet natural death of their child? One would surely be innocent. But then she supposed that's what Joanne was arguing: she was that one innocent woman.

Carla scanned the files, taking a mouthful of cold coffee brought in from home. Each one seemed pretty standard: pathologist file attached, judge's comments at the end. She checked again. No, she was wrong, one of the reports was missing. She checked the case. Shit. Joanne. Why was the pathologist's report missing from Joanne's case but was attached in all the others?

She felt a rush of adrenalin – what if Joanne was right and Eve *had* faked her reports to apportion blame to the parents? But why on earth would someone do that? It seemed an extraordinarily cruel thing, and even if she had, why would Eve remove just one report from the files and not all of them?

Frustrated, she saw Bremer coming and wondered if she should run it by him now or wait for the debrief. The look on his face as he walked into the office told her it should be the latter.

'I've got Eve to come in, but my God it was hard work.' He threw his leather briefcase on the floor and sat down. 'Gerry was determined she shouldn't come to the station. "She's a pathologist," he kept saying, as if pathologists have the right to some sort of special treatment. He's in the job, for God's sake, so he knows full well we have to cover all bases, and anyway,' he rolled up his shirtsleeves, 'Eve doesn't exactly strike me as the kind of woman who needs a minder.'

Carla almost laughed. But she didn't. 'He just loves her, I guess.'

'Enough to argue with a superior officer for twenty minutes?'

Twenty minutes? Gerry really mustn't have wanted Eve to be brought in. 'Maybe he's worried about the risk of upsetting her when we mention the miscarriages?'

Bremer sighed in clear frustration. 'Possibly. Anyway, I want you in on the interview. Nell and Paul are with Joanne and it might help Eve loosen up a bit if she's there with someone she knows.'

Carla doubted anything much could loosen Eve up, and she was irritated to be rolled out as the friendly face of the force yet again, but she knew Bremer well enough not to bother arguing. 'Sure,' she said, 'just let me know when she arrives.'

Eve accepted the coffee with a sharp nod, took a sip, and didn't wince at the heat. 'White, one sugar – well done.'

Bremer got straight to the point. 'Eve, we understand you have been receiving threatening letters?'

'Plural? I gave you one.' She smiled, then stopped almost immediately. She looked to Carla. 'Oh, Gerry. I suppose he gave them to you?'

Carla nodded.

'We have Joanne Fowler in the station now,' Bremer said.

Eve turned back to him, not bothering to hide her surprise. 'Because of the letters? I really don't think it justifies that. I'm quite able to handle it myself. And anyway, how do you know she wrote them?'

'Not just about the letters, about the murder of Connor O'Brian too.'

'But what has that got to do with my letters?'

'We are pursuing a line of enquiry which suggests Joanne wrote a note to Connor's partner, Kelly-Anne, telling her you were going to falsify your report in order to make it appear she killed baby Georgie.'

'Did she now.' Eve took a sip of the coffee and nodded, more to herself than them. 'And you know this how?'

'Pardon?'

Eve placed her coffee on the table. 'How do you know she wrote the note? Have you had it tested for fingerprints? Done forensics on the ink used or the handwriting?'

'Not yet, no. As you are aware, forensics in a murder inquiry can often lag behind the real-time investigation.'

'So you don't know she wrote them. But you've dragged the woman in here anyway. That's what you're telling me.'

Why was Eve defending the woman threatening her? 'Is there a reason you don't want us speaking with Joanne?' she asked.

'Of course I have a reason.' Eve looked as if it should be self-evident. 'I made the biggest mistake of my career. That woman suffered because of it and now, quite understandably in my opin-ion, harbours a deep sense of injustice, which she, again rightly, directs at me. You bringing her to a police station, only months after she was released from what I imagine was a living hell, is only going to make matters far worse for all concerned.'

Bremer considered her for a moment. 'But if she is writing the letters, why don't you want her caught?'

Eve tipped her head back, clearly frustrated. 'Caught for what, exactly? Using a pen? It's not a crime I'm familiar with.'

'Do you know the identity of the person writing the letters?'

Eve folded her arms. 'No.'

'And why didn't you report them to the police?'

Eve studied him before speaking. 'They contained personal information I didn't want thrown into the gossip mill. If you must know.'

Carla braced herself for Bremer to mention the miscarriages, but instead he said, 'OK. So back to Connor. Could you tell me where you were the night he was killed?'

Eve looked taken aback. She'd clearly also been expecting a different question. 'In the lab.'

'People there with you?'

'No. But the signing-in book will show I was there.'

Carla knew all that showed was someone had signed in and out, not that it was Eve. Bremer would want more than that.

'CCTV at the lab?'

'Are you doubting my word, Detective Inspector?'

'Detective *Chief* Inspector.'

'I stand corrected. And yes, there is CCTV.'

'Good.'

Eve studied Bremer for a couple of seconds before speaking again. 'Why do you think I would kill Connor, Detective Chief Inspector? Why would I waste my time on scum like him?'

The words felt aggressive in the confined space. Carla glanced at Bremer, but he seemed unfazed.

'Scum,' he said. 'You surmised that from the brief time you saw him?'

'You're telling me you don't know a criminal when you see one?'

'Maybe. But I'm a policeman and you're not. Why did you think he was scum?'

Eve leaned towards the table. 'Because he murdered his child, Detective *Chief* Inspector. If someone like that isn't scum, I don't know who is.' She held his stare for three seconds before leaning back and folding her arms. The tension was almost unbearable. Carla glanced nervously to Bremer, who was looking unwaveringly at Eve.

'I was under the impression you told Sergeant Jackson you believed the mother had killed the child?'

'Yes. And I still maintain that.'

'But you just said Connor did.'

When Eve next spoke, it was as if to a small child.

'It was self-evident. The man had clearly groomed the poor girl to be with him. I mean, she was, what, seventeen?'

When Bremer didn't reply she continued.

'The man clearly targets vulnerable young women. He'll have form for it, no doubt, and he'll probably have a history of domestic violence.'

Carla flinched. Eve nodded to her, acknowledging she was right.

'He moved on to a younger model and controlled her to the extent she questioned her sanity: "Did I come on to that bloke?" "Was I really to blame for the argument because I didn't put the washing out right?" Men like O'Brian thrive on that shit. They don't always know they're doing it, but they make sure the woman they are with is crushed. She cannot put anything above him, and that includes a child.' Eve paused and Carla could see she was trying to check herself, bring her feelings to heel. When she resumed speaking, her voice was level.

'Men like O'Brian see a child as a threat to their control of the woman they're with. If she puts the child's needs above his own, he feels ignored, pushed out. Kelly-Anne may have killed her child, but she did it because Connor wanted her to. He might not have explicitly stated it – he'd have given her little cues she knew how to read. Codes, if you will. That's why Connor is scum.'

Carla couldn't fault her argument, but she'd never felt comfortable about writing someone off. Was the world a better place without Connor? Possibly. But not for the people who loved him, however misguided they were thought to be. Finding Connor's murderer wasn't just about justice for him, but for those left behind. Gloria would never fill the hole in her heart left by his death and whilst Kelly-Anne was young enough to find a new man, Carla doubted she'd ever see life the same way again. Their grief deserved an ending so their new lives could begin, and Carla wasn't sure Eve got that aspect of justice at all.

'You seem to be quite invested in the O'Brian case. Do you often get emotionally involved?' Bremer asked.

'Oh please. I'm not being emotional. I work with facts and the fact in this case is that Connor coerced Kelly-Anne into killing their child.'

'I'm not sure the Fowlers would agree you only work with facts.'

Eve's stare grew colder, blue eyes unblinking.

'Do I need a lawyer, Detective *Chief* Inspector?'

Bremer smiled before replying. 'No, of course not. I think we're done here now. You're free to go.'

And with that, it was over.

Thirty

Then

It's Alf who hears about the social workers first.

'They are sniffing around – why?' He's pacing the café but stops to put the question to us. I feel myself shrink back.

'What do you mean?' Aoife asks.

'Why are social workers getting it into their heads something is wrong with the pair of you?'

I'm suddenly angry he's suggesting it's somehow our fault. What did he think was going to happen when we rocked up at the care home off our faces at two in the morning? But as quickly as it comes, the anger goes, replaced by a chest-gripping fear they'll stop us seeing him.

'How should I know?' Aoife replies. 'They haven't bothered us for years, so I haven't a clue why they're bothered now.'

I think of my social worker – Harriet – how nice she is and

how much I like our sessions together. She reminds me this is all just temporary, that even though it feels like no one loves me, or I'll always be the one with hand-me-down clothes and the 'special ticket' for school lunches, I can be more than this.

And then I remember. When I was with Harriet last week she'd mentioned my dress, one Alf had bought me.

'It's very pretty,' she'd smiled.

I'd smoothed over the soft material. 'It is, isn't it.'

'Where did you get it?'

I didn't know which shop, so I said, 'It was a present.'

'How lovely.' Another smile. 'Who from?'

I'd panicked. 'My mum. She left it for me to make up for missing me so much.' The lie hurt because I'd wanted it to be true. I fiddled with the dress, avoiding Harriet's stare, knowing she knew it wasn't true. I hated my mum at that minute, hated her for making me sit in the office where a woman judged me for my lies, and pitied me.

'Mary,' Harriet eventually said, 'workers at the home have said you and Aoife have been getting a lot of nice clothes recently.'

I stayed silent.

'They are worried about you both.'

Anger built. No one was worried about us, that was a lie, they barely checked we got home at night. They were jealous of the clothes, that was all. Jealous because the money they got to be zookeepers wasn't enough to get them nice things like me and Aoife had.

Harriet had sighed. 'OK then, Mary. Let's meet again next week. But please take care of yourself.'

I'd bolted from the room. I should have gone and told Aoife they were suspicious, but my anger got in the way. I ran home, consumed with hatred for my mum, dad, the care-home staff, but mostly for myself for being so worthless that all I deserved was pity from a woman paid to look after me.

So, by the time I got back to our room, I'd forgotten about the clothes and what Harriet had said. I only remember when Alf talks about the social workers, and watching Alf's anger, I'm not about to mention it now.

Alf stops pacing. 'OK, we'll just be more careful. The police aren't going to be interested in a pair of girls like you.' He isn't looking at us so doesn't see Aoife flinch at the truth of his words.

'So it will blow over in a couple of weeks.' He turns to look at us, his face set, tight. He points at each of us in turn. 'They ask you anything, you stay quiet, yeah?'

We nod. His eyes flash – disgust, hate, I can't tell.

'One word you've talked to the police and I'll find you and kill you, got it?'

We nod again. Both desperate to show him we wouldn't; both equally certain he would.

Thirty-one

'Eve is hiding something. I just know it.' But what? That was what Nell couldn't figure out.

'Do you think Eve knows who wrote the letters?' Paul asked Carla.

'She seemed sure it wasn't Joanne, but other than that I couldn't say.'

'I'm going to stick my neck out and say she does.' Bremer was tapping his pen on the desk. Nell wished he wouldn't. She was irritated enough as it was.

'Are we any further with Connor's phone bills?' she asked.

Carla shook her head. 'I'll chase.'

'And when you do, ask for Eve's and Joanne's phone bills, so we can see if they have been in contact.' Nell turned to Bremer. 'I want to go and check out the husband. I can't think of better revenge than getting the woman you hate wrongly convicted for murder, and car salesmen are dodgy as hell.'

'Generalisations, Nell,' Bremer warned, but he looked interested. 'OK, you and Paul do that, Carla check for calls and dig some more on Joanne and Eve. See if there's anything in their backgrounds that suggests a connection prior to Joanne's arrest.'

But Nell was out the door before he'd finished speaking.

The showroom, selling every make of car imaginable, was on an industrial estate right by the station. They found Ian Fowler sitting behind a large glass desk in a room filled with shiny new BMWs, and the frosty reception they received told Nell he knew they were police.

'DS Jackson, DC Mackintosh. We'd like to have a few words about your wife, if that's OK.'

'No, that's not OK. I'm at work and it's not going to be a selling point having a couple of coppers here.'

Nell smiled and looked around the empty showroom. 'Well, you're very welcome to come down the station – you know where it is, after all.'

Ian looked thunderous. 'If anyone comes in, we stop, got it?'

Nell didn't reply, just took a seat.

'Frankly, I'm surprised the police have the resources to bother so much about a couple of letters. But then,' he clasped his hands together, the tips of his index fingers touching, 'she's one of your own, isn't she? So I imagine you can find the money for that.'

'We're not here about the letters.'

Ian's face grew hard. 'I see. So what are you going to fit my wife up with now?'

'Murder, actually.' Nell got it, but his attitude was still annoying her. 'What was your wife doing two nights ago, Mr Fowler?'

Ian glared at her before reeling off a description of that night that matched Joanne's almost word for word. Working together, then, Nell thought.

'Your wife said she often wakes at night.'

'That often happens when you've had a bereavement, especially one whose subsequent police action denies the time to grieve.'

'Do you wake when she does?'

'No, not always,' he replied. 'I suppose I've got used to it.'

'So if she left the house that night, you might not have noticed?'

'I assume you mean "if she left the house to kill a man"? In which case, I think I would have noticed her returning covered in his blood, don't you?'

'We didn't say the victim was a man, Mr Fowler. Nor did we mention blood.'

Ian waved his pencil dismissively. 'Murder always involves blood. Unless you're in an Agatha Christie novel where the butler uses poison, or whatnot. And I just reverted to default when I mentioned gender. But hey,' he held his hands up, 'arrest me for misogyny if you must.'

He was good, Nell had to give him that.

'Do you know Connor O'Brian?'

Ian frowned. 'No, why would I?'

'He's never bought a car from here?'

Ian stared at her. 'I'd have to check my records.'

'That would be very helpful, thank you.'

'Seriously?' His tone was scornful.

'Seriously.'

'For God's sake. Fine. I'll check my records. This is going to start to look like police harassment if you're not careful, Sergeant.'

'I'll be sure to bear that in mind. Would you say you were a supportive husband, Mr Fowler?'

'My wife spent years in jail for a crime she didn't commit, and I fought every day to get her out so she could be allowed to grieve for her the death of our child. I'd say that was supportive, wouldn't you?'

'If something was bothering Joanne, you'd do what you could to help her, yes?'

'Of course.'

Nell nodded. 'Does your wife know anyone called Mary?'

Ian's jaw tensed, a tiny move, but Nell clocked it.

'Not that I'm aware of.'

'A friend she met in prison maybe?'

'My wife didn't make friends in prison. They don't take kindly to child killers in there.'

Nell thought he was probably right. 'I suppose they all felt a little bad when they found out she was innocent.'

'I bloody hope so. They made her life hell. She was in there with murderers, for God's sake.'

'Handy set of contacts to have, one might say, especially if they felt they owed your wife a favour.'

'So you've gone from thinking I killed this O'Brian person to make her happy to saying she hired a hitwoman to do the job for her? I'd stop fishing if I were you and come back when you know what you're talking about.'

'Did you or your wife know Ms Graham prior to the death of your child?'

'Don't be ridiculous.'

'Answer the question, please.'

'No. I'd never seen Ms Graham in my life before the day my daughter . . .' he paused, stumbling on the word, '. . . died.'

'And your wife?'

Ian's eyes flashed with an anger so vicious Nell thought for a moment he was going to lunge across the desk and hit her. She felt Paul tense.

'No. My wife had never met Ms Graham before.'

'To your knowledge,' Nell corrected.

'Why would she not tell me if they'd met before? And more importantly, why do you seem so convinced they had?'

'Well, I've always thought it a little odd your wife should become so fixated with the pathologist who gave evidence against her. I mean, even if Ms Graham was wrong and this resulted in your wife going to prison, well, people make mistakes.' She shrugged, deliberately irritating him, wanting him to lose more control so he slipped up.

'Why not just ask for an apology,' she continued, 'go through the proper routes for compensation? Then these accusations could stand up and be scrutinised, as could the actions of Ms Graham.'

Ian watched her, stony-faced. She hadn't got him yet, so she went on.

'I just wondered if maybe her grudge goes beyond the fact of her imprisonment.'

Ian remained silent.

'Your wife was adopted, wasn't she?'

No reply.

'Does she know anything about her birth parents?'

'No. And she has no desire to find them.'

That you know of, Nell silently added.

'And besides, she has a very loving and supportive family right here. Me.'

'I'm sure she does. But the urge to know where you come from is probably a hard one to fight. Might she have looked into her history without telling you?'

'Joanne tells me everything.'

'Really? Well maybe she didn't want to upset her family. Maybe that's when she met Mary?'

'There is no Mary!' Ian was shouting now. 'Leave Mary out of it.' He stood. 'I'd like you to leave. Neither my wife nor I have had anything to do with O'Brian's death and we haven't written any letters to that woman. Maybe you should ask her about all this, seeing as she's so good at writing false reports. She would probably find writing a couple of letters to herself a breeze.'

'Why would she write the letters herself?'

'Why would she write a false report accusing Joanne of killing our child?'

'I'm sure Ms Graham wrote up what she believed to be true from the evidence she saw.'

Ian leaned across the desk and placed his hands close to Nell. She didn't move.

'The reason we won the appeal was because that report magically went missing. So they had to examine the evidence again and lo and behold, everything she'd written in the report was a lie.

'Now I have nothing more to say on the matter and in future, should you wish to speak to me or my wife, we will require a lawyer.'

Thirty-two
Then

We sit holding hands, Aoife and I, while the first police officer speaks and the second looks on with bored indifference. Turns out the police did care about us after all and I don't know if we are more scared of them or of Alf when he finds out.

'Do you know Alf Waites?' the officer asks. The interview room feels hot, claustrophobic. The smell of smoke seems ingrained in the wooden edges of the worn tables, and the stale stench of previous occupants permeates every pore.

We nod.

'How did you meet him?'

Aoife squeezes my hand. 'He owns a café we go to, by the front.'

'Do you spend a lot of time there?' He smiles, trying to disguise the importance of the question.

'Yes, after school mostly. Why do you want to know?'

'Your social workers have raised a few concerns over the . . .' he pauses, '. . . relationship you have with Mr Waites.'

'There's nothing wrong with it. He's a friend. We are allowed friends, you know.'

'Were you ever there alone with him after closing? Or say, at his flat?'

I freeze. How could the social workers know we go there? I try to think of anything we could have done to give the game away, but we always look clean, we don't have bruises and we don't skip much school. And anyway, why do they care – being at Alf's means that we're out most of the time, so surely that's two less problem kids to deal with?

Our hands feel hot, sweat sticking them together. The policeman repeats his question. 'Do you ever go to Mr Waites's house?'

'Sometimes.' Aoife's tone is guarded and rightly so, as I catch a flicker of interest in the second officer's face. I give Aoife a look to warn her, but whether she doesn't see or she doesn't care, I don't know.

'Are you ever there alone with just Alf?'

'Yes. What of it?' Aoife replies.

I've heard that tone so many times before I know it means the mist has come down, that whatever happens next is not going to be under her control.

'What did you do when you were there after closing?'

Aoife takes her hand out of mine, leans across the table. 'Fuck,' she spits.

The lack of shock on the police officers' faces should tell us something, but all I can think is, *Aoife, don't ruin it. Don't take it away from us by telling. They'll separate us and I'll be alone again.*

The police officer asks more questions but by now Aoife's anger has made her mute and the fear in my belly has rendered me the same. What is Alf going to say? Will they arrest him? Will he send people to hurt us because we told? But then I have a thought – it wasn't me who told. I was asked by Harriet and I didn't say a word. I did what he asked; it was Aoife who didn't, she is the one to blame.

And in that second, the seed of doubt which has been growing with the baby – the fear she will love me less, the baby more – turns into a gap, just a chink, but I know it can grow to divide us: me one side, Aoife the other, Alf in the middle. Which way will I jump – towards her, or him? And sitting here in the stuffy room with two leering policemen staring at us like specimens in a jar, panic tearing at my heart, I don't think I know.

Thirty-three

Needing nicotine, Carla headed outside, but as she turned the corner by the entrance to HQ she saw Eve standing there. Deep in thought, she was leaning against the wall staring upwards, a cigarette held loosely by her side. Shit. She'd have to ditch the idea and come back later, but just as she was about to turn back, Eve looked over and raised a hand of acknowledgement.

'Carla,' she called over, 'come and join me. Lung cancer is far more palatable when it has company.'

With no way to get out of it, Carla walked across and accepted the offer of a lighter.

'That DCI of yours is a charmer, isn't he?' She stared down at Carla. 'Don't go falling for his smile, Carla Brown.'

'I won't. He's OK really. Just a bit . . .' She searched for the right word.

'Arrogant,' Eve decided for her.

'Yeah. Well, he is ex-Met.'

Eve raised an eyebrow and blew smoke upwards. 'Is he now. Well that explains it then.' She gave Carla a smile before taking another drag. 'I'm sorry if you found that awkward, in there.' She nodded towards HQ. 'Put you in a difficult position I would imagine.'

'Because I'm friends with Gerry, you mean?'

Eve looked surprised. 'And me, I presume?'

Carla wanted to crawl away and hide. God, the woman intimidated her. It would never have occurred to Carla that Eve would want a friend, let alone her.

'Yes, sorry . . . it's just, I mean . . .'

'I know what you mean.' Eve patted Carla's arm, but it was more of a 'stand down' gesture than affection.

'You've been Gerry's pet project since day one. Loves a project, does my husband.' She paused for a drag. 'And I suppose I was just along for the ride.' She smiled again.

God, Carla wanted this to be over. It was far easier to deal with standoffish Eve than this warmer version.

'And it's been nice for Gerry.' She looked down at Carla. 'I think he's enjoyed helping someone other than me.'

'How does he help you?' She hadn't meant to ask, but it would never have occurred to her Eve needed help.

'Without him I wouldn't be where I am now – in my profession, I mean. I was so determined to make it and at first he wasn't convinced, but when he saw I wasn't giving up, he threw everything into it, just like me.' She stubbed out her cigarette and pulled out another. 'Dirty double.' She gave Carla a wink and flicked open the lighter. 'It's a big thing for a man to do that.' She sounded thoughtful. 'Whatever they say, men mostly want their wives to be less successful than them. It's the mothering issue – they all expect you to keep their lives running smoothly while they do the "real" work. Otherwise they get jealous and that sort of resentment just keeps getting bigger.'

Carla laughed. 'I can't imagine Gerry being jealous, it doesn't seem his style.'

Eve frowned. 'No. I don't think he has ever displayed that emotion.' She sighed. 'I really wish he hadn't shown you the letters. There was no need and all it's done is further aggravate Ms Fowler – unnecessarily,' she added.

'But surely that was the obvious conclusion to draw? That Joanne wrote the letters?'

'Maybe, but obvious doesn't always equate with right, now does it?'

Carla had to concede. 'What did you hope we would conclude?'

'I'm not sure I know. And really it was Gerry who first suggested the idea I tell you. He doesn't like keeping secrets, least of all from you.' She stubbed her cigarette out as Gerry rounded the corner in his car.

'Here's my ride,' Eve said as Gerry pulled to a stop and rolled down the window, giving Carla a wave.

Eve looked down at Carla and smiled. 'See you soon, no doubt.'

Carla nodded. 'See you soon,' and she waved as Gerry drove Eve away.

Bremer was waiting for her, arms folded, when she got back to the office.

'I saw you having a nice friendly chat with Eve. Get anything out of her?'

'No, she just chatted about Gerry really.'

'He's an odd one, that bloke. What is he – nearing retirement and still only a PS?'

A little harsh. Not everyone wanted to climb up the ranks, and besides, being a sergeant wasn't exactly a failure. 'I get the impression they put Eve's career first.'

Bremer's look made it obvious what he thought about that. 'He doesn't strike me as the sort to do anything without her say-so.'

Carla was irritated now. Bremer didn't even know Gerry, so who was he to make judgements about his marriage? 'He gave me the letters without her say-so.'

'But did he? We only have his word for that.'

'I can't see that it matters who decided to. We got them, that's all that counts.'

'Is it? I'm not too sure. Eve's got something to do with this case and if Gerry does whatever he's told, that could make things difficult.'

'In what way? Gerry's not even on the case.'

'Yes, but you are.'

Carla was too furious to reply. Bremer unfolded his arms and spoke carefully.

'I don't mean you would say anything deliberately, but I know he's an important person in your life and that could make things awkward.'

Yeah, like when you drag me into an interview with his wife, she wanted to say.

'I just wouldn't want your friendship with Gerry to comprom- ise the investigation,' he finished.

'My friendship with Gerry will not compromise anything.' She knew her voice was shaking and she hoped he knew it was from anger.

'Good. Thank you.'

Carla went to her desk and sat down. Her whole body was shaking with anger – he'd made her get far more involved in this case than she had in any other and now he had the cheek to ques- tion her ability to do her job? She was about to go to his office and tell him she wasn't going to do anything more than sit at her desk and do the work she usually did, when Nell stormed into the room, a bemused-looking Paul following seconds later.

'I'm telling you, he's lucky I didn't punch him.' Nell threw her bag under her desk as Paul mouthed 'Ian Fowler' to Carla.

'And did you hear what he said at the end?' She placed her hands on the desk and leaned back against it. 'He said, "There is no Mary! Leave Mary out of it." She looked expectantly at Paul and when he didn't answer, continued.

'How does he know there isn't a Mary? If he knows as little

214

about this case as he's saying, then how does he know Mary doesn't exist? And –' she was animated now, hands gesturing as she spoke, '– if he doesn't think there is a Mary, then why do we need to leave her out of it?'

She had a point. Why would Ian Fowler tell them to leave Mary out of the investigation if she didn't exist? Which begged another equally obvious question. 'Why is he so keen for us not to pursue Mary in this investigation?'

Nell pointed at Carla. 'Exactly. The only reason he wouldn't want us investigating Mary is if it would harm Joanne. Which means they know who she is – a real person not just a pseudonym for Joanne – and why she is connected to Connor and Eve. Hell,' she raised her hands in the air, 'Mary is the link we've been looking for all along.'

Carla picked up the phone. If Nell was right, there had to be a trace of Mary somewhere in the phone bills, and if there was one, Carla was damn sure she'd find it.

Thirty-four
Now

I wish my husband had never given me her number. He should have known I would use it to torture myself, that I couldn't resist calling her. And now they will find the call I made to her, and slowly it's all going to unravel, just like I want it to.

That's the part of all this my husband doesn't understand. Why I am sabotaging my own life to be rid of hers. But it's more that he doesn't want to see it. His fear of losing me, of not having me in my life, makes him blind, but even he would acknowledge this is no way to live a life. Constantly fighting to be rid of Eve, to battle every day the demons of our past. No, better to be gone from here, for good this time, than continue as we are.

So I made the call. Right before I killed O'Brian. I feel no guilt for that; the man showed no compassion towards his child, so why should I to him? And I wanted to warn her she might end up the same way if she gets in the way.

But what I found out from that call was her desire to be rid of Eve matches my own. Her determination to get to the truth as insistent as mine is to hide it, because Aoife's blood runs through her: wilful, powerful, beautiful Aoife. So as we both race to the finish line, it's up for grabs who'll get there first, but either way it's Eve who will be the final prize.

Thirty-five

The Telephone Unit had finally come good. Carla opened up Connor's phone bill: row upon row of calls he'd made and received, all presented in order of date and time, the duration of each marked down to the second.

She got the familiar buzz from knowing this was going to move things forward and sorted the lists by telephone numbers. She then highlighted all calls to or from telephone numbers belonging to the four women: Joanne, Gloria, Kelly-Anne and Eve.

She drew blanks for Joanne and Eve, but Connor's phone had made calls to Gloria and Kelly-Anne's phones not long before he died. Carla checked the times: the call to Kelly-Anne's phone was timed at 22:02 and the one to Gloria's, at 22:28.

She opened Maps on her phone and typed in the travelling

times from the women's home addresses to the flat where Connor was killed. It was impossible for either to have travelled the distance to the flat between their phone call and his death at approximately 23:00.

Carla reordered the data by time and date and searched to see the calls made and received in the time leading up to Connor's death. Other than the two calls made by Connor's phone, there were only two calls in any of the phone bills made around the time of his death: at 22:59 to Connor's phone, but one at 22:45 to Joanne's.

What if that was the killer calling to check Connor was in? But why call Joanne just before? Carla ran the number through the rest of the phone bills, but found no other calls to or from it, and a quick Google search drew a similar blank.

'Shit.' She was going to have to submit a request to get the name of the phone's owner, which meant another call to the Telephone Unit.

Bremer called out from his office. 'Problems?' He appeared at his office door, sleeves rolled up, collar undone.

'What you got?' He nodded towards the phone data. 'Anything?'

She pointed to the number highlighted in red. 'Someone called Joanne right before they phoned Connor on the night he died.'

He walked over to the screen and peered at the numbers. 'Have you run it through the databases?'

'Yes, and Google. It comes back blank.'

He stared at the screen, nodding. 'Could it be our killer?'

She didn't want them to get ahead of themselves. 'Let's wait to see who it comes back to.'

'Was the call answered?'

'The one to Joanne was, the length of the Connor call suggests not.'

'So why would the killer be calling Joanne?' He held up his hand to stop her correcting him. 'I know. We don't know it's the killer yet. But we've been working with the assumption that Joanne is in on this somehow, and she wouldn't call herself.'

'So maybe she isn't our killer.'

'But the killer knows her and Connor. So there's definitely a link.'

'Looks that way, yes.'

'Could she have hired the killer? Maybe the call was to confirm that Joanne wanted her to go ahead?'

Carla considered this for a moment. 'Could be. I'll request financial records for her, see if she made any big withdrawals around the time of his death.'

'Good.' Bremer looked down at the call data. 'Anything to link the phone number to someone called Mary?'

'Impossible to say until I do a check on it. But there are no other calls from this phone to anyone else, so if this is our Mary, she's very good at covering her tracks.'

'Not as good as she thinks.' He pointed to the screen.

'Yeah, well, that's the other thing. This investigation has been as sterile as they come. No forensics, limited call data. It looks like whoever murdered Connor knew what they were doing, so why make such an obvious mistake?'

Bremer considered the screen. 'Run it through the Telephone Unit and tell them to do it on the hurry-up. If this is our killer, I want to know who it is ASAP.'

Thirty-six
Then

It takes us three weeks to pluck up the courage to go and visit Alf. We know he's been questioned by the police because they told us not to go near him. What we don't know is what he's going to do about it.

We hold hands as we walk across the beach.

'He's going to be so mad,' Aoife says.

'Do you think he'll . . .' I stop talking.

'Have found other girls?'

I nod.

'Don't be silly. He'll have been pining for us – how could he not!' She laughs and drags me across the beach towards the wall, where we sit and share the McDonald's we picked up on the way. Aoife dips chips into my strawberry milkshake while I eat the

Filet-O-Fish I only got because it reminds me of Mum. We watch the wind pick up the sea.

'Do you think he'll hurt us?' I ask despite our silent vow not to speak about the things he does to us we don't like.

Aoife looks unsure and runs her finger over the scar on her wrist. A scar that wasn't there before Alf.

'Maybe we shouldn't go back?' As the words come out I know I shouldn't have said them because Aoife turns and looks at me with total disbelief, which soon turns to anger.

'It's all right for you, you've got your mum.' She holds up her hand to stop me speaking. 'No one is going to turn up in my life and rescue me like a bloody fairy princess.' She holds her stomach. 'I've got this to think about now. It's his baby – he's going to have to love it.'

We both know that's not true; we are both examples of the lie that every parent loves their child. But what if he does? What if Alf does want the baby and him and Aoife become a family? Where does that leave me?

'I'm going to tell him,' Aoife says, 'about the baby.'

My stomach lurches. I put down what's left of my food. I try to be calm. On the one hand it's getting obvious, so it would be better to tell him before he guesses. Then we'll be in control. But on the other we risk losing him before we've even got him back and I'm not sure I'm ready for that just yet.

But there has been an absence in Aoife recently, like she's gone to a place I can't visit even if I wanted to, because that place is curled up around the baby in her womb. I miss her and some-times it feels like I've lost her already and that thought takes all the wind from my lungs.

'Come on, let's go.' Aoife stands, trying to brush away the mood that's fallen, but we walk towards the café in silence. When we see its lights, she stops and takes my hand.

'I won't let him hurt you. If he tries, I'll go to the police myself. There won't be more fists or burns. I promise.'

I try not to cry. I think of the mark on my shoulder that has never gone away, branding me as his, and the bruises on my thighs which come and go like night and day.

'Aoife—'

But before she can answer, the café door opens and there's Alf in the doorway, blocking out the light.

'Nice to see you, girls.' His voice feels as familiar as my own, like coming home to a warm cosy fire and a cup of hot chocolate in front of the TV. My shoulders relax and I let myself be hugged, burying my face into his jumper, smelling cooking and cigar-ettes, whisky and wine.

As Aoife hangs back I gesture for her to come forward.

I feel sure in this moment it is going to be all right. Alf loves me too and nothing, not even a baby, is going to get in the way of that.

Thirty-seven

While she waited for the telephone number to be checked, Carla started to dig into Joanne's and Eve's backgrounds. She opened Google – police databases were good, but they couldn't compare with the World Wide Web – and it didn't disappoint: ten minutes in and she'd got more via the press than ten hours of searching on Thames Valley's system could ever have achieved.

As Carla scanned the articles she grew increasingly intrigued; it was as if Joanne Fowler's and Eve's histories were mirror images of each other, but with hairline cracks that diverted each intended course. But what if those cracks had converged, as Nell believed? Was it possible their paths had crossed before Joanne's child had died?

Carla wrote down what she knew. Articles written during Joanne's trial told her the woman had been taken into care at birth. She'd spent two years in a foster home – three miles from Eve's childhood home – before being adopted by a schoolteacher and a university professor, both upstanding members of the community. The articles asked repeatedly, 'How could a woman from such a family become the evil murderer we see now?' All relied on lazy stereotypes about the genetics of evil – 'some people are just born that way'. Carla didn't believe that. For her, actions stemmed from life experiences, not a dodgy gene pool, and if the last eight years as an analyst had told her anything it was that criminals came in all shapes and sizes, from all sides of the class divide.

The papers told her Joanne had met her husband at university in Solihull and they'd married soon after graduation, living for three short months in a rented property on Cowley Road, Oxford. They hadn't come to the attention of the police until the death of their child, which was seemingly when Eve entered their lives.

Information on Eve was harder to come by. HR held some, but it was limited and incomplete. What Carla did find was that Eve had been admitted to a Portsmouth care home aged fourteen after her stepfather's abuse had landed her in Portsmouth General and concerns for her welfare had become too loud to be ignored. After two years Eve left the home, moved to Reading and a few years later began work as a civilian in the police – forensics, but low level, due to her lack of qualifications. After marrying Gerry, at some point Eve must have gone back to school, because ten years later she had a university degree and a job with the Home Office. But the gap of ten years was unaccounted for. Eve had not been employed by Thames Valley Police or the Home Office, and there was no account of when she had moved to Oxford, or why.

Carla turned to Google. Eve's names – both maiden and married – drew blanks, save for cases she'd worked on after qualifying as a pathologist, so Carla typed in the care home's details. One article appeared and she scanned it, hand poised over a mug of coffee.

The article had been written thirty-five years ago and had only found itself on the Internet after an intern – so the paper's website told her – had studiously uploaded all past stories from the *Portsmouth Chronicle* onto the World Wide Web.

It detailed a gruesome murder that had rocked the seaside town. A young care-home girl had been lured to the beach by Alf Waites, a man three times her age who'd pummelled her head with a rock before setting her body on fire. No motive was given, but Waites still went down for twenty years.

The lack of a name bothered Carla and not just because it frustrated further research.

'So invisible she wasn't even worthy of a name,' she muttered, noting the date of the murder. She checked Eve's HR record – Eve would have been at the care home at the time Waites murdered the girl. She must have known her, or at the very least known of her.

Before she could google contact details for the care home, her phone rang and the number on the display told her it was the Telephone Unit.

'Carla Brown speaking.'

'Hi, I've got the details of the phone number you wanted checking, but it's not good.'

Shit. Pay-as-you-go, then.

'It's a phone box.'

'What?'

He gave the address. 'I've checked either side of the two calls you identified and there were no others made from the phone box within a two-hour period either way.'

Carla didn't need any more. She'd got her killer. No one else would have called both the victim and Joanne otherwise. She thanked him and hung up, then dialled Nell.

'Those calls came from a call box on the street where Connor was murdered. Someone must have seen the person who used it.'

'Right, Paul and I will do a door-to-door. You'll tell Bremer?'

'Yeah, will do. And there's another thing. I think there's a connection between Eve and a murder which happened thirty-five years ago. She'd have been fifteen, sixteen.'

'And that helps us how?'

Carla looked at the screen showing details of the care home. 'I don't know yet, but I'll let you know as soon as I do.'

Thirty-eight
Then

Alf looks to Aoife as she hangs back in the shadows.

'Aoife?'

I nod to her but she shakes her head and it suddenly occurs to me she's unsure of his reaction, not towards her but to the baby, and this fills me with an anger as hot as molten iron. She's choosing the baby over herself and if she's doing that now, then what is she going to do to me after it arrives? What role will I play?

'Aoife's pregnant,' I blurt out, ignoring the look of horror on her face, 'and it's yours.' Of course none of us knows if that is true or not, but it makes no difference to Alf and I see immediately he clearly realises the implications. Soon there will be living proof of his crimes and a couple of days in a cell will turn into a hell of a lot more.

Alf removes his arm from around me, walks to the window

and looks out to sea. He says nothing, but the atmosphere around him changes in that weird way it can shift molecules so they charge or go still, and Alf's are charged.

I wish I hadn't told. I wish I could take it back and look at Aoife to say sorry, but she won't catch my eye.

Slowly he turns around to face us, his expression a mixture of disgust and hate, and I know how bad my mistake is, but it's too late.

'Get rid of it,' he snaps. 'Privately. I'll pay.'

Aoife is whiter than I've ever seen her. Her eyes stand out above the hollows of her cheeks, her pregnancy simultaneously expanding her and causing her to shrink.

'I can't,' she says, her voice tiny. 'I'm too far gone.' She places a protective hand on her stomach and I see Alf flinch.

'Then I'll fucking get it out.' He moves towards her and my heart is beating so fast I think I'm going to vomit it out of my throat. I move sideways, towards Aoife, and as I place a hand around her shoulders I realise for the first time how very scrawny she's become; as if by becoming smaller she can somehow disappear from the world, taking her baby with her.

'No, you won't.' My words sound more confident than I feel, and as Alf's face stretches into a bastardised version of a smile, I feel any confidence I may have leave me.

'Mary, come over here.'

'No.'

'Mary, I'm not asking you, I'm telling you. Come over here.'

Those words have been said to me so many times they may as

well have been branded on me with burning metal. I obey, because I've made my mistake and now I have to live with the consequences, whatever they may be.

Alf puts his arm around me and relief at his acceptance quells some of the panic I feel whirling like the sea outside.

'Mary, listen to me. If this baby sees the light of day there will be no more "us". No more new clothes or nights out – I'll not be allowed near you. Is that what you want?'

Everything is unravelling too fast and I don't know what to do. Alf pulls me in and as tears run down my cheeks I move in closer, desperate for his warmth and size to block out the fear I'm feeling.

'So, you'll help me get rid of it, yeah?'

I look at Aoife, but the panic in her eyes, like a cornered wild animal's, makes me run from her.

'Yes.'

His arm relaxes across my shoulders; he kisses my hair. 'Good.'

'No.' Aoife's voice is bigger than she is; it fills the room as she stands and shouts, 'You will not kill my baby!'

And there it is. Admission it's hers, not 'ours'.

Alf strides across and pushes his face in hers. 'Then I'll bloody kill you,' he says. But this time, Aoife doesn't shrink or buckle under his threat; instead she says:

'Go ahead. Kill me.'

So Alf obliges and slams her head into the table.

Thirty-nine

Nell unclicked her seat belt and picked up her notebook from the footwell. She looked down the street where a lone man was walking his shopping home, shoulders hunched from the weight. She nodded to the phone box across from the flat. 'That must be the one, but check the number just in case.'

'Will do. Positioned well, if you wanted to check on the occupants of the flat,' Paul added.

'Have you got the picture?' Nell had two printouts of the still from the CCTV, the best they could get of the woman who had entered Connor's flat, but she didn't hold out much hope they would jog anyone's memory.

Paul waved his copy at her. 'I'll take the right, you take the left.'

Outside the air was thick with heat; a shimmer covered the road, suggesting pools of water that weren't there.

'If this heat doesn't end soon I'm going to die.' Paul's face was already glistening, and Nell held her hair up, glad of the smallest brush of air on the nape of her neck. Cars passed slowly, windows open, radio DJs unwittingly competing to give their week's song a shout-out.

Paul crossed the road, leaving Nell to approach a peeling red wooden door, with its broken buzzer and sealed-up letter box. She knocked and waited before knocking again. When she heard footsteps she took out the CCTV picture and her warrant card and held them up.

A woman in a headscarf peered through the crack in the door, metal chain in place. 'Yes?'

Nell shoved her warrant card through the gap. 'DS Jackson, Thames Valley Police. Can I ask you a few questions?'

'Yes?'

The woman didn't move. Nell smiled.

'Can you open the door for me?'

The woman hesitated, then shut the door and Nell heard the scraping of metal on metal.

'You're here about the dead man?' the woman asked.

'Yes. We'd like help identifying this woman.' Nell held up the picture. 'Do you recall seeing her in the days leading up to his death?'

The woman examined the picture, then said, 'I can't see her.'

'I know it's a poor image, but if you could think back to see if you remember a woman with long brown hair, it would be really helpful.'

The woman slowly shook her head. 'No. I mean, I haven't seen her.'

Nell looked at the carpeted staircase ingrained with the dirt of years. 'Is there anyone else who lives here?'

The woman instinctively pulled the door towards her a little. 'Why?'

'Because maybe they saw this person?' Nell could see her trying to judge whether it was a trap.

'My husband and child. But he's at work and my son is too young,' the woman replied.

Nell nodded and pulled out a card. 'Can you ask your husband to get in touch if he remembers anything?'

The woman looked unsure but took the card.

'Will you do that?' Nell asked.

The woman read it, glanced up at Nell, then back down. 'Yes.'

'Thank you. Have a good day.'

The woman had shut the door before Nell had finished speaking.

Nell saw Paul was further along the road, so she was playing catch-up. Four more doors with no answer and she was matching him.

'Any joy?' she called over, knowing he would have said if there was.

'Not yet,' he called back.

'OK, let's keep going to the end, then we'll try the backstreets.'

Nell knocked on two more doors, feeling the case slipping away from her as each time she was met with silence. Two doors left and she checked on Paul, deep in conversation with a male occupant. She felt relief that at least someone was home and was about to knock on the last-but-one door when she heard her name being called.

'DS Jackson?'

Nell turned to see the woman she'd spoken to earlier hurrying towards her, the gold flecks in her ankle-length dress catching in the sun.

'DS Jackson, I think I remember something.' The woman came to a breathless halt on the pavement beside Nell.

'I forgot before – I remember the woman with the brown hair.'

Nell suspected she hadn't. Rather she'd gone back into her flat and her husband had agreed she could remember the woman.

'I only saw her once, across from our flat,' the woman continued. 'She was standing under a street light so that's how I noticed her.'

'And when was this?' Nell took out her notepad and started to write.

'The night before the man died. I remembered it when I saw the police the next day but didn't think it could be important.'

'But important enough for you to notice her?' Nell got it, people didn't like to speak to the police unless they had to, but it sure as hell didn't help them do their job.

'And what was she doing?' Nell asked, when the woman didn't reply.

'She was standing for a while but then she went to that phone box.' The woman pointed to a phone box opposite the flat. 'She was looking around under the phone and then she made a call. Two maybe. I thought it was odd because no one ever uses the phone box, especially not so late at night, and also she was there for a while but I couldn't see her speaking to anyone.'

That would fit with the fourteen-minute time lag between calls. 'Can you describe her for me?'

'I'm not sure. It was dark.' The woman shrugged apologetically. 'She was maybe, tall?'

'How about her age, any sense of that?'

'I would think about fifty, maybe older.'

It wasn't much but it was something. Nell took down the woman's name, thanked her, then called Paul over.

'I've got confirmation the woman from the CCTV made the calls. Check the number so we can confirm that it's the same as the one on the phone bill.'

'Will do.' Paul's armpits were ringed with sweat as he jogged across the road to note the number. Nell watched him pull the pen lid off with his teeth before she turned to look up at the flat. Something was niggling her and it took a moment for her to identify what it was. Everything was so clean. So far the flat hadn't revealed one bit of DNA, which, considering the amount of men traipsing in and out of it, was a surprise in itself, and now they knew the killer had used a phone box?

This was someone who knew police procedure. Someone who knew what traces could be made and what a call from a mobile phone could reveal. But then, thanks to the plethora of crime novels and TV dramas revealing every secret the police had, everyone was now an armchair expert in police procedure. So did this mean anything?

Paul ran back across the road, slightly out of breath. 'Got it. It's the same. Want me to ring it in to Carla?'

'No, we're done here. We can take it back with us.'

'What's up? I thought you'd be happy to finally have a lead.'

'Doesn't strike you as odd there's so little forensics to go on? I bet you that phone box is as clean as a whistle too, yet we know she placed the £500 there for Gloria to find, so you'd think there'd be a trace.'

'Maybe, but you can't wipe out a phone call.'

'Yes, but what does that tell us? We know she made the call because we have a witness who matches her to the CCTV print-out. But that's all we've got. We can't do the usual checks on the call data because it's a phone box, so it's just random people making random calls.'

'Possibly, but Carla can work wonders with phones. I wouldn't give up hope yet.'

He was right, but she wasn't sure even Carla was that good. 'OK, let's get back. We're late for the meeting as it is.' And with one last look at the phone box, she got in the car and jacked up the air conditioning.

Forty
Then

Aoife is on the ground, her body still. The cut from her head has started to bleed onto the floor. I scream and Alf slaps me, his face ashen.

'Shut up.'

We stand there, staring at her, and my legs are shaking so much I think I'm going to fall down. Alf moves to the door and for a minute I think he's going to leave me there alone with her and I panic. But then he turns the lock in the door and pulls down the blind, and I look back to Aoife.

I can't see if she's breathing. I try to go towards her but my body won't move. 'Aoife,' I call.

'I said, shut up. Let me think.'

I wait.

'Fuck.' He's rubbing the back of his head, hard, staring down at Aoife.

'Shouldn't we call an ambulance?' I dare to say, then freeze as he glares at me.

'No.'

No? Anger starts to push away at the edges of my panic. *No?* 'We can't just leave her – she needs help.' I start to walk towards her, slowly, judging Alf's reaction with each step.

I'm standing above her and looking down at her red hair, pale face. Her eyes are closed, mouth slightly open, and I notice her hand is cradling her stomach, fingers frozen in an attempt to protect her child.

I bend down and smooth her hair aside. 'Aoife?' I whisper. 'Aoife, it's all right, I'm going to help you.'

I lean in, aware of Alf's stare on my back. Her face is so white I'm afraid to touch it. 'Aoife,' I whisper in her ear. 'Aoife, I'm sorry, I'm so sorry. I love you – please wake up.'

I can't see her chest move so I reach out to feel a pulse, pressing hard into her neck, desperate to feel her heartbeat against my fingers.

There is nothing. I pull my hand back and sit on my heels. The muscles in my body have gone to jelly and the room starts to spin.

'You've killed her.' I look at Alf. 'You've killed Aoife.' Why isn't he doing something? Why isn't he helping us?

He's shaken and this makes me want to hit him – he did this, he took my only friend, it is all his fault. But something inside me whispers, 'It's yours.'

I feel the hysteria rise in me. 'You've killed her!' I repeat, before feeling the back of his hand on my neck, sending me crashing to the floor beside Aoife.

'Shut up! Let me think.'

I stay lying down, staring at Aoife's shut eyes. I remember her eyes shining, blue sparks of light dancing as she laughed. The idea of not seeing those again crushes my chest and forces a cry out into the room. I hear it as if it comes from someone else and I wish more than anything it came from Aoife. How can I live without her? What will I do?

I reach out and stroke her hair, pushing it away from the blood congealing on her scalp. 'I love you,' I say, and as I do, she flinches.

I hold my breath but there it is again. The slightest of movements to tell me she's alive. 'Aoife,' I whisper, frantic now. 'We have to get out of here. I'm going to get you out, OK?'

I look at Alf, who is pacing by the window, then look to the door. Can I get her there? I look back at Aoife, but there is no way I can get her to the door and even if I could, Alf would easily stop me.

Alf is walking towards us. He crouches down beside me and reaches to Aoife's neck. I push his hand away.

'Don't touch her,' I yell, 'don't you bloody touch her.' He mustn't feel her pulse, can't know she's alive or he'll finish the job, I'm certain of it.

He pulls back and gives me a look of something I think is pity.

'I'm sorry,' he says.

I'm breathing heavily, thoughts running like scattered ants, trying to think how I can save her. But then Aoife makes a gurgling noise as if blood is rattling in her throat. I catch Alf's eye. He heard it too.

I reach to put my arms around her but he pushes me away. I scramble up and grab at his back, trying to pull him off her but he yanks me away and I fly halfway across the floor.

'Please,' I shout, my shoulder throbbing from the fall. I grab it and wince in pain. 'If you let us go I promise we'll go away from here and you'll never see us again. Please don't kill her.'

'Help me lift her,' he barks, pulling at Aoife's jumper so her stomach, in all its milky whiteness, is revealed. The baby. I could still save the baby.

I don't move.

'Help me,' he barks and I crawl quickly towards them.

'We're taking her to the beach.' He starts to pull her out of the room, blood smearing the floor as he does so. He gets to the door and reaches to unlock it, and while he does I run to the kitchen and grab the knife from the counter.

Tucking it in the waistband of my skirt, I run to the door. 'Why are we going to the beach?'

'To bury her.'

I stand stock-still. He can't mean that. 'But she's alive!' I go to pull Alf's arm away from Aoife, but he shakes me off.

'She won't be by the time we get there.'

'But the baby?' As soon as I say it I wish I hadn't because it reminds him it's there.

Alf is holding Aoife's legs mid-air. 'We need to get rid of it.'

I look at her swollen stomach. For eight months that baby has grown and grown. We have spent months hiding its shape as Aoife grew its fingers and toes, scared the care-home staff would find out, more terrified Alf would. And we did it, we kept it safe for this long, and so even though I have no idea how I'm going to do it, or even if I can, I'm going to save that baby and I'll kill Alf if he tries to stop me.

Forty-one

Finding nothing more of interest in O'Brian's phone bill, Carla was relieved to see an email from the Telephone Unit arrive in her inbox: *I got you a bit more historical data, hope it helps.*

Attached was call data from all the phones, but from the weeks leading up to Connor's death rather than the one week she had analysed already. Ordering them again by phone number, she methodically checked for every number she knew: Gloria, Kelly-Anne, Connor, Eve, Joanne and her husband, Ian. Then she checked to see if any number had called this group. Half an hour later she had determined one hadn't.

Frustrated, she took a more general look at the calls, noting all calls and texts between Gloria and Connor, then those between him and Kelly-Anne. She pictured the messages – *where r u?* and *come home* – but call data didn't give her words, just slowly built a picture in which every piece of the jigsaw remained blurred and uncertain. She double-checked the phone-box number against Gloria's and Kelly-Anne's call data, but found nothing.

Switching to Joanne's call data, she was about to do the same when a number caught her eye. The last four digits were familiar, but after checking them against all the others she drew a blank.

Her heart started to thump. *It couldn't be?* Carla pulled out her phone and scrolled down her list of contacts. And there it was. The number on Joanne's call data was right there in her own phone.

She dropped the phone and gripped the edges of her chair, trying to ride out the wave of nausea crashing over her.

Gerry.

Carla only just made it to the toilet before she threw up. Gripping the toilet bowl, she waited until her stomach had nothing more to give, then rocked back on her heels and wiped her mouth with her hand. Why had Gerry called Joanne in the days leading up to Connor's death? Hell, why was he calling her at all? Was he warning her off, telling her not to contact Eve? But surely he knew how dangerous that would be to any future case they might have against Joanne?

She stood, steadying herself against the cubicle wall, before going to the sink to wash her face. Her thoughts were a mess: should she ask Gerry about the call, confront him and ask for an explanation? But that would reveal they were looking at phone data, which would mean he'd know they were checking on Eve, and Bremer would kill her if she did that. But she could trust Gerry, couldn't she?

The thud in her chest told her otherwise but she railed against it; surely she owed Gerry enough to tell him? A second thought pushed out the first. Maybe she could delete the call from the spreadsheet – who would ever know?

'Jesus, Carla.' She looked in the mirror. 'You do that, you might as well quit the job.' She felt ashamed. Start tampering with evidence, you lose any right to be in the job, she knew that.

She walked out of the toilet straight into Nell.

'Hey!' Nell looked annoyed, but then stared at Carla. 'You OK?'

Should she tell her? 'Fine, thanks.'

'Not pregnant, are you?!' Nell laughed. Carla felt vomit rise again. Nell put a hand on her arm. 'I was kidding, you know?'

'I know.' She tried to paint on a smile. 'Find anything at the scene?'

They started walking back to the office as Nell explained they'd got a confirmed sighting at the phone box.

'Well, that's brilliant!'

'It's a start.'

'That's what I love about you, Nell,' Carla said as they reached the office for their briefing. 'Your endless positivity.'

Bremer looked at Carla. 'Go.'

Carla recounted the facts about the telephone number, the phone box and how it linked to Joanne and Connor, before giving a summary of the backgrounds of both Joanne and Eve. She then explained about the murder on Portsmouth beach around the time Eve had lived there.

'And you've got nothing more on it than that?'

She wanted to reply, 'Give me a chance,' but instead said, 'No. I need to get hold of the social worker and the senior investigating officer on the case first. See what they can tell us. There's nothing more about the case on the Internet and police files weren't computerised back then, so I can't even request the case file from Hampshire Police. It'll have to be someone who worked on it.'

Bremer looked at the clock. 'We're pushing it for time. Carla, see if you can get hold of social services. Nell, you contact Hampshire and get the SIO's details. But on the understanding we're probably going to have to leave it until tomorrow until we get them in.'

Nell wheeled her chair over to her desk and picked up the phone at the same time Carla picked up hers.

'Social services, how may I help you?'

'Hello, this is Carla Brown from Thames Valley Police and I'd like to speak to someone about a Portsmouth care home.'

'Is that a complaint or an enquiry?'

'Enquiry.'

'Hold the line, please.'

Carla listened to the elevator music with increasing irritation. There was no way they were going to give her information over the phone; the most she could hope for was a snippet of information to take her forward, but how likely was that going to be?

'Hi Carla, Belle speaking, how can I help?'

The warmth in Belle's voice took Carla by surprise.

'Hi. I'm just hoping to get some info about a girl who was looked after about thirty-five years ago.' Carla gave the details of the Waites case. 'Anything you have would be really helpful. Especially the names of the child who was murdered and the second girl? The one who was with her when she was murdered.'

When Belle spoke again, her tone was serious. 'I wasn't old enough to have worked on that case but we all know about it. It's the one we have training on the minute we start work.'

'It's particularly the second girl we are interested in. A name if possible.'

Belle paused before replying. 'It's going to take us hours to dig out the file and then every one will need a signed authority to release it, which could take us into next year. So I wonder whether you'd find it more helpful to speak to the social worker in charge at that time?

'She's still with you?'

Belle laughed. 'God, no. Harriet left years ago. But she's the one who does the training on the Waites case.'

Carla noted down the address and thanked her.

'Any luck?' Nell called over.

'Got an address of the social worker. Retired, but moved to Princes Risborough.'

Nell looked impressed. 'I'm having a nightmare with Hampshire. Seems they don't know their arse from their elbow, let alone who ran the Waites case.'

'Maybe the social worker would remember?'

Nell glanced at the clock. 'How far away is that?'

'Forty minutes.'

'Fancy a trip out? I'll drop you home after.'

Carla thought about her empty flat, the phone call she wished she hadn't seen from Gerry. 'Sure. Why not.'

Forty-two
Then

The beach is cold and I shiver. I look down at Aoife and want to curl up with her. Is she dead yet? I daren't check. The waves crash behind me and I wish they would scoop me up and take me back out with them.

Alf has brought the container of petrol he uses to fire up his generator. It's blue, like Aoife's eyes. I can see the liquid in the moonlight settling now the container is still. At least she will be warm, I think, and then I feel a surge of laughter rise in me. I am not really here, I tell myself, this is not really happening. If I say it long enough maybe it will be true.

'What about the baby?' I have no idea how to save it and I feel hope turn to panic. I scramble to order my thoughts but they jump around my head like ping-pong balls.

Alf leans over and pulls the knife from my skirt. 'Cut it out, of course.'

I stand there, speechless. Shocked he knew it was there, panic-stricken at what he is about to do.

'Then we take it away from here and bury it somewhere different,' he says, 'so the two bodies can't be linked.'

I want to say 'I'm not doing that,' but my mouth won't form the words. I feel as if Aoife's stomach is watching me, waiting for me to act in its defence, but the only defence I can offer it seems to be inaction and that's no help at all.

When Alf kneels next to Aoife's stomach, I turn my back. *Please be dead, please don't feel pain when he cuts you. Please be dead.* I repeat this in my head until I hear the smallest of noises from behind me.

I turn and scream. The blood has stained the sand red and there's so much of it I feel it could drown me. My head swims and I sit down hard against the dunes.

Then I see it. This red little bit of life trying to cry out into the world, trying to wriggle free of Alf's arms, and I think, *You've got Aoife's spirit, my little thing.*

Alf is staring at it, its cries getting stronger as it learns to breathe. I stand. 'Give it to me.'

Alf doesn't respond so I push myself up and run to him, pulling my cardigan off as I stumble towards them. I take the baby from his hands, wrapping it as I pull her away from him. He just watches me. I clutch it to me, trying to make sure it's warm, and then I see she's a girl. Her eyes open a little, deep blue stones staring up at me, and I pull her closer. She is bigger than I thought she would be, strong, healthy. She mews in my arms.

'Take it back to the café and I'll deal with it later.' His tone is distant.

'Her,' I say. Alf pauses, his eyes flittering unwillingly over the baby I'm holding. I hold my breath. Maybe he's changed his mind and he'll let her live; maybe there's a father in him after all. But the thought of him touching this baby makes my blood run cold.

'Take it and make sure you're not seen.'

This is my chance. I hug the baby close to me, fearful of dropping her, then I turn my back on Aoife and hurry our baby away.

Forty-three

Harriet Arnold's house was simultaneously neat and chaotic. Everything seemed to have a place, but those places extended to the whole house, which was covered in a blanket of books, candles and hanging objects that provided a tinkling background hum. Harriet herself mirrored the house: neatly dressed in an array of purples, blues and reds, she was adorned with a variety of heavy silver jewellery ranging from chunky rings to a statement necklace. After asking them to sit on the frayed brown sofa, she fiddled absent-mindedly with a clutch of silver bangles on her wrists.

'So you want to know about the Waites case?' she began. 'Not our finest moment. We all knew, you see, what was going on. But what can you do when teenage girls insist on avoiding all forms of help?' She continued without waiting for an answer. 'We contacted the police and they did their bit, but the truth of the matter was these girls "loved" the man who was abusing them, because they had no other experience of love to compare it to.

'Quite a striking pair they were,' she continued. 'All long legs and big eyes, but with an awful haunted look, making you want to take care of them even more than you usually did with that sort of girl.'

'That sort of girl?'

Harriet gave a heavy sigh, which felt weighed down with the memories of all the struggling teenagers she'd dealt with over the years.

'Sometimes a girl came to us from a family that was functioning, to a certain extent anyway, but which had reached a crisis and needed short-term help, or maybe long-term, but either way the building blocks, though flimsy, had been stable. For the most part,' she added. 'Those girls were easier to help because they had things we could work with, an understanding of social norms, of consequences. But some girls came to us with none of this. They had no blocks on which to build a life. They were, to risk using a tabloid trope, feral.'

'Which types were these two girls?'

'Well, Aoife was a girl who'd had no foundations whatsoever. Her family – and I use that in the loosest sense of the word – had been chaotic and in crisis more often than not. She'd been in and out of care since she was one, but she also had a sensitivity which hadn't been beaten out of her, despite all attempts. In contrast, the other child was one we thought would only be with us for a few weeks, but as the months went on and her mum didn't want to have anything to do with her, we lost her. I don't think she could ever get over her mum choosing her dad over her, and she kept expecting her to turn up any day, which of course she never did.'

'Aoife was the murdered child, yes?'

Harriet nodded. 'Yes. So very tragic. Aoife was one of those girls who pretends they don't care about anything because that way no one can hurt them. But with Mary she was different, maternal even, so it was especially lovely to watch the two of them form such a bond.' She gave a short laugh and settled back in her seat, teacup in hand.

'Mary?' Nell looked at Carla, who was clearly as stunned as she was.

'The second child on the beach was called Mary?'

'I will never forget those two children as long as I live. So yes, I'm quite certain she was called Mary. Mary Balcombe.' She smiled. 'From the moment the girls met they were inseparable. We used to joke in the office. "Who's seen the duo today?" we'd ask, and one of us would always have seen them – on the beach, at McDonald's, in town.' She looked down at the floor and shook her head.

'What happened to Mary, after Aoife died?'

'Well, naturally we all thought she'd fall apart. But she seemed to gain some inner strength and after the initial grief, she pulled through quite well, all things considered. Worked hard at school – turned out she was as bright as a button when she put her mind to it – and scored almost the highest in her year in her end of school exams.'

'Was Mary ever implicated in the death of Aoife?'

'Good Lord, no, the pair wouldn't have harmed each other for all the money in the world. No, Mary stayed around in Portsmouth to do her exams then left.'

'She left? Did you look for her? Put out a missing persons?'

Harriet's face was deliberately calm. 'She was sixteen when she left – the day of her birthday was the last day we saw her. In those days, sixteen was the legal age to leave the care home, so she did.' She paused. 'We know we failed her, I don't need you both here to tell me that. We failed both of them. But all I can say is, we tried. Sometimes that's all you can do.'

'And you never heard any more from Mary after she left?' Carla asked.

'No. Sadly not. I thought a lot about her over the years, wondering what she'd grown up to be, trying not to wonder too hard in case I was right.'

'But you said she had good grades?'

'Grades mean nothing when you're as lost as she was. She'd lost the one person she loved and who loved her, so if I were to hazard a guess I'd say that was pretty much the end of any chance she had of a normal life. I can't even bear to picture where she ended up.'

'We'd like to find out about a girl who may have known Aoife and Mary,' Nell asked. 'She'd have been the same age as them – called Eve?'

Harriet narrowed her eyes, thinking, before shaking her head. 'No, I'm sorry, that name doesn't ring a bell. And really, no one hung out with Mary and Aoife.'

'Are you sure you can't remember a child called Eve? Surname Wilkes?' Nell gave Eve's maiden name, hoping to jog Harriet's memory, but she shook her head again.

'I'm sorry, but I can't. Although,' Harriet gave a short laugh, 'are you sure you're not looking for Aoife?'

Nell glanced at Carla, but she just shrugged.

Clearly amused by their confusion, Harriet said, 'Aoife is the Irish for Eve.'

Nell stared at the woman. Aoife. Eve. They couldn't be the same person – one was dead and the other wasn't. But if there was no record of Eve at the care home, then who the hell was she and where had she come from?

Forty-four
Then

I feel my heart beating against the baby. I look to the wall where Aoife and I had sat just hours before and wonder, should I run? But he told me to go. He was giving me a way out without me needing to find one.

'Stop!'

I freeze. Alf's voice is right behind me. I clutch Aoife's baby closer to me.

'There's a bloody cop.'

I follow his finger and see a uniformed officer walk slowly past the café. An orange street light catches the metal on his hat and it glints sharply.

'We'll have to wait until he's gone. I can't set the fire or he'll see it and I need her to be good and crisp before they find her. And you can't be seen with a newborn or they'll haul you in.'

I feel my heart thud faster. This is my chance. The copper will help me and if I can get to him maybe I can also save the little bit of Aoife I have left.

I hear Alf's heavy breathing as we crouch in the grass growing tall out of the sand. I could outrun him. I am younger and fitter than him. I look down at the baby to see her nuzzling for food, her mouth turned sideways as she tries to suck milk from the wool of my cardigan.

I suddenly panic. Do they need food straight away? I have no idea what a newborn baby needs only minutes after birth. Am I killing her now by not feeding her, causing her to die in my arms?

The thought makes me stand.

'Get down,' Alf hisses.

But I'm done with his demands.

I start to run, trying not to slip or drop the baby, who cries in protest at the sudden movement. I can hear Alf start out behind me so I run faster, slipping slightly on the seaweed as it clings to the rocks.

I reach the steps, taking them two at a time before I slip. The cardigan slides off the baby's head and she looks at me, surprised.

'Sorry,' I whisper, picking myself up. 'Not long now.'

I glance back to see Alf bent over, hands on his knees, dragging in breaths. I turn again; the copper has almost disappeared behind the café wall.

'Come on,' I pull the baby close, 'let's go.'

I reach the copper. He looks down at me, at once confused and horrified, and I realise how awful I must look with my face covered in blood – both Aoife's and mine.

'Jesus.'

'Take the baby.' I can barely speak as the air slices my throat. I look over my shoulder to see Alf climbing the steps; the man follows my stare.

'Take it,' I say, shoving her into his arms, arms that instinctively receive her.

'Make it safe.'

'Hold on,' he says as I start to run off. 'Hold on, you're safe now.' He is reaching for his radio, struggling to hold the baby and call for help.

But I will never be safe. Not now, not ever.

The copper catches up with me. Alf is standing by the sea wall, watching us. The policeman puts a hand on my arm. 'I've called for help.' His voice is the kindest voice I've ever heard and suddenly I want to cry. But if I start I don't think I'll ever stop.

Alf takes a step forward and then we see it – the glint from his knife in the orange glow.

'Run and hide.' The policeman's voice is urgent now. 'There's a bin behind the shop – climb in it and I'll be back with help.'

'But don't tell anyone about the baby,' I beg.

He shakes his head, dragging me by the arm towards the bin.

'Hurry,' he says, his body shielding me from Alf.

I scramble to lift the lid but it's so heavy I can barely manage.

The copper is walking towards Alf with one hand out, offering reassurance if he will just put the knife down.

I shove my foot into the gap I've created and heave my body over into the rotting food below. I bury myself as deep as I can go and then shut my eyes and listen.

I hear sirens getting louder, multiple ones, all competing to be heard. I hear the copper's voice as he yells for Alf to stop and from his tone I think it's Alf running away, not running towards him and the baby. I let myself feel the smallest stab of hope, which grows as I hear the baby cry.

The sirens are deafening now and they drown out her wailing. I hear voices shout, directions being given. Then I sense the bin lid being lifted and despite knowing it can't be Alf, I freeze in fear.

'Hello?' It isn't the copper's voice, but neither is it Alf's. I don't move.

'Hello?' the voice repeats and when I still don't move, he calls out, 'There's no one in here – are you sure it was this bin?'

'Yes.'

This time it's the man from the beach, the one with Aoife's child. His voice is distant, but I hear it as clearly as if it was being whispered in my ear. I start to push my way out; a light shines down on me, through the gaps in the rotting food and broken plastic.

When I reach my hand up to feel the air, he grabs it. 'I'm here, you're safe now.'

I emerge into the evening air much as Aoife's baby did,

screaming and yelling, terrified of what I will find. But what I find are the man's strong arms around me; he is whispering words I can't discern, but I feel comforted and it makes me never want to leave him.

'The baby,' I say, my breath on his cheek.

'She's safe,' he whispers back.

Forty-five

Carla looked up at the windows of her flat. They were depressingly dark, which meant Baz wasn't home. The car engine was still running and she knew Nell was waiting for her to get out, but her legs weren't playing ball.

'Would you like to come up for a beer?' she said, before her brain had time to question it. 'Or wine.' She suddenly realised she had no idea what Nell drank.

Nell hesitated, then took the key from the ignition. 'Sure, why not.'

Despite the darkness of the flat, Carla immediately knew Baz had gone for good. She spent ten minutes scouring every inch of the place for a sign he'd once lived there, but his shaver was gone from the bathroom, clothes from the bedroom, even his morning mug from the kitchen, until it felt like the only thing left to prove he'd ever lived there was the faintest smell of his aftershave.

Carla sat on the small sofa. Nell had opened a bottle of wine and was standing by the kitchen door.

'There's a letter,' she said.

Carla looked at the envelope on the coffee table, the familiar writing scrawled across the paper in black. Pulling her feet under herself, she dragged a blanket around her shoulders, using it to cover her face too. That couldn't be it. Surely he wouldn't leave her after everything they'd been through, all the history they shared?

Nell walked over and sat cross-legged on the floor, cradling the wine and two glasses.

'What's going on?' She poured Carla a glass and then one for herself.

'He's left me,' Carla said, having downed half the glass in one before explaining.

'Look, this is just a blip, OK?' Nell said. 'He's making a grand gesture to show how upset he is before coming back with his tail between his legs to beg for forgiveness.'

'You don't know Baz. He's as stubborn as they come.'

'No, I don't.' Nell waved the bottle, swaying slightly. 'But I know men. They're kids, the lot of them. As soon as you know that, you can handle them. How do you think I manage Paul? I think of him as a poor lost toddler and work from there.'

Carla laughed. 'Maybe I should have been a lesbian.'

Nell shook her head, digging out her cigarettes from her jacket. 'Big hetero misconception – that there's a choice. Or that it's any easier,' Nell added, holding up her lighter. 'Do you mind?'

'Out the window,' Carla said, picking up her tobacco.

'For God's sake, have a real one for once, live a little.' And pushing a Marlboro into her hand, Nell headed to the window seat.

As they smoked, they watched the last of the night's drinkers stagger home, kebabs in hand. The cool night air was a welcome relief after the day's heat, and as clouds began to gather, the air became lighter.

'What do you think about the whole Mary thing?' Nell asked her. 'Is she our chief suspect?'

Carla didn't know and in truth, right then she didn't care.

Nell sighed into the night. 'I need to get a life, don't I?'

'Yeah, you do. Anyone on the horizon?'

'Nah. Hard to meet people in this job, you know?' Nell dropped her cigarette into the street below.

'Have you tried a dating site?'

'God, no. I'm not really a big sell, am I? Cop, out more hours than I'm in. Drink more than I should, and can't make a washing machine work for love nor money.'

Carla laughed. It felt good. Made her feel lighter. 'You're gorgeous, Nell. You'd have everyone queuing up in a second.'

Nell lit another cigarette. 'Well, you're pretty hot yourself. I mean that in a totally platonic way, of course.'

Carla grinned. 'Of course.' She accepted the cigarette Nell held out for her and took a mouthful of wine.

'I'm sorry if I've been a nightmare to work with.'

Carla looked up, surprised. 'You've not.'

'Yeah, I have, a little. Well, sometimes more than a little.' Nell held up her forearm, street light catching the lines of hot pink skin. 'Seems I haven't put the attack to bed in quite the way I'd hoped I had.'

Carla looked at the scars. She knew about the attack, they all did; the whole station had been on alert for days until they knew she would survive.

'I'm sorry the analyst missed the knife.'

Nell covered her arm. 'Wasn't your fault. And I'm sorry if I took it out on you.'

They sat for a while, backs against the window frame. Carla closed her eyes. She felt good. Maybe it was going to be OK. Being without Baz. She yawned and thought of Mary. Where was she now? Out there somewhere, in Oxford, but how were they going to find her if she'd disappeared without a trace?

'No one just disappears,' she said.

'What?'

'If it is Mary from the beach, we need an address, a telephone number, a car licence plate, just something to start us off. It's got to be there, we just haven't looked hard enough yet.'

Nell smiled.

'What?'

'Even in the midst of heartache, you remain an analyst first.'

She leaned in and pointed her empty glass at Carla. 'Remember that, Brown.' Then she pulled back. 'Now to bed. We have a woman to find in the morning and I've a feeling this one's going to be a challenge, even for you.'

Forty-six
Now

He is asleep. I listen to the sound of his breathing and feel the slow rise and fall of his chest. Then, when I'm sure, I get up and leave.

I walk to the kitchen, pull open the fridge and pour more wine, then sit at the table and drink.

'Hey there, still on the wine?'

'Don't be mean, Aoife.' I'm not in the mood for her teasing.

'Oh, dumbo, I'm just kidding.'

'Our baby is back.'

Aoife is silent.

'And I don't know what to do. Tell me what to do, Aoife.'

'Is she pretty?'

I want to tell her she is beautiful like her mother, with hair the colour of sunset and eyes as big as the moon, but instead I say, 'She wants to meet us.'

'I see.'

'Do you want to?'

'I'm not sure. Let me think.'

While she does, I drink more. I finish the bottle and open another. As I pour, Aoife replies.

'I don't think it's a good idea.'

I feel relief. 'No, I don't think so either.'

'I don't see where it would get us really. I mean, it's done now, isn't it? We can't be her mum like we planned, so what's the point?'

'I agree.'

'Did she say why she came to find us?'

'Just to thank us, I think, for saving her.'

'Hmmm. Is that the real reason, though?'

'That's what I said.'

'To your husband?'

'Yes.'

'Well it doesn't surprise me he's taking the easy option. Weak, that man. I've told you before.'

'He's not.' But I don't say it emphatically. It will only wind her up, and then she'll go on for hours.

'All men are the same. They say they love women, but they're scared of us. They know that if they let us out of our boxes for long enough, we'll find out how crap they really are. We're their mirrors – they project the image they want to see onto us, but they know it's only a matter of time until the mirror breaks and they see themselves for what they really are.'

I've heard this so many times it almost lulls me to sleep.

'I'm sorry, am I keeping you up?' she snaps.

'No. It's late, I should go to bed.'

'Not until we've decided what to do about the baby.'

I suddenly have a thought. 'Do you miss her, Aoife? I do. Well, the thought of what she could have been, at least.'

'No, I don't. How can I miss something I never had?'

I want to remind her she had her for eight months, hidden in her stomach, but I know Aoife well enough to realise when she's put the wall up it's far too high for anyone to climb over.

'You're going to have to get rid of her.'

'But how?'

'Hasn't Eve been any help?'

'No. All Eve cares about is protecting her own back.'

'Well, she's another one we need to get rid of, but first let's sort the baby. You just need to use your initiative like you did with Connor. Which, by the way, I didn't know you had in you. Well, obviously that's not true, but I thought that ship had long since left the port, if you know what I mean.'

'I didn't enjoy it, Aoife.'

'Really, not even a little? Not when you pictured Alf's face there instead of Connor's?'

I hadn't seen his face. I'd attacked from behind. Once a coward, always a coward. He'd been out cold from the get-go, helped along by alcohol, no doubt, and it hadn't felt like I was killing a man. He hadn't moved, save for the movement from my blows, and so it felt more like killing a rat than a human – the way you keep on hitting even after you know it's dead, just to make sure it doesn't jump up and bite you.

I take the empty bottle to the sink and open the cupboard below. Taking out a plastic bag, I wrap the bottle in it and shove it far to the back before putting the half-full one back in the fridge.

'Night, then.' She sounds sulky, but I'm too tired to care.

'Don't be mad at me, Aoife. I miss you.'

'I know you do.' Her voice is softer now. 'I miss you too.'

I stand in the kitchen, moonlight catching the edges of the sink. 'I'll find a way to sort our baby.'

'Thank you.'

'I'm sorry.'

'I know you are.'

I want to cry. To lie on the floor and howl like I did in the home, sobbing until I was so exhausted I fell asleep, the crusty old carpet poking into my skin. I want oblivion.

'Go to bed, my lovely,' Aoife whispers in my ear. 'See you in your dreams.'

Forty-seven

Nell woke to the sound of workmen drilling the pavement outside, a taste of alcohol in her mouth, and an imprint of the sofa on the side of her face. Pulling herself upright, she took in the discarded wine bottles and the makeshift ashtray on the window seat, all of which brought with them seeping memories of last night.

'Hey, you're awake. I've got you a coffee.' Carla held out a mug and smiled. Her hair was perfectly styled, her lips red, and Nell cursed her for being so together after all they'd drunk.

'Thanks.' She took the coffee and sipped, wincing at the burn on her tongue. 'You OK?'

'Yes, I think I am.' Carla sat down next to her and Nell shifted slightly away, aware she must smell of alcohol, fags and sleep.

'Thanks for last night.'

'You're welcome. Thanks for coming up.'

Nell took another sip, this time braced for the heat.

'I've been thinking,' Carla said, her expression suddenly thoughtful. 'If Mary has been targeting Eve, and was involved in Connor's murder, I bet there's something in the phone bills I got from the Telephone Unit that will identify her. I mean, stalkers – which is what she basically is – evolve. The contact they have with their victims has to be sufficient to sate their desire, so although originally happy with letters – maybe the odd glance through a front-room window – gradually that will cease to be enough. They'll need more contact – braver contact, more direct – to get that same feeling of satisfaction. Eve started to get the letters months ago, right?'

Nell's hangover was struggling to keep up so she just nodded.

'So, I don't think Mary would have been content to stick with that for all this time. I think she'd have wanted a different form of contact, and I think somewhere in the investigation we've already come across it, we just didn't know it when we saw it.'

'You think something in the investigation already tells us who this Mary is, and why she killed Connor and is obsessed with Eve?'

'Yes. We have all the pieces; we just need to put them together to make the right picture.'

Nell thought for a moment. Carla's theory might be right, but there was a nagging feeling she couldn't get rid of, one that meant their investigation was about to get a lot more complicated.

'Do you think Eve is in danger?' she asked. Carla's lack of surprise gave Nell her answer.

'I've been thinking about that all night. I think we have to assume she is. If Mary is fixating on Eve, who knows how far she'll go.'

Paul and Bremer were already in the office when Nell and Carla arrived. Carla hurried over to her computer and within seconds was immersed in every check possible to identify Mary. Bremer called Nell over and handed her a takeout coffee.

'Thought you might need it. I certainly do.'

Nell didn't even want to think what Bremer had done the previous evening to warrant a strong black, but she accepted the flat white offered to her.

'Anything good come out of your visit to the social worker?' he asked.

'Well, I'm not sure it's good news, but she was adamant there was no Eve Wilkes at the care home where Mary grew up.'

'What does that mean?' asked Paul.

'It means Eve Graham didn't go to the care home with Mary,' Carla called over her shoulder. 'I'm going to try to confirm, but don't hold your breath – their records are a nightmare.'

'So if the connection between Eve and Mary isn't the care home, what is?' Paul asked.

'And why does Eve's HR record say she attended the home when she didn't?' Nell added.

'Could it be Mary thinks Eve is someone else?' Bremer asked.

'Too coincidental,' Carla called over. 'The person who killed O'Brian has links to Eve and Joanne, we just don't know what that connection is yet, just that they're called Mary.'

'Are we assuming Mary is our prime suspect?' Paul asked. Nell looked at Bremer, a deep frown across his brow.

'I think it's worth giving that some consideration. Carla, what's the likelihood of finding anything out about Mary?'

'Low to zero.' She swung her chair round to face them. 'She disappeared from Portsmouth in 1984. I'm going to be lucky to find anything on her, and then of course she could have changed her name. I've already checked voters and there isn't a Mary Balcombe anywhere near the age Mary would be now.'

'How about a picture?' Bremer asked. 'Can we get one from social services?'

'As I said, their files are bad enough when computerised. Mary's file will be buried in some warehouse so even if we can find it, it's going to take a while.'

Nell felt her mood drop a notch. 'And then we'd have to get an artist to make her look, what, fifty? And then what are we going to do, put out a media appeal?' The idea was ridiculous; not only would it take too long, it would be like looking for a needle in a country-wide haystack. Hell, she might even have gone abroad and then what would they do, get Interpol involved? She could feel the atmosphere in the office dampen, the realisation that without a photo, an address, a phone number or number plate, Mary was going to be virtually untraceable. And if that's what the sixteen-year-old had hoped for, she'd made a damn good job of it.

'I think we need to speak to Joanne,' Carla said. 'Get her to tell us what the phone call was about on the night O'Brian died.

We also know a woman paid Gloria for access to her second flat. We know Gloria hasn't managed to identify that woman from the CCTV as Eve, so that leaves us with Joanne and Mary. If Joanne is working with Mary, and it seems to me to be a legitimate assumption at this stage, then we need to start with her.'

'Agreed.' Bremer pointed to Nell. 'Take Paul and go pay a visit to Joanne – surprise her, so she doesn't have a chance to run. Carla, you get the SIO for the Waites case on the phone and pull him in. If they're working together, we need to find Mary ASAP before Joanne can warn her.' He paused. 'What about Eve? Do we think we need to notify her? Is she at risk?'

'I think we need to at least warn her. Maybe make sure her husband stays with her, seeing as he's a cop. I don't think we need to do anything more yet. The less we make our lines of enquiry public the better.'

Bremer nodded. 'Agreed. Carla, after you're finished with the SIO, get hold of the husband and ask him in for a chat. Nell and Paul, we'll see you later, and if you've any doubt over Joanne's story, bring her in.'

Forty-eight
Then

All I want is to see the baby, know she's OK. But it's been hours now, so all I can do is sit on the hospital bed waiting for a social worker to take me to the police.

No one has mentioned her – why has no one asked me about her? I pick at the rough bed sheet and list the things that worry me: the baby; what will happen to me now; whether I will be in trouble for helping Alf; will I go to jail? My mind buzzes with thoughts and I bite my lip until it bleeds.

'Hey, don't do that.'

I look up and find the copper who rescued me smiling down at me. He hands me a tissue and I dab it at my lip. I suddenly want to cry. I'd forgotten how gentle his voice is, how it wraps me up and makes me feel safe.

'Where's the baby?' I whisper so the nurses can't hear. He comes and sits on the bed and takes my hand.

'Your baby?'

I hesitate. If I say she's mine maybe they'll let me keep her? But if I keep her Alf can find her and I don't want that to happen. It suddenly strikes me I shouldn't want her found either. She links me to Aoife's murder just as much as she links Alf.

I'm filled with sadness that I can't be with her and wish I could have held her for a little longer in the hope she might remember me.

'No,' I say, 'she was Aoife's. My friend.' He nods and I see he knows this already. Of course, I think, they will have found her body by now. I'm consumed by grief and guilt.

'Shall I tell you a story?' he asks. I nod, my throat too filled with tears to reply.

'My mother was sixteen when she had me. Just about your age. She'd been in care all her life and she saw me as the start of her life. The proper life she should have had but didn't.'

I want to lean into him, rest my head on his shoulder while he talks, but I don't.

'She had me in the toilet of the care home she was in. She wrapped me in the blanket she'd bought for me and took me to her room. My mum fed me as she lay on the bed, singing softly. She told me a light breeze came in through the window, making the curtains flutter and a wind chime tingle. It was, she said, the most peaceful she had ever felt and she knew this was why she had been born. To have me.'

He stops for a moment and I stay quiet, understanding that he's remembering her.

'She kept me hidden for three days.' He speaks with pride. 'Three days she went downstairs for breakfast, lunch and dinner before returning to give me mine. Then one day, the girl in the next bedroom to my mum told the staff she'd heard a baby cry.' He takes a deep breath and lets his shoulders fall as he exhales.

'They found me and took me from her. I can't even begin to know the pain she must have felt, having her life snatched away like that. She told me she screamed and fought and begged them to leave me, but they took me anyway, bundled me into the back of a car, and the last she saw of me was my face wet with tears as they drove me away.'

He seems to run out of breath, so I squeeze his hand just as Aoife used to squeeze mine.

'But you found her?'

He brightens. 'I did! Three months ago I managed to track her down after years of searching. She's lovely. I worried she wouldn't be my mum, you know?'

I nod. Because I do.

'But she was my mum right from the off.' He says this with such love I am almost overwhelmed by it.

'You see the thing is,' he suddenly becomes serious, 'she didn't handle the separation well and there are scars on her wrists to prove it. And when I saw you, running to me with this little baby in your arms, I could only think of my mum and what she would have wanted a man to do to help her if she'd managed to save me like you saved Aoife's baby.' He looks down at his hands. My heart is pounding.

'I wanted you to have a chance to know her.' He looks at me and his eyes are blue like the sea. 'I wanted to keep her safe for you so you didn't have to go through what my mum went through.'

'Where is she?' I whisper.

'With my mum. She's caring for her and I promise you there's not a thing my mum won't do to help her and you.'

'She is mine. Mine and Aoife's,' I say, firmly.

He nods.

'Well, I've sort of got myself in a bit of a hole now anyway. They know there's a baby and they're looking for it. So I've got to keep her hidden for now, anyway.' He suddenly looks lost and I think how handsome he is. How old can he be? Twenty, twenty-one? I can see the emotion has exhausted him – not just from finding me but from finding his mum too.

I want to tell him I'm grateful and I am, in part, but she is still proof of what I did, so I could never keep her. I could see her, though? Say goodbye properly. Tell her about her mum and send her out into the world with all the love I can give her.

'Thank you,' I say, kissing his cheek. 'It is the nicest thing anyone has ever done for me.'

Forty-nine

As Carla began dialling Hampshire Police she saw Gerry appear at the door with two takeout coffee cups in his hands. She hung up.

'I thought I'd bring the coffee to you rather than make you come to it.' He offered her a cup, then handed her a sugar.

'Thanks.'

'You OK?'

He sat opposite her, his back to the wall listing the people of interest in the O'Brian case. She glanced at Bremer's office. She needed to get Gerry out of there.

'Yeah, sorry, just busy.'

'Any new developments?'

'No, just plodding on, you know how it is.'

'How was Eve in the interview?' He took off the plastic lid and stirred in three sugars.

'Prickly.'

Gerry laughed. 'She's mad at me because I gave you the letters.'

'Why did you? Give them to me, I mean?'

Gerry kept stirring the coffee. 'I thought it might help you in the O'Brian case, seeing as the author had mentioned it, but I suppose I also hoped you'd find out who was sending them.' He looked at her.

'We're no further forward on that – sorry.'

'That's OK.'

'Are you worried about them? About Eve?'

'A bit. They're unsettling. It's making Eve distant and I'm not used to that.' He smiled. 'I always thought it might be nice to be a bit more independent of each other, but it turns out I quite like us being joined at the hip.'

Carla took a sip of her coffee. She should ask him about his phone call to Joanne. He could clear it up, tell her he was just warning her off, no crime in that. So why wasn't she?

'Did you find anything more on Mary? How she's linked to the O'Brian case?'

'No. Drawing a blank there too.'

He nodded.

'And you're sure there's nobody Eve knows, past or present, called Mary?' she asked.

Gerry suddenly looked sad.

'Gerry?'

'No, no one. Or if there was, she's long gone.'

'So, there was someone?'

Gerry shook his head but before she could press him further, Bremer opened his door, looking thunderous. He strode over to the desk, glaring at Gerry.

'How can we help you, Sergeant?'

Gerry looked surprised. 'Just popping in to say hello to Carla, sir. You know us sergeants, always wanting to look after the team.'

'She's not on your team, she's on mine. Are you suggesting I don't look after her?'

Her? The cat's mother? Carla fought the urge to intervene. Bremer looked as though he was going to blow at any moment and she'd rather not be the focus if he did.

'Not at all, sir.' He stood, smiled down at Carla and said, 'I'll see you later. Hope the coffee helps.' He glanced at the wall behind him. Bremer moved to block his view.

'Sergeant, please leave.' Bremer still hadn't looked at Carla but anger radiated off him.

Gerry turned to face him with a look Carla had never seen before. 'Is there a problem with me asking how an investigation involving my wife is progressing?'

'Yes.'

Gerry put his coffee down. 'I'm getting the sense you think we're involved somehow? All I did was give you letters that might assist you. If you can't find out how they could help the case, I would suggest you try looking a little bit harder.'

'Your wife is involved in the death of Connor O'Brian. I repeat, please leave.'

'Involved?' Gerry held Bremer's stare. 'How is she involved other than by doing her job?'

When Bremer didn't reply, Gerry continued. 'Do you have evidence or are you just fishing?'

Carla stood. 'Gerry, please. Leave it.'

He didn't look at her. 'Come on, tell me what evidence you have?'

Bremer stepped closer to Gerry. 'I gave you an order to leave.'

'And I'm not following it.'

'I will remove you if you fail to leave.'

They stood, face to face, for what felt like minutes before Gerry grabbed his coffee.

He left without saying a word and after he'd gone, they remained silent. Carla was shaking. She'd never seen Gerry like this before. What the hell had happened? He knew Eve was involved in the case because he'd damn well told his wife to give Carla the letter that indicated she was. So what the hell had made that kick off?

Bremer turned to face her, before sitting down next to her. 'Carla—'

'I couldn't stop him,' she interrupted. 'He just walked in. I couldn't tell him to leave.'

He nodded. 'I know. And I'm sorry he put you in that position. Do you understand how inappropriate it is for him to request information on the case?'

'Yes.'

'He's using your close relationship to get information he shouldn't have access to.'

She wanted him to shut up. She got it, she really did.

'That's abusing a friendship. That means he's putting his interests above yours.'

Was he? No, he just wanted to help his wife. That was a normal reaction to have.

'He should respect your work and not pressure you into saying things you don't feel comfortable with.'

'He didn't.' But of course, he had.

'OK.' Bremer smiled, but a soft smile, not the normal full beam. 'Have you rung Hampshire Police yet?'

'No. I was just about to when . . .' She stopped.

'OK, well get on to it now.'

'Will do.'

When Bremer had gone back to his office, Carla sat very still, trying to detangle her feelings. She was annoyed to have been a pawn in their power struggle; she was annoyed Bremer had seen fit to step in when she could have dealt with it; but mostly she was annoyed Gerry had even come to the office in the first place. Surely he should know it wasn't on?

Her mobile bleeped. Checking it, she saw a message from Gerry. *Sorry.*

She stuffed her mobile in her bag, sick of the lot of them, and picked up the phone to Hampshire Police.

Fifty

Hampshire Police gave Carla the phone number for the senior investigating officer in the Waites case. They also told her he'd retired to a village in the Cotswolds, only twenty minutes away from HQ.

'Mr Eyre? Carla Brown, analyst from Thames Valley Police.'

'Analyst? They're getting you to do their work for them now, eh?' His voice was warm, not chiding, an upper-class accent Carla thought more suited to the military than the police.

'Mr Eyre—'

'Call me William.'

'William, we were wondering if you could come in to speak to us about the Alf Waites murder case you were in charge of back in 1983?'

'That's a long time ago, Ms Brown. My memory is about as

much use as my waterworks these days.' He laughed and Carla couldn't help but join him.

'Well, we have toilets here, if that helps.'

More chuckling, which turned into a cough. 'Sorry, lungs took a battering during the 1980s. Forty a day on the crime squad does that, you know.' His tone became wistful.

'The Waites case?'

'Ah yes, sorry job that one.'

'Could you come in? Say, about midday?'

'Well, I'll have to check my schedule. I have an important cribbage match to win.' He laughed again, awkwardly. 'But yes, I'll be in to see you shortly.'

When Carla collected him from the front desk, William Eyre was exactly as she had imagined. Dressed in tweed, with a wooden walking stick, his face ruddy from spirits, and his stomach round from good food. What she didn't expect was how easily he slipped back into detective chief inspector mode.

'So,' he said as they walked towards the office, 'have you got a lead?'

'A lead?'

'On Mary Balcombe. I was always convinced she was up to her eyes in it, so I assume the case has been reopened?'

'Not exactly, no.'

Eyre stopped walking. 'Then why am I here?'

Carla waited for a uniform to pass before replying. 'We think it may be connected to another case, a more recent one.'

'Ah . . .' He continued walking, nodding, as if proved right about something. 'So she's struck again, has she? They always do – once a killer, always a killer. Although I expect you know that.'

Carla didn't reply, just held the door open for him, for which he thanked her.

'Of course it's not me you should really be speaking to, it's that young lad who made it his mission to "save" her.' He shook his head. 'Most unbecoming.'

'Young lad?'

They'd reached the office, but as she held another door open, they both stopped. Eyre tapped the side of his head.

'Memory isn't what it was, but I'll dig around for the name.'

'Thanks, that would be really helpful.'

'You're very welcome, my dear.'

Bremer had a cup of tea waiting and Eyre seemed slightly put out. Not used to being a witness, she thought, taking the seat next to him. Bremer smiled his smile. Eyre looked unimpressed.

'Thank you for coming at such short notice, sir.'

Carla noted the reference to his past rank; a clever move, she decided, when Eyre reacted with a nod.

'I'd like to speak with you about Mary Balcombe. We'd like to know a bit more about who she was, where she went.'

Eyre let out a short laugh, but unlike the one Carla had heard earlier, this was pointed. 'I think if either of us knew where she went, we wouldn't be sitting here now.'

'You said in the corridor you assumed we'd reopened the

Waites case because we'd found evidence on Mary. Why do you think she was involved in Aoife's murder?' Carla asked.

Eyre sat back in his chair and placed his hands over his stomach.

'It just never really sat well with me – you know the sort of case.' He looked to Bremer, who nodded. 'The kind you know is cut and dried on paper, but something just doesn't feel right.'

'Did you look into Mary?' Bremer asked. 'When you had this instinct there was more to it?'

'Of course.' Eyre seemed offended. 'But it was man grooms girls, kills girl whose pregnancy proves his guilt, involves other groomed girl, who is left traumatised by the whole experience.'

Bremer was silent, waiting for Eyre to continue.

'We see it now more than we did back then,' he went on, 'organised groups grooming girls for sex parties. But back then it was all new to us. We tried hard to unpick it, but it felt like trying to find one end of a roll of wool from another. And of course social services were no help; they were too busy conducting their own internal review of what'd gone wrong to think about helping out the police.' He rolled his eyes. 'Arse-covering reigned back then, especially where social services were concerned.'

'It's no different now,' Bremer agreed.

'So you never found out where she went?' Carla asked.

Eyre turned to her. 'No,' he said, 'by then the perp was behind bars and we had no need to look for her.'

'You suggested to me earlier you always expected to hear about Mary again. Why was that?'

Eyre looked impressed she had remembered. 'Because her

story never quite added up. She was covered in blood – not her own, Aoife's, as well as unknown DNA that seemed to link back to Aoife, but not sufficiently for us to prove another person was involved.'

Bremer frowned. 'I don't understand. You found DNA linked to the victim, but it wasn't the victim's?'

Eyre looked steadily at him.

'Aoife had a child?' Carla asked; it was the only thing that made sense.

'We believe so. Aoife's stomach was slit from side to side. The post-mortem showed she'd been pregnant, but there was no sign of the baby. We couldn't prove the child's gestation, so defence would have argued conjecture if we'd presented it, but the whole team felt it was relevant.'

'But why was this not made public?'

'It was. There were a few reports of it in the local news but we asked the media not to over emphasise it.'

'Because if someone knew it had survived, they might go after it?'

'Exactly. And why else slit a young girl's stomach in two?'

'And you'd be looking because that child would have been proof of the abuse?' Bremer offered. Eyre lifted his left shoulder slightly, an attempt at a shrug.

'That's what we decided. Aoife showed signs of significant gestation, possibly up to eight months, so any baby delivered would have been hard to get rid of. And you can't tell me, in all this time, it wouldn't have been found by some dog walker or

amateur archaeologist by now? So whoever took it, kept it alive –
but why?'

'Do you believe Mary had something to do with it?'

'Yes, but why she didn't allow it to die like its mother, we
never understood. And how did she rescue it between leaving the
beach and hiding in the bin? We timelined the hell out of it and
couldn't make it work.'

'What about that young man?' Carla asked. 'The one you said
was unbecoming in his involvement. Could he have helped get
rid of the child?'

'We wondered that too, but then why would he? There was
nothing to suggest he'd ever met Mary before that evening, so
how could we believe he got rid of a child for her before calling
for help? And if he did, there was only a maximum of twelve
minutes before backup arrived, so where could he have taken it?
We checked every hospital, charity and care home in a five-mile
radius. Nothing.'

'Are you sure he didn't know Mary before that night?' Carla
asked. It seemed impossible to her that a man would help steal a
child with someone he'd only just met. But then people did all
sorts of unpredictable things, often for unfathomable reasons.

'We checked it all out and there was nothing to link the two.'

'Did you ask him if he saw a child?' Bremer asked.

'Of course we asked him. We weren't completely incompe-
tent! But he maintained he'd met Mary as she ran off the beach,
saw the man he assumed was attacking her, and told her to hide
in a bin while he radioed for help.'

'And you believed him?'

'I had no reason to disbelieve him.'

'Why?'

'Because he was one of our finest young officers.'

Fifty-one
Then

I sit with Aoife's baby in my arms and cry. It's so amazing to hold her and see how solid she is, how alive, but it reminds me Aoife has gone and that I'm alone.

'Can't we keep her?' I look up and see him sadly shake his head.

'How can we do that? Someone will notice her, put two and two together and we'll be arrested.'

He's right, but I still wish we could. Aoife was right, babies love you no matter what you are, so why can't I have that love? In Aoife's place.

'We haven't got long; the home will check on you soon.'

I lift her up and smell her soft pink skin. I hold her close and shut my eyes, imagining the warmth of her body is Aoife's. 'What shall we call her?'

'What?'

'While we have her,' I open my eyes to look at him, 'she has to have a name.'

He looks frustrated, but I know he'll relent. I've learned that about him in the last week since Aoife died. He is kind and gentle and when I see him I get a lot of little butterflies dancing in my stomach.

'What would you like to call her?' he asks.

I look at the baby. What is her name? I try to think what Aoife would have called her and feel frustrated she didn't tell me. I kiss the baby's hair, so fine I worry it could rub off.

'I think I'd like to call her Joanne. After my mum. Do you think that's OK? Jo for short.'

He comes over and smiles down at her. 'Hello, little Jo.'

I try to cross my fingers under her blanket – maybe now she has a name, he'll let me keep her.

The police keep talking to me and we're both worried they will find out about Joanne. I've been working hard at school so as to make the social workers, who watch me like hawks, think that I'm behaving myself, but it's still hard to sneak out and see her.

'Why don't we run away with her?' I say when I'm next at his house. 'Just take her and go somewhere no one knows us.'

He's washing Joanne's bottles, his back to me. 'A twenty-year-old man and a sixteen-year-old girl with a baby in tow will look suspicious wherever we go.'

I dangle a toy in front of her face and watch as her eyes try to focus on it, mesmerised.

'But *we* could go?'

I look up. He's staring at me with an odd look on his face, his hands covered in soap suds.

'What do you mean?'

'Well, you're sixteen now, you can go where you like. I can move anywhere really – transfer to another force, so we could be sure of an income.' He's becoming animated. 'I mean, what's for you here?'

'My mum,' I say immediately, even though I haven't seen her in over a year.

He doesn't miss a beat. 'We can invite her to stay with us, away from your dad. It would be like a new little family.'

The word makes my heart twitch. I look at his kind eyes and the brown hair that never looks brushed and wonder what it would be like to be a family with him.

'But Joanne . . .' I say.

He turns back to the bottles.

'We can't, Mary. I'm so sorry.'

And I know he's right, I know he is sorry, and I also know he's not going to change his mind.

The night he is to take Joanne away, rain is battering the windows.

'You can't go now, can you?'

I see him wince at the hope in my voice. He comes across to me and looks down at Joanne in my arms, then kisses the top of my head. I haven't had human contact other than Joanne for so long I feel electricity jump through me. He places his hand on my shoulder; it's warm and heavy.

'Let me have her, Mary.'

I pull her closer. 'No. I want to go.'

'There's more chance of us being seen if there are two of us.'

I look down at the baby, who is perfectly asleep, a small bubble of milk on the side of her lip. I dab it with the blanket.

'You know I'm right. And then after the court case, we'll go too.'

'Will she be safe, where you take her?' My voice is so small I can barely hear it.

He nods.

'And you have the bag with all her stuff and the note explaining which toys she likes?'

Again, he nods.

'Do you think she'll ever come looking for us?'

'Maybe.'

'What would we do?'

'I honestly don't know. I suppose it would depend on what she wanted from us.'

I look at Joanne, who is starting to wriggle, and wonder what she will be like when she's big. I get a sudden punch to my heart at the thought she'll meet a man like Alf or that her new mum won't want her when she's older. I start to cry. I can't stop anything bad happening to her, just like I couldn't stop it happening to Aoife.

'Mary . . .' He's speaking softly in my ear. 'I'm going to have to go.'

I hiccup back a tear and look at Joanne. 'I love you,' I say. 'I love you so much, and your mummy was the best thing to ever happen to me. But she was wrong when she said you are our baby. You're not, you're hers, and all I can do is make you safe.' I stroke the top of Joanne's head, hair soft like down. 'She would've loved you to the moon and back every single day and so would I. I'm so sorry I took her away from you and that I won't be there in her place. Please don't hate me when you grow up and please don't try to find me, because I'm not worth it.'

I start to cry again, so much I find it hard to breathe. I kiss her on the head, tuck the blanket in tightly around her, and hold her up to him. He leans down to kiss my cheek, but I turn my head and our lips meet. We stay like that for a moment, holding on tight to each other, with Joanne close between us.

Then he's gone, and with him the only thing holding me to this life.

Fifty-two

Ian Fowler flung open and door and glared out at them. 'What?'

Nell decided to match his directness with her own. 'There's been a development in the O'Brian case.'

'And?'

'So we'd like to speak to your wife, please.' It wasn't a question and Fowler knew it.

'She's asleep at the moment.'

Nell put her hand on the door and a boot into the hall. 'That's OK, we'll wait while you wake her.'

Ten minutes later Joanne appeared, dishevelled and bleary-eyed, wrapped in a blanket.

'Hello, Joanne,' Nell said. 'We'd like to ask you about a phone call made to your house on the night Connor O'Brian was killed.'

Ian glanced down at Joanne. It looked innocent enough, but

Nell knew it was a question, one that told her he wasn't the one who had taken the call.

'Joanne,' she asked, gently. 'Did somebody phone you the night Connor was killed?'

Joanne didn't move; it was as if she couldn't even hear them. Nell looked to Ian.

'It's hard for her to have you here. The trauma of the last few years is still very real and we've barely undergone therapy for it.'

His tone was gentler than before and Nell nodded. Leaning forward, she tried to catch Joanne's eye.

'Joanne,' she said softly. 'We don't think you did anything wrong. We think the killer has involved you in this by mistake. I know you want to avoid all mention of it and pretend it didn't happen. And I understand you don't trust us, but if you know anything at all about that night, please tell us.'

Nell thought Joanne was about to cry, but the woman surprised her by wiping her face with the palms of her hands before sitting upright.

'Someone did call here.' She ignored the questioning look from her husband. 'I don't know who it was. They hung up before I could speak to them.'

'The thing is, Joanne, we know the call lasted three minutes. So, are you telling me the call was just three minutes of silence?'

Joanne opened her mouth to speak, then shut it. Ian stared at Nell, his arm still around his wife.

'Can you tell me what relevance this has to anything?' he asked.

'The killer called the victim and one other person – that other person was your wife. I'd say that was pretty relevant, wouldn't you?'

When he didn't answer, she turned back to Joanne. 'Was the woman who rang you called Mary?'

Joanne's head shot up. 'Why do you ask that?'

'Why don't you answer that?' Nell replied. 'Do you know someone called Mary?'

'No.'

'Was the woman who contacted you on the night Connor was murdered called Mary?' Nell repeated.

'No.'

'Are you working with Mary?'

Joanne gave a small laugh. 'Working for what?'

'I don't know, I'd hoped you'd tell me that. Maybe you want to frame Ms Graham for Connor's murder?'

'No.' Her tone was one Nell imagined she'd learned in prison: hard, defensive.

'But you do want to pay back Ms Graham for what you consider a miscarriage of justice?'

Ian opened his mouth, but Joanne put her hand on his arm, silencing him.

'I want Ms Graham to pay for what she did and why she did it. I don't want to do that by framing her for a crime she didn't commit. How would that be any better than what she did to me?'

'So why did she do it?'

'Pardon?'

'Why did Ms Graham frame you for the murder of your child?'

Joanne winced as if Nell had slapped her.

'You'd have to ask her that.'

'I'm asking you.'

'Because she found proof, Sergeant, proof that gave her crimes away.'

Nell felt adrenalin kick in. 'Crimes?'

When Joanne remained stoically silent, Paul took over.

'Joanne, what did Mary say to you on the phone?'

Joanne hesitated before answering, clearly deciding whether to admit her role or stick to denial. She chose the former.

'She said nothing. I asked if it was her, but she didn't reply.'

'But you thought it was her?' Paul asked.

'Yes. She's done it before.'

Nell made a mental note to get Carla to check further back on Joanne's phone bills.

'So you've spoken to Mary before?' Paul continued.

'No. But I have spoken to her husband. And I think Mary has called me. I get odd late-night calls when no one speaks.'

'You never told me that,' Ian said, lowering himself onto the seat next to her. Nell held up her hand.

'You've spoken to Mary's husband?'

Joanne looked frustrated she had to explain. 'Mary isn't yet ready to speak to me, so her husband does.'

'What were the conversations about?'

'Just chatty, asking how I was, that sort of thing.'

'And you contacted them?'

'Yes.'

Paul glanced at Nell, who nodded for him to continue.

'And why was that?'

'Because Mary and her husband saved me – they're the reason I'm alive.'

Nell couldn't believe she hadn't seen it coming.

'Joanne,' Nell said, 'did Mary save you from the beach?'

Joanne looked at her. 'Yes.'

'Was your mum called Aoife?'

'Yes. I just wanted to find out who had saved me, so I searched all the papers for clues of an abandoned baby around the time I was born, but the only thing I could find was a reference to a missing baby. I did look everywhere for more information and finally found a mention of a policeman who had looked after me the night I was born. I traced him to Thames Valley but when I contacted him and asked about Mary he explained she wasn't ready to acknowledge her role in my mum's death, so we were biding our time, trying to coax her to face up to her past. And mine.'

'Joanne,' Nell leaned in again, keen to get her full attention, 'did you collude with Mary to kill Connor O'Brian?'

'No.' She was assertive now. 'I had no reason to hurt him.'

'But Mary did?' When Joanne didn't reply, Nell glanced at Paul. 'Joanne, I'm going to have to take you in, do you understand that? There is a lot we need to go over and I think it's best we do that at the station.'

'No!' Ian's face flushed with anger. 'I won't let you do this to her again. I promised to care for her, to look after her, and so far, thanks to you, I've failed. But not this time.' He stood. Paul did too.

'Please take a seat, Mr Fowler.'

'No. This time I'm coming out fighting, so no, you may not "take her in" unless you have a damn good reason to do so.'

'Would accessory to murder be good enough for you?'

'My wife hasn't murdered anyone – not Connor, and most definitely not our child.'

Nell hadn't wanted it to, but she'd guessed it would end like this, and if they were going to continue to obstruct the investigation she really had no choice. 'Joanne Fowler, I'm arresting you for—'

'NO!' Ian launched towards her. His hand connected with her cheek, but before she could react, Paul had him on the floor. 'Ian Fowler, I am arresting you for attacking a police officer—'

Joanne let out a howl. 'Not again, not again not again not again . . .' She began to hit her hands against her temples, harder and harder, until Nell grabbed her wrists.

'Stop.'

Joanne struggled against her, both their arms in the air. 'I didn't do anything.' Her face was wet, tears and mucus merging to form a shiny film. 'Please, I just wanted to find my family.'

Nell felt Joanne's arms go slack, so she loosened her hold, pulling them downwards to Joanne's waist. She spoke gently, as if to a child.

'Let's go to the station and I'm sure we can clear it all up. We just need to find Mary, Joanne, before she hurts anyone else. Before she hurts you.'

Joanne was shaking her head, looking at the floor, and Nell doubted she'd heard her.

Fifty-three

Eyre sipped at his coffee and continued. 'I don't remember the officer's name, I'm afraid, but the boy was conscientious, if a little too empathetic for my liking. Seemed to have developed an emotional attachment to Mary, you could see that straight off at the scene. Might have been his way of dealing with the trauma of the event, but even so . . .' Eyre trailed off.

'Do you know if he's still on the force?' Carla figured if he was new to the job at the time of Aoife's killing, there might be a chance he was still on active duty. And if he was, maybe he'd know what happened to Mary.

'No, and that's probably why I can't remember his name. He left soon after the case went to court. Gave his evidence, then transferred to another force.'

'Which one?'

'No idea I'm afraid.'

HR would know.

'Was there anyone else on the beach that night, anyone who might have taken the baby for Mary?' As Carla saw it, between Mary leaving the beach and meeting the unknown officer, she'd managed to hide the baby, which meant if it wasn't him, someone else must have helped her.

'Not that we documented, but remember we weren't on the scene until at least twelve minutes after she'd left the beach.'

'Yes, but she met your officer much sooner than that, didn't she?' Carla said.

'Yes, three to five minutes, if that.'

'So it's just impossible it was anyone other than him who helped her hide the baby.' It didn't help, but it closed a blind alley.

'If it was hidden,' Bremer said. 'We are assuming the child lived, but what if Waites got rid of it while Mary was running for help?'

'Impossible,' Eyre said. 'He wouldn't have had a chance to bury it anywhere other than the beach, and we searched every last inch of it.'

'Impossible to search every last bit, though?'

'True,' Eyre conceded, 'but he'd have had to dig pretty far down to hide it from us, and we saw no sign anywhere of digging, other than at Aoife's makeshift grave. Plus,' Eyre added, 'the tide has a marvellous way of revealing secrets of the sand, and it never has. Not to my knowledge, anyway.'

'So we're back to the baby being alive when Mary left the beach and our unknown officer colluding with her to hide it,' Carla said. 'What was the timeline between him meeting Mary and calling for help?'

'He said he met her, rushed her to the bin when he saw Waites coming up the steps, and then ran back to his patrol car. He estimated four minutes between meeting her and radioing in.'

Carla wished Eyre was as good at names as he was at the rest of the case details. But then a timeline would have been pored over time and again; a junior officer, not so much.

'But we've only got his word for that?' Bremer asked. 'The time he took.'

'Yes. It could be he took longer, but I doubt it. We found Waites near to the scene, and even taking into account his size slowing him down, he'd only managed a distance of about ten minutes.'

'And Waites never admitted there was a baby?'

'No, both he and Mary denied any knowledge of it.'

Bremer looked thoughtful. 'I wonder why she saved it.'

'Proof,' replied Eyre.

'Proof?'

'Yes. She'd been abused by this man who'd killed her best friend in front of her. The baby was proof of what he'd done and taking it was like some sort of insurance policy.'

'But that would require careful thought, wouldn't it?' Carla said, 'and I can't imagine a fifteen-year-old being that savvy moments after her best friend was killed. Maybe she wanted to save it because she loved Aoife.'

The men shared a glance but Carla didn't care. Something was irritating her, something she couldn't remember, but which she had a feeling mattered to the case.

'When did you say the officer left Hampshire Police?'

'Right after the case went to court, so about a year.'

'And you say he'd been in the police for about two years by that point?'

Eyre nodded, watching her carefully.

'And his age at the time he transferred?'

'I'd say around twenty-one.'

Carla stood. 'Can I use your office?'

Bremer looked questioningly at her, but when she didn't reply he said, 'Sure.'

Carla grabbed her notebook and with an apologetic smile at Eyre, went into Bremer's office and closed the door.

She rang HR. Three short minutes later, she heard what she'd hoped against hope she wouldn't.

'And you're sure? He transferred from Hampshire Police?'

'Absolutely sure. The third of September, 1984.'

It was Gerry. She'd remembered him telling her he was lucky he was only going to have to serve twenty-eight years to get his pension and it hadn't occurred to her to ask why not the usual thirty. But now she knew. He'd transferred from Hampshire Police, bringing his pension with him, at precisely the time Mary had gone missing.

Gerry was the officer on the beach. The age fitted – Gerry was coming up to fifty-five, so at the time of the murder thirty-five years ago he would have been twenty. Then she remembered the phone call to Joanne.

Joanne who was thirty-five. Joanne who was adopted because she'd been abandoned.

Carla had no idea what to do. She'd kept the phone call a secret and now that call was the one thing to link Joanne to the O'Brian murder. And what about Gerry? The man who'd helped her so much over the years, and not just in work but in life, too. He'd been the first person she'd told when Baz asked her to marry him and the first she'd confided in over her fears of having a baby. She put her head in her hands. She couldn't lose another person from her life, not now, not after Baz had gone.

Bremer knocked on the door and opened it. 'You looked like you had a lead there?'

Carla looked up, startled. 'Not sure, still firming it up.'

Bremer looked interested. 'OK, I'm going to take Mr Eyre to his car. Let me know when I get back.'

When he'd gone she just sat and stared at the desk, trying to ignore the conclusion she'd already drawn.

Joanne had come back to find the policeman who'd saved her and Gerry had tried to cover it up. But why? And how far had he gone to make sure they weren't linked?

And then she realised. If Gerry carried Aoife's baby to safety, then Gerry must know the person who handed her to him.

Mary.

Fifty-four
Now – Eve

I pull petals off the roses Gerry brought me. 'My husband loves me, my husband loves me not,' petals fall on the kitchen floor, 'my husband loves me, my husband loves me not . . .'

'Eve?'

I close my hand round the head of the rose and crush it. 'My husband loves me not.' I turn to face him.

'What's the matter? Has Mary been here again?'

'Why would you think that?'

His face is one of studied concern. 'You just seem angry.'

'I'm not angry. I'm annoyed we've got ourselves into a position where the police are now circling.'

'And you blame me for that?'

'It was your idea.'

'But you agreed.'

He's right. I did. When Mary sent her latest creation, it felt different from the others. Like she was stepping up her attack. So we agreed it made sense to wrong-foot her by going public. 'But I didn't agree to the rest, did I?' And that is the crux.

Gerry sits down. 'I had a run-in with Bremer.'

I stare at him. This just keeps getting worse. He is pale and his hands are shaking. I soften. We are, after all, in this together and if we fight we're doing Mary's job for her.

I put the kettle on. 'Or would you prefer a glass of wine?'

'A beer would be good.'

I open the fridge and take out a bottle of wine and a beer. Popping the lid, I hand it to him before getting myself a glass and joining him at the table.

'What happened?'

'I went to see Carla and he told me to leave. I refused.'

I am lost for words.

'He thinks you have something to do with Connor's death.'

'What? That's absurd.' I almost laugh.

'Is it?' Gerry's eyes don't leave my face, searching it for the answer he wants. I take a mouthful of wine.

'I need a cigarette.'

'No, please, Eve, answer the question.'

'Are you seriously asking me if I murdered a man?'

'Yes.'

I stand, grab my wine and pull open the kitchen door. Gerry follows me. After a couple of drags I'm able to reply.

'Why do you think I killed a man, Gerry?'

He looks pained. 'Because since Mary's come back you've been distracted, distant, and I feel like you're slipping away from me and I don't know what to do about that.'

He's right. I have been. But that's to be expected. It was a shock to hear from her after all this time. It was Joanne's fault, coming back and bringing Mary with her.

I take his hand and hold it up to my cheek, then kiss it. He smells of soap but tastes of salt after a hot day in the office. I kiss it again.

'I'm sorry. You're right. And we need to be together on this one or it's going to go very wrong. But you can't seriously think I would kill a man and then go and work the crime scene immediately after?'

Gerry shook his head. 'No, of course not.' I see him hesitate and I'm about to get angry when he says, 'I think they know I called Joanne.'

I let go of his hand. I told him not to contact her. I told him no good would come of it and we needed to cut her out of our lives, not bring her into it.

'The phone bills?' I say.

'Yes. They may have got Joanne's call data and it would show up. Carla would recognise the number, I'm sure of it.'

'But she hasn't said anything to you?'

'No.'

I relax a little. 'Well, then. Carla would have told you. She adores you and your friendship would matter more to her. She'd definitely put you first.' I take a couple of mouthfuls of wine and start to feel better. Maybe this is all going to work out OK. We just need to get rid of Mary first, then deal with Joanne afterwards.

I feel a laugh brewing at the absurdity of it all. Me chasing Mary, who's chasing Eve, and Joanne chasing all of us. I think I may be drunk. I take another mouthful of wine just to make sure.

'Anyway,' I say, 'the point is, Carla mustn't know yet that you called Joanne, so what we need to concentrate on is getting rid of Mary.' I can see he's still hurt, but we don't have time for nicey-niceness.

'Eve,' he says. I stub out my cigarette.

'Yes.'

'Do you think Mary killed Connor?'

And there we have it. He's finally figured it out.

'Yes. I do.'

'Why did she kill him?' The pain in his expression is almost unbearable.

'I have no idea. Best you go and ask her that yourself.'

Fifty-five

'What do you mean, you won't charge her?' Nell was standing, hands on the custody sergeant's desk, wishing she could grab the charge sheet and fill it in herself. The uniformed sergeant stared coolly back at her.

'As I said just a second ago, charge her with what?'

'Withholding evidence, resisting arrest, to name but two.'

He looked at Joanne, who was standing next to Paul, looking at the floor, her face streaked with tears.

'I must say, I've never seen a more compliant subject, Sergeant.'

'Well she is now, but half an hour ago she was screaming bloody murder.'

'That's not true,' Ian shouted, his handcuffed arms held lightly by Paul. The sergeant raised an eyebrow at Nell and she knew she'd lost.

'Are you going to be the one to tell my DCI you've let his suspect go, or am I?'

'You are, Sergeant Jackson, and you might ask him to train his officers not to waste my time while you're at it.'

Nell didn't answer. Turning to Paul, she said, 'You OK to book him in?' She nodded at Ian.

'Sure.'

'I assume you're going to let us book him for resisting arrest?' she asked the custody sergeant.

'That one I'll do for you.'

'Much obliged.' And she didn't bother hiding the sarcastic tone.

In the office, Nell sat down in her chair and leaned her head back, staring up at the ceiling. The custody sergeant had wound her up so much she needed a cigarette, but feeling in her pocket, she realised she'd left them in the car. 'Just fucking typical.'

Carla came to the door of Bremer's office. 'What?'

'I've just had a run-in with a job-pissed custody sergeant and now I've got no cigarettes. And what are you doing in there?'

Carla looked tired. The trademark red lipstick had worn off; it made her look younger.

'Want me to roll you one?'

Nell couldn't think of anything worse than a rolly, but her nicotine craving overrode her disgust. 'Sure, thanks. Join me?'

'Yeah, why not.'

Outside was cooler than it had been in weeks. Clouds passed

the sun, shutting out light before suddenly revealing it again. Nell took a drag of the roll-up.

'Not bad. Smooth.' She watched a cloud, the underneath of which carried rain past them, and felt the anger of the last half-hour pass with it. 'What were you doing in Bremer's office?'

Carla looked uncomfortable.

'What's wrong?'

Carla let out a sigh that felt to Nell as if she was giving in, offloading something into the air, allowing it to drift away with the smoke.

'I think Gerry is the policeman who saved Mary and the baby.'

'What? The fat sergeant? Eve's husband?'

'Yeah. And I also think Joanne could be Aoife's baby.'

'How did you get to that?' Nell listened as Carla explained the timeline. She wasn't convinced. 'But that could just be a coincidence. That Joanne's the same age. There's nothing really to link her to Gerry, is there?'

She could tell from Carla's face there was.

'Jesus. What is it?'

'He called Joanne.'

'Gerry called Joanne?'

'Yep. A few days before O'Brian was killed.'

'Jesus Christ, Carla, when did you find that out?'

'Yesterday?'

Nell stared at her. 'Are you kidding?'

'No. I was hoping it was a coincidence.'

Nell didn't bother to reply. Flicking her cigarette into the road, she turned to go. 'Come on, we need to tell Bremer.'

Nell nodded for Paul to join them as the team gathered by Carla's desk.

'Go on,' she said. Carla relayed her theory about Gerry and Joanne. She clocked Bremer staring hard at her as she spoke.

'This phone call Gerry made to her. When exactly did you find that?'

'About two minutes before I walked in the door,' Nell said before Carla could reply. 'That's why we went for a cigarette break, trying to work how it all fits.'

Bremer looked satisfied with the reply. 'So we now think Mary is the main suspect for Connor, and Gerry and Joanne are linked to her?'

'Looks that way, yes,' Nell said.

'You brought Joanne in, didn't you? Let's go and ask her.'

'The custody sergeant refused to book her. Said there wasn't enough evidence.'

'So where is she now?'

'On her way home, I imagine.'

'Jesus.'

'But the husband's tucked up downstairs,' Paul pointed out.

'Yeah, but he's not going to land her in it, is he? Not after everything they've been through.'

'I'm not sure Joanne will know anything anyway,' Carla said. 'I've checked and checked, but there are no calls to Joanne and

Gerry from the same number. Which you would expect if Mary was in contact with them. I'd have seen a pattern, a triangle of calls, if you like. But there just isn't one.'

'Are we any closer to finding out where Mary is?' Bremer spoke quickly, his face one of measured concern.

'No. When she left Portsmouth she disappeared and left no trace that I can find. It's like she disappeared into thin air.'

'What if we're on the wrong track?' Nell said. She went to the board and picked up a pen. 'Mary disappears in 1984. From Portsmouth,' she wrote as she spoke. 'Eve's HR file says she was in Portsmouth at this time, but we can find no record of her there. The next time we get a record of Eve is when she went to university, right?' She looked at Carla, who nodded. Nell looked at them all to see if they got where she was going. They didn't.

'What if Mary is really Eve?'

'And that would mean Joanne has been right all along about Eve deliberately fitting her up?' Carla started to speak quickly. 'She approached Gerry and he told Eve, who wanted to get rid of her because—'

'Of her "crimes",' Nell finished for her. 'Joanne alleged Eve had committed a crime in her past that Joanne's presence threatened to expose. And we know Mary was implicated in the death of Aoife.'

'Right,' Carla went on, eyes bright. 'So when Joanne's baby died, Eve saw a way out. There's only four pathologists, and they write their cases on a board so everyone knows who is doing what. What if Eve saw it and asked to be assigned the case, then faked the evidence to get Joanne put away?'

'But why would she then take the report just before the appeal?' Bremer asked. 'That action directly led to Joanne's release.'

'Gerry,' Carla said. 'Maybe he felt guilty about what Eve had done and wanted to right a wrong.'

Bremer held up his hand. 'I get your train of thought, but I'm very conscious of the fact we have a potential threat to life against Joanne and Eve. If Mary is Eve, and I'm far from convinced she is, I don't see how Eve can be in danger, but Joanne still is. So our priority, Nell, Paul, is to ensure Joanne is safe.'

They nodded.

'How long ago did the custody sergeant let her go?'

Nell checked the clock on the wall.

'Half an hour, give or take five minutes.'

'How far away does she live?' Bremer asked Carla.

'An hour, maybe hour and a half at this time.'

'So if she's gone home, she'll still be on her way now. Nell get over there, I'll get uniform to back you up and if Mary's there, consider her dangerous and proceed with care. Ditto Eve,' he said, as an afterthought.

Nell grabbed her jacket and keys.

'I'm going to send someone to Eve's home address, as we have to assume she is linked somehow, and if Gerry is at either address,' Bremer said, anger flashing, 'I want him arrested on the spot.'

Fifty-six
Now – Mary

'Where are you going?'

I keep my back to him.

'Mary,' he begins, quietly. I know what he's going to say next but it won't help. 'Please don't go.'

'I have to.' I keep my back to him because I know if I don't he'll persuade me.

'It's all going wrong,' he says.

The hall feels very still, like time has stopped for a moment. I almost daren't breathe in case I disturb it.

'If you leave I know something awful will happen. Are you going to find Joanne? Because that's just not fair. She's innocent in all of this – she was just a baby, she can't be to blame.'

'It's all her fault. If she hadn't come back, if she hadn't contacted you –' I swirl to face him, '– and if you hadn't agreed to meet her, then maybe we could have found a different way. But now there is nothing left. She is proof of what happened that night on the beach.'

'But she isn't. She has no idea what really happened. She thinks you saved her life, Mary, and you did.' His tone is rising with his sense of urgency. 'You carried her to safety and saved her from harm.'

'And look how she's repaid me.'

Gerry throws up a hand and turns from me. 'She just wanted to connect with the one person who knew her mum. Aoife.'

Hearing her name makes my heart shiver.

'Please don't do anything to hurt her.'

I wait for him to turn around but he remains with his back to me.

'She has Alf's blood running through her. Blood never lies, Gerry.'

When he doesn't reply, I say, 'I'm sorry,' and leave.

It doesn't take much to get into the house and as I walk around Joanne Fowler's home I wonder what Aoife would have made of her daughter's neat and ordered rooms. I walk in silence, studying every bit of proof she is alive: her pictures, the baby she lost, the husband she loves. I study the baby – can I see her grandmother in her? I believe I can, but I know it's probably because I hope to.

A little further into the house I find her baby's room, left untouched. I run my hands over the baby blanket, carefully laid over the edge of the cot, and turn the mobile above until it chimes. Love mixes with loss of hope in this room and the weight of it forces me to leave.

I wander back to the front room and sit on a sofa, the softness of which pulls me in. I lie back and close my eyes, succumbing to it. Could I have had this life, if Alf hadn't owned me? What would it have looked like? Roast dinner on Sundays, holidays in France and walks in the mountains with dogs we had rescued? There's no point in dreaming, I decide. The life I was given is the one I've lived – regardless of my origins. And I haven't done too badly, except for the babies, and I deserved to have them taken. No woman deserves a baby when they've taken one from another, I know that now.

I hear a key in the door and panic. I grab my bag. I'm not ready for her yet. I look around for somewhere to hide and find a corner by the curtain I can just about fit into. I stay there, barely breathing, as I hear Joanne walk to the kitchen. She seems to be speaking to someone yet I sense she is alone; is she on the phone?

'They've kept him in – can you do anything?' Silence as she listens, which makes me think I'm right about the phone.

'But what about Mary? When can I meet her? Surely it's time?'

I know who she's speaking to now and I feel a stab of anger. Gerry. He's become attached to Joanne, as I'd feared he would. I think about texting him from my hideaway, but what would that achieve? I must wait for Aoife. That's the plan; that's what I must do.

While I wait, I listen as Joanne clatters in the kitchen, all the while speaking to Gerry. She's starting to sound scared.

'But what if she comes here first? What if she's angry like you said she might be?'

I almost snort my disgust. *Judas.* When Aoife finds out what he's said, she'll make him pay. I hear a click as Joanne pushes the kettle button down.

'Mary.'

'Aoife?' I whisper.

'Shhhh.'

I exhale my relief she's here.

'What's Joanne doing?' she asks.

'Talking to Gerry.'

'Always weak, that man.'

I feel a stab of something – protection? It was Gerry, after all, who saved me.

'He's on our side, though,' I say.

'I've told you, never trust a man. It's only the two of us we can trust.'

'Yes,' I say, before hearing Joanne move into the living room. I freeze.

'Not long now,' Aoife says. 'Be strong. We can do it – together we can do anything.'

I listen. Joanne is on the sofa now. There is silence.

'Have you got the knife?' Aoife asks. I look at the knife in the waistband of my skirt, just like it was all those years ago.

'Yes,' I whisper back.

'Good. Then it's time.'

'Who's there?'

I can almost see Joanne now, upright on the sofa, scanning the room for the origin of the sound.

'Come on.' Aoife's tone is urgent and she's right; we're only going to get one shot at this.

'Let's go,' she says. 'Let's eliminate the proof once and for all.'

I stand. Joanne sees me and pushes herself back against the pillows she neatly stacked the night before. I pull the knife from my skirt.

'Mary?' Joanne asks.

It must be strange for her to see me after all this time. I nod.

'Mary, Gerry is coming to help you.' Her face is white, eyes taking in the room, searching for her phone.

I spot it first and in three steps I have it in my hand. I stand and hold it up as if in a victory salute, before I drop it to the floor and smash it with my foot. I hear Aoife giggle and I feel pride in making her happy. It emboldens me.

'Mary,' Joanne repeats. 'Can we wait until Gerry is here?'

'No.' My voice sounds distant and unlike my own, but I cling to the words as if to a lifeboat in a raging sea.

Joanne speaks again and I know she's trying to buy herself some time. I'm not stupid.

'Gerry says you saved me. Is that right?'

Clever, pulling on my heartstrings. I stay silent. Sirens are in the distance; she hears them too: her look is hope, mine panic.

'Get her – now,' Aoife hisses, and as Joanne turns to run I'm on her.

'Get her out and in the car,' Aoife says as I wrestle Joanne to the floor. Her breathing is hard because my knee is against her neck, but all I can think about is doing what Aoife wants. Paying her back for what I did.

I pin Joanne's arms behind her.

'Come on,' Aoife says, opening the door, 'get her to the car.'

I comply, dragging Joanne towards the entrance, acutely aware of the sirens getting closer.

Once outside I open the boot and push Joanne inside.

'Hurry,' Aoife calls.

The sirens are so loud now they almost drown out Joanne's shouts from the boot. I try my key in the ignition and fail.

'For Christ's sake, hurry,' Aoife says, her voice cross and urgent. I panic, shoving the key in as hard as it will go and turning it. The engine roars into life and I feel triumphant.

'Now where?' I ask.

'The beach,' she replies.

Fifty-seven

Nell, Paul and the uniform backup had found no evidence of Joanne when they'd arrived at her house. Looking through a window, they'd seen a handbag on the floor, its contents scattered, and requested permission to gain entry. Carla and Bremer were now bent over the radio as it crackled on her desk, both listening for updates on the operation's attempts to gain access to Joanne's home address.

'Entry gained,' the radio told them.

They'd broken down the door, but Carla knew that was when the danger began. The first potential flashpoints were the front room and downstairs toilet.

'Downstairs empty and secured.'

Carla bowed her head in relief. She'd never managed to move from paper analyst to real-life operations, the fear her analysis might result in an officer's death being too much to bear. But hearing that the downstairs was empty came with feelings of relief and frustration, because that meant the upstairs had to be searched – a far more precarious scenario – as well as the possibility that Mary had managed to evade them.

She leaned forward, her ear close to the radio, willing it to reveal their current situation. It crackled.

'Upstairs bedroom to the left, empty and secure.'

They'd managed to escape, despite the speedy response. Joanne was gone.

'Upstairs bedroom to the right, empty and secure,' came another voice, and she gave up hope.

'Bathroom, empty and secure.'

'Carla?' Nell's voice echoed into the office.

Carla pressed the response button. 'Go ahead.'

'The house is empty. I need you to give us another viable alternative.'

Bremer held up his hand to indicate she shouldn't respond.

'Stand by,' Carla said into the radio, looking to Bremer.

'Call Gerry,' he said.

'Gerry?'

'When I told him we were concerned about Eve he went white as a sheet. Wherever he's gone now, it's to find her, and wherever she is, Mary and Joanne will be.'

'But why would he tell us?' He's lied so much already, she wanted to add, but couldn't bring herself to betray him so openly.

'It's worth a go.' He picked up the radio as she reached for the phone. 'Nell, Paul, stand by. We're looking at other possibilities.'

Gerry's phone rang until Carla thought it would go to answerphone, then:

'Hello?'

'Gerry, it's Carla. We're worried about Eve. Do you know where she is?'

'I'm at our house now,' he sounded out of breath, 'but no one's here.'

'Is there anywhere else she may have gone? Anywhere you can think of?' The briefest pause told her there was. 'It would really help us, Gerry – and Eve.'

Gerry didn't reply. Carla listened to his deep breathing, her frustration growing because his silence told her he knew something.

'Come on, Gerry, Eve could be in danger.' Why wasn't he more concerned?

'Portsmouth,' he said, finally. 'There's this café she used to go to. I think she might be there.'

'Address?' She wrote it down and held it out to Bremer, who went to the other side of the room to radio Nell.

'Thanks, Gerry.' She wanted to ask him a million questions – about why he had been talking to Joanne, who Mary was, what she had to do with Eve – but she knew they didn't have the time. 'I'll let you know when we find her.'

'OK, thanks.'

As Gerry hung up, Carla sat there, dead phone in her hand. Something didn't feel right: his manner, the shortness with which he spoke to her, stilted almost.

'Wait,' she called to Bremer, who paused, his hand on the communication button. 'What if he's sending us to Portsmouth because Mary's making him?'

Bremer walked back across the office. 'Go on.'

'He didn't sound right – something was making him reluctant to speak. What if Mary's there with him and making him say that to throw us off the track?'

'So we send Nell to the Grahams' home address?'

Carla shook her head. 'Can you give me twenty minutes?'

Bremer looked unsure.

'Fifteen,' she said.

He gave a short nod. 'Fifteen, but if you've not got something by then, I'm sending Nell in.'

Carla ran down the corridor to the Telephone Unit. 'I need cell site, and I need it now.'

Sarah the analyst looked up from her desk, her face briefly studying Carla's before she replied. 'Number?'

Carla read out the numbers for Eve, Joanne and Gerry, waiting as the analyst dialled.

'Yes, I need an urgent cell site on the following numbers.' Reading them out, she clicked open a map, preparing to plot the coordinates that would tell them where the phones were located. Carla knew it was a long shot. Cell-site analysis would only tell them where the phones were within a mile radius, the phone masts creating a triangle within which they could be located, but if they were lucky they could narrow it down to an area around an address. All she needed now was to know if they were heading to Portsmouth or were still in Oxford.

Sarah noted down coordinates and gestured to the computer for Carla to input them. As soon as she noted the first one, Carla had her answer – they were still in Oxford. As Sarah thrust more coordinates at her – each specific to the different numbers Carla had given her – it became obvious that Joanne and Eve were headed to the Grahams' home address.

Sarah hung up. 'All three in the vicinity of Jericho, two currently travelling, one stationary. Does that help?'

Carla looked at the Grahams' address, bang smack in the centre of the triangle where the phones sat. 'Yes,' she said. 'It helps a lot.'

She ran back down the corridor, aware her fifteen minutes was almost up. Pushing through the door she saw Bremer on the radio.

'Don't send them to Portsmouth. Joanne, Gerry and Eve are still here.'

'Where?'

Carla beckoned for the radio. 'Eve's,' she said, as Bremer handed it to her.

'Nell?'

'Go ahead.'

'They're in the vicinity of the Grahams' home address. We've only got a mile radius, but they've pushed it as far as they can and it seems Eve is on her way there now.'

'What's the address like, do you know?'

Carla had already opened Google Street View. 'Very open. Terraced street, so hard to be covert. Garden runs down to canal, so multiple escape routes. I'd say park a street away and assess.'

'Can you find me an OP?' Nell asked.

'An observation post?'

'Yeah, try to get one across the street where I can see into the house before we go in.'

'OK. Stand by.' Carla put the street name into the police database, hoping to find someone who'd entertain a cop or two while they hid in an upstairs bedroom. She got two hits: one for a domestic, which she wrote off straight away, and one old lady whose cat had gone missing and she'd been worried it had been stolen. It was as good as a gift. She pressed the button.

'Nell, I've got a Mrs Hardacre. Sixty-nine years old, living alone. Looks like she's a possible and it backs on to the Graham house, so you should get a good view of the rear of the property.'

'Great, I'm on my way. Text Paul the address and let me know when Hardacre's given us the go-ahead to proceed.'

Bremer took hold of the radio. 'Be careful as you approach, Sergeant. Stay back until you're sure it's safe to go in.'

The radio crackled in response, but Nell was already gone.

Fifty-eight
Now – Mary

I pull the car into St Margaret's Road, near Jericho, and turn off the engine.

'What are you doing?' Aoife asks.

'I can't go to the beach, Aoife. I can't see another person hurt there. And I don't want to be near Alf.'

Aoife snorts. 'He's in prison, dumbo.'

'You know what I mean.'

Her silence tells me she does.

I watch a homeless woman pick a cigarette butt off the ground, her battered trousers and falling-apart shoes a marked contrast to the grand houses rising up behind her, and I think: *Could that have been me if Gerry hadn't saved me?*

'Well, where do you want to go?'

'Home,' I say. 'I want to go home.'

*

We pull up outside and I scan the street for signs of police. I note each parked car, every pedestrian who walks by, but see nothing to make me think they're here.

'Come on.'

I hesitate by the boot, scanning the street again. I have no idea how I'm going to get her out without being seen, but she's kicking against the metal of the car and if I don't she's going to be heard.

'Joanne,' I say, loud but not too loud. The movement stops. 'I'm going to take you inside now. I'm going to open the boot and if you scream or do anything to attract attention, I'm going to push you back in and drive you to the sea where I'll burn your body on the beach.'

She is saying something but I can't hear what.

'I've done it before and I'll do it again.'

Aoife is stifling a laugh. 'You're very good at this,' she says and I want to tell her to shut up, I'm concentrating. We still risk Joanne kicking off the minute I open the boot and I have no idea if I can trust her or not.

'Gerry,' Aoife says.

'What?'

'Tell her Gerry is in the house and he'll help her.'

I do and when Joanne remains silent I open the boot.

Her face is smeared with tears and her hair is half pulled from her bun. She is cowering, legs pulled up, arms wrapped around her knees. Her eyes flicker left and right before settling on me.

'Please, Mary.'

'Do you want to come and speak to Gerry and we can sort this all out?' I'm quite pleased at how reasonable I sound and I know Aoife agrees.

'Yes, please.' She starts to uncurl.

I say, 'Wait,' and lower the boot slightly as a man walks past with a tiny grey dog. He glances at me and I smile, but he doesn't return it and after he walks past he turns back to look at me.

'Police?' Aoife asks.

'I don't think so.' But it's exactly what I'd thought too. 'Come on.' I help Joanne out of the boot and with another quick check of the street, I half push, half pull her up the steps and through the front door. Only when it's closed do I take a breath.

I'm holding Joanne's arm tight and at an awkward angle. She winces but I hold it there. To tell her who's boss. She is whimpering like she did the night she arrived on the beach and I want to smack her head in to shut her up.

'Mary?' Gerry appears. He looks at Joanne and turns as white as the sheets on our bed. 'Jesus Christ, what have you done?'

'Making things right again.'

'How is this making things right?'

He's shouting now and Joanne shrinks in the face of it.

'You're scaring her.'

He laughs. 'You're bloody kidding me, right? I'm the one scaring her. Jesus God.' He stops speaking and we all stand there for a moment, unsure what we will each do next. I hear a sob come from Joanne and yank her arm.

'Please shut up.'

She looks up at me, eyes wide, then over to Gerry, whose face softens.

'Always was a sucker for the younger model,' Aoife says.

'I'm going to put her in our bedroom now and lock the door. I will have the key with me, so it's no use trying to be the hero and letting her out.'

'And then what?' he asks as I begin to push Joanne up the stairs.

'Then I'm going to pour myself a glass of wine and decide what to do next,' I say.

'Good move,' Aoife says.

'Thank you,' I reply.

Fifty-nine

Mrs Hardacre let Nell and Paul in with only the briefest of glances at their warrant cards.

'I'll bring you some tea,' she said, after settling them into the upstairs bedroom. 'With biscuits,' she added.

The room was a spare but the bed was still neatly made, unused towels set out on the washstand, untouched. It smelled of perfume or talc – Nell couldn't decide which – and the street light outside poured a pinkish acid glow through the lace curtains. The house was perfectly positioned behind and to the left of the Grahams' house, giving Nell a good vantage point of the garden, the kitchen and the back bedrooms.

'You've got to hand it to Carla, she's pulled this one out of the bag pretty sharpish.' Paul was looking through a sliver in the curtains, his binoculars trained on the back door.

'See anything?' Nell pulled the nightstand across from beside the bed and stood the radio on it.

'No, house appears empty, all the lights are out. Maybe the cell site was wrong?'

'Well, it only gives us a mile radius to work with.'

Paul removed the binoculars. 'But where else within this mile would they be?'

'Exactly. So they must be here. We just need to wait, and when we're sure, we go in.' Nell held out her hand. 'Here, let me have a look.'

Paul moved aside to let her sit on the window ledge and took out his phone as Nell focused the lenses. Paul was right, the house was in darkness. She moved the binoculars slowly across each window, pausing as she reached the kitchen. Squinting, she could just about make out an empty bottle of wine on the side by the sink. No wine glasses, though, she noted, cursing the lack of moonlight to assist them.

Paul placed his phone next to the radio as it crackled for their attention. He picked it up. 'Go ahead, Control.'

'We've had a sighting of Eve by the boot of her car outside her house. Officer on foot. Noted the boot was half open.'

'Did the officer see where she went?'

'No, he didn't want to hang around. Just got a positive ID, then left.'

'Ask if she was alone,' Nell called over.

'Control, was the subject with anyone?'

Bremer's voice broke through static.

'OK, thanks, Control.' Paul put the radio back on the table. 'Just Eve. Looks like you may have been right.'

Nell went back to watching the Grahams' house, her eyes following the slope of the garden downwards to where it met a small, thin stream. She was about to look away when a shaft of moonlight escaped the clouds and she saw it hit silver objects hanging from a tree whose branches curled downwards, as if to protect what lay underneath. What were they? Bells? Did this mean anything? Frustrated, she focused the binoculars on the neatly tended space below the tree. Four tiny silver crosses sat in a row, equally spaced; whatever lay under them must have been equally small. Shells covered the soil on top of each one.

Before the moonlight could be pushed back behind the clouds, she handed the binoculars to Paul.

'Look, beneath the tree, end of the garden. What do you see?'

He followed her finger, pausing when he reached the spot. 'Graves?'

'That's what I thought. Baby-sized graves.'

'Grim.' Paul moved slightly to the right, chewing his bottom lip in concentration. He trained the binoculars back on the house. 'Do we risk entry?'

Could she risk it? The house was in blackness and they didn't even have a floor plan. They couldn't enter without knowing the exit routes, and that garden would be a nightmare to contain: no light; access across the stream. And they had no idea what Eve had done with Joanne. Entering too quickly could put her in greater danger. But for how long could she justify waiting?

Nell reached for the radio. 'Control?'

'Go ahead.' Bremer's voice echoed around the room.

'What are the chances of a police helicopter on our address? This darkness won't allow a safe entry. I'd rather know what we're up against than go in blind.'

'I'll get on to the duty inspector, see what I can do. No other sightings?'

'None. Is Carla there?'

'Carla here. Go ahead.'

'Carla, can you do a risk assessment on Eve? See if there's anything we need to worry about.'

'OK, although I've researched the hell out of her and nothing suggests she's used violence before – not on our systems, anyway.'

'Can you just double-check?' They'd be wearing stab vests, but it was preferable to know what you were up against before it came at you.

'I'll have a dig, see what I can find,' Carla replied before the radio went dead.

Nell put the radio back on the nightstand. Nothing to do now but wait.

The radio crackled. Nell let go of her phone.

'Sergeant Jackson?' Bremer joined them in the room again.

'Jackson here. Go ahead, Control.'

'I've got the helicopter for you. Five minutes. It's the best I could do. It will be with you in fifteen.'

Five minutes wasn't long, but if they shone the light right, it might be enough.

'Thanks, Control, we'll await their arrival.' And turning down the radio, Nell leaned back against the wall, closed her eyes and waited for the hum of the helicopter.

Sixty
Now – Mary

The kitchen is in darkness, clouds having smothered the moon so not even a shaft of light escapes. I listen for sounds from the upstairs bedroom, but all is silent. I pour a glass of red from a bottle on the side. I'm so tired my blood feels as thick as cement, crawling through my body with a slowness matching my thoughts.

Where is Aoife? She's been gone too long and I need her here to settle me. I take a mouthful of wine and enjoy the quick hit of the alcohol. What if she's up there with Joanne? What if she chooses her child over me, just like she did all those years ago? I feel panic start, so I down the wine and pour myself another. No, this is about me and her now, getting back to where we always should have been. She wouldn't betray me. Not when I'm trying to show how sorry I am for betraying her.

Gerry appears at the door. He scans the room but finds only me.

'Mary?'

'Obviously.'

His shoulders look tight and anxiety practically jumps from him, electrifying the room.

He gives a short nod. 'Where is Eve?' His tone is tight.

'I don't know.'

'Don't lie to me, Mary. Where is she?'

'Why do we always have to talk about Eve. Eve, Eve, Eve.' I mimic mouths speaking with my hands.

Gerry takes the seat opposite me. He clasps his hands in front of him, making a church steeple. 'You know when we went away – from the beach – and we decided you should be called something else. To help you put the past behind you?'

'Yes.' I do, of course, although I'm not sure why that's relevant.

'And you wanted to be called Aoife so she would always be with you – do you remember that?' He's speaking carefully, as if worried his words are like stones on glass.

'Yes.'

He looks at me, but I don't know what he wants me to say, so I drink my wine.

'Mary.' His expression is one of measured patience and I want Aoife to hurry up and get back here.

'Mary, it's been thirty-five years since Aoife died and in that time I've watched you work yourself almost to the grave trying to live enough life for the both of you.'

I stare into the glass. I don't want to hear him. I don't understand why this matters now.

'And you did it. You made an amazing life with an amazing career and you did it all while using her name.'

I stay silent.

'But then things seemed to get a bit confused when—'

'When Joanne came back,' I finish for him, triumphantly. 'So if we get rid of her, we get things back to how they were again.'

He looks at me sadly. Where is Aoife? I see his eyes glide over the table, resting on my phone. He pulls his from his back pocket and nods to mine. 'Turn it off.'

'What?'

'They'll be able to trace where we are, so turn it off.'

I nod and do as I'm told, but suddenly Aoife is back and she's angry.

'Don't tell her what to do. We've both had enough men telling us what to do and look where that got us,' she snaps.

'Where is Joanne now, Mary?'

'Don't tell him,' Aoife says. 'Just get outside and dig the hole.'

I stand.

'Where are you going?'

'I have to dig a hole.'

He stares at me. 'For *what*?'

'Joanne.'

Gerry stands. 'For fuck's sake, Mary, this is ridiculous.'

'Aoife and I just want to start our lives again, lives as they should have been.'

'Aoife and you?'

'Yes.'

He studies me for what seems like ages before shaking his head and grabbing a wine glass. 'I don't know what to do any more. All these years I've stood by you, protecting you, and now I'm honestly at a loss as to how to help you.'

I'm unsure which of us he means.

'Stood by us both,' I correct. Gerry stares at me from over the rim of the wine glass. He's drinking mouthfuls as if it's squash. Aoife won't like that. She doesn't like a drunk, Gerry should know that.

'So what are you going to do now, now that you have Joanne?' He places the half-empty wine glass on the table and wipes his mouth with the back of his hand.

'Kill her, of course,' Aoife replies.

'Kill her, of course,' I repeat.

'And then what? You're just going to ride off into the sunset and believe the police won't come after you?

'Mary?'

I've been lost in thought, unsure what Aoife intends us to do after we bury her. 'Yes?'

'Joanne is Aoife's baby, she's her child. And Aoife agreed for her to be your child too. Joanne is *your* baby, my love. Do you not remember holding her in your arms and begging me not to take her from you?'

I do remember. Like I remember all the other babies I lost as punishment for keeping her alive. 'All my babies are dead, Gerry, you know that.' I hold his stare. 'They're buried at the bottom of the garden without so much as a funeral. Four little bodies, neatly lined up in a row.'

'Joanne's not dead.'

'And that's worse because she, of all of them, deserves to be dead.'

'No person deserves to die because of how they were conceived.'

'She wants to hurt us, Gerry.'

He slams the wine bottle to the floor sending shards of red-stained glass across the tiles.

'There is no "us",' he shouts, his face puce. 'Aoife died thirty-five years ago and I helped carry her body off that beach. There is only one person, Mary, and that's you.' He moves towards me and I withdraw.

'Mary, I love you, I'll do anything for you. But I won't do this. Joanne does not deserve to die.'

There is silence, and then Aoife tuts.

'We should never have trusted him.'

I nod my agreement.

'And now,' Aoife says with a sigh, 'we're going to have to kill him too.'

Sixty-one
Now – Mary

After the rolling pin hits Gerry over the head, I hear the crunch of bone on ceramic as he hits the floor, arms splayed as if hugging the tiles. I stare at him: face down on the floor, rolling pin rocking silently by his side.

'Come on,' Aoife is saying, 'we need to hurry now.'

I can't stop staring at the pool of blood gathering beside Gerry's head. It creeps from him, as if testing how far it can get without being caught.

'Mary.' Aoife's voice is harsh and it jolts me away from Gerry's blood. 'Focus,' she says. 'Don't let me down now. We need to finish digging that grave.'

I still hesitate and when she next speaks, her tone is conciliatory.

'Mary, have I not been with you all these years? When you

weren't sure if you could go to medical school, wasn't it me who convinced you that you could? When you wanted to give up because it was so hard, didn't I talk you through it? And what about when you lost a baby like I lost mine? Didn't I whisper to you while you lay in bed, tears so bad you could barely breathe? I lost Joanne thirty-five years ago, but because of you she's still here. I want my baby back, Mary. I want to rest with her in my arms like it always should have been.'

'But then you'll leave me.'

'I said I would never leave you and I won't. But you owe me this. You helped kill me, Mary, and then you took my baby.'

I bite my lip.

'So don't mess up again now, OK?'

I nod and stand, stepping over Gerry to get to the back door. 'OK, I'll do it.'

The bottom of the garden is dark and it's hard for me to hold the spade when my hand is still shaking from her words. My mind is a whir of questions, but I ask the one that matters most. 'Did you come back for me or Joanne?'

'What?'

'Did you come back to get Joanne or to be with me?'

'I came back long before Joanne arrived.'

'Yes, but you would have known she'd come looking for us, wouldn't you? That she'd trace Gerry from the press coverage, which would take her to Eve, and then us. Did you come back to wait for her?'

Aoife's silence tells me the answer. I stop digging.

'What's the matter?' Aoife asks.

'You never cared about protecting my secret, did you? About what her being here means for me. You just want her dead and all to yourself.' I'm fifteen again, jealous, bitter about the baby. 'You said she was ours.'

'She is. But you gave her up, Mary, so I've come to take her back.'

When I don't reply, she snorts. 'You're such a let-down, Mary,' echoing my mother's well-worn words.

I clench my jaw.

'Dig that hole,' she yells. 'Dig that hole and give me my baby back!' She's shouting now, but I don't move.

'Our baby,' I correct.

And then there's a sudden absence.

'Aoife?' I stand. What can I hear? I glance up to the bedroom window and in a rare slash of moonlight, I see Joanne standing there, her face staring down at me with a whiteness that matches the moon's.

We lock eyes. The sound is getting nearer, and as the moon goes back behind the clouds, an unnatural light floods me.

'NO,' I shout, ducking underneath the tree. I look up at Joanne, her eyes locked on the sky. This can't be the end. And throwing down the spade, I race back towards the house.

Sixty-two
Now – Mary

I sprint across the garden and the helicopter finds me as I reach the back door. I glance up, the pilot and crew a patch of dark behind the beam of the spotlight. Slamming the door behind me, I run to the kitchen sink and reach behind the plumbing, behind the plastic bags and the kitchen rolls, to find the rolled-up cloth I stuffed there.

I pull it out and unroll the faded yellow duster, the weight of its contents filling me with relief. Keeping low, I move quickly from the kitchen, pulling the door closed behind me to shut out the light and their view.

I take the stairs two at a time, my eyes searching for evidence that Joanne has escaped from the room I put her in. But as I reach the landing I see it remains closed, the rope around the handle and the latch still firmly in place. I untangle the knot and push open the door to see Joanne by the window, her hands up against the glass, mutely calling to the pilot and his crew who circle above us.

I know she's heard me but she doesn't turn, so I walk slowly towards her, the gun in my hand heavy and full.

'Get away from the window.'

Joanne remains still, so I jab the gun in her kidney. She cries out in pain and half falls, half turns towards me.

'Sit.' I jerk the gun towards the bed and she does as she's told. When she's seated, I try to compose my thoughts, but the constant flashes of light into the room distract me. I need Aoife; she'd know what to do. I feel fifteen again, unsure, reacting to, not deciding, events, which are beyond my control.

'Mary?' Her voice is small and childlike, soft and gentle; light catches her face, like the burst of a Polaroid flash I saw when I was young.

'Gerry told me I have you to thank for my life. How you saved me that night on the beach and carried me to safety. I came back to thank you. To ask you about my mum and what she was like when she was young.' Her hands are shaking, her voice barely able to form the words as she pleads with me.

'What was she like, my mum?'

I am back on the beach and I am cold. I have Aoife's blood on my hands and I want to get it off so I rub it hard across my jeans, harder and harder until her blood mixes with my own.

'Stop it, you stupid cow,' Alf says.

I want to cry. I want to curl up next to Aoife's body and make it warm again, wipe her face clear of death, breathe a smile back to her lips.

I am back on the beach and I am cold and I have Aoife's blood on my hands. I can't keep her warm; I can't restart her smile, because I have failed us both.

'Mary, I don't want you to blame yourself.' Joanne's voice joins me on the beach. But I am still cold, so very cold. Where is Aoife?

'I know why you, I mean Eve, put me in prison. I know your fear was if I came back, Aoife would somehow leave you. That she'd choose to go with me. I know you thought you'd be put in jail for your part in her death. But you must remember, you saved her child. You saved me.' She tries to smile.

'I'm cold,' I say. The sea wind has reached my bones and they chatter to each other, telling the story of my betrayal.

Joanne slowly stands. She reaches behind her, her eyes all the while on my face, and pulls a blanket across.

'Here.' She offers it to me.

Sand from the beach is in my mouth, each grain like a tiny pill of salt. Alf is on top of me, his arm against my neck as I flail against him, trying to tell him I can't breathe, but the sand gets in the way.

I'm on the floor. I try to tell Joanne I can't breathe, but all I can do is cough up sand, over and over until the beach is underneath me.

An arm is round me. Aoife? I move my head a little and there she is, wrapping the blanket over my shoulders, saying soothing words I can't hear but whose sound feels like a lullaby.

'Forgive me, Aoife?' I ask.

'I forgive you,' a voice whispers in my ear. Tears fall onto the sand, the cold steps back a little, and in the sound of her voice I close my eyes.

Sixty-three

'I need to know the dates Eve Graham had off for maternity leave or sickness.'

The HR officer listed four occasions when Eve had spent time off work, then read out a fifth.

'Oh, no, cancel that one. It was wrongly inputted as sickness rather than firearms training.'

Carla stopped writing. 'Firearms training?'

'Yeah, but it was four years ago, so she wouldn't be authorised to have a gun now.'

'Why would a forensic specialist need firearms training?' She said it more to herself, but he replied.

'How should I know? All it says was it was authorised and she spent three days in training.'

'Which officer authorised it?'

'Um, hold on. OK, here it is. PS Graham.'

Oh God, Gerry, what did you do?

What possible need could Eve have had for firearms training? Unless he'd felt Mary was such a threat to her that he wanted to make sure she could protect herself? And then, of course, what point would there be in training to use a firearm without having one to fire?

'Bremer?'

Bremer came to his office door. 'Helicopter arrived?'

'I don't know, but I think we may have a problem. I think Gerry or Eve may have access to a firearm—'

Before she had finished speaking, Bremer was on the radio to Nell.

'DS Jackson?'

'Come in, Control.'

'Where are you?'

'Still in the OP.'

'OK, don't leave until I get you armed backup. Carla has found reason to believe there may be a firearm at the address. You are not to enter the premises until armed response have arrived. I repeat, you are not to enter the Graham address until I give the go-ahead.'

'But, sir –' the whir of helicopter blades sounded in the distance, '– the helicopter has arrived. If we've only got five minutes of light to work with, we won't have time to wait for armed response.'

'Armed response will be there in five minutes. You are not to enter, whatever happens.' Bremer's face was tense. 'Do you understand, Sergeant?'

'Yes, sir.' Nell's voice told them both what she thought, but Bremer was already in his office by the time the radio went dead. Carla sat for a second, staring at it. Nell wouldn't go in, would she? Carla knew she wouldn't put Paul in danger, or the uniforms waiting for her direction to enter, but would Nell risk it herself? Bremer's voice shouted loudly from the office, directing armed response to get to the Grahams' house. In five minutes it could all be over. If Nell could wait that long, she would be safe.

Nell had seen Eve sprint across the lawn, seen her give a short shout, her eyes fixated on the bedroom before disappearing inside. What had Eve noticed?

'How long until armed response get here?' she asked Paul.

'Four minutes? Minimum,' he added.

'Shit.' Four minutes was a long time. 'So we just leave Joanne in there? That's what Bremer is saying? We leave her alone with Eve?'

'No, he's saying we wait until we're sure who's in there, and until firearms can back us up.' The tension in Paul's tone over-rode his reasonable words.

Nell jabbed her finger at the Graham house. 'I know who's in there.'

Paul hesitated. 'Bremer is right,' he said finally. 'We can't help Joanne if someone in there has a gun.'

'But we don't know there's a gun. Carla just flagged up the

fact the address *might* contain one.' Nell was losing patience. She grabbed her stab vest.

'I'm going in. You get there as soon as armed response arrives.'

'Jesus, Nell, I'm not letting you go in on your own.' He was already pulling on his stab vest before she caught his arm.

'Constable, I'm telling you to stay by the radio. I need you to coordinate firearms when they arrive.'

Paul shook his head. 'No way—'

'Constable,' she interrupted him, 'that's a lawful order.'

Paul stared at her. 'That's fucking low.'

Nell knew it stung to have her pull the superior-officer card – they were a team, equal despite the sergeants' exam between them – but right now she didn't care. She wasn't going to risk his life just because she was risking her own. 'I'll see you in four minutes, OK?'

Paul's look told her all the things he wanted to say, so he just nodded. 'Stay safe, Jackson.'

The radio crackled. Bremer appeared at the door. 'Carla?'

She looked up at him.

'You OK?' He looked concerned. The radio crackled again.

'Control? Come in, Control?' Paul's voice came into the room and from Bremer's expression, Carla knew his first thought was the same as her own – where was Nell?

Carla pressed the button. 'Control here, go ahead.'

'The suspect has been sighted. DS Jackson has gone in. Where is armed response?'

Carla could hear the tension in Paul's voice. She caught Bremer's eye, his look a mix of anger and concern. Striding across the office, he took the radio.

'DC Mackintosh, what do you mean DS Jackson has gone in? Gone in where?'

'She's headed to the Grahams' address, sir.' The helicopter was so loud in the background, it almost drowned out his words.

'I told her not to go in without armed officers. How long ago did she leave?' Bremer checked the clock.

'One minute ago, sir.'

Bremer's finger hovered over the button. He looked at Carla. 'That leaves three minutes at least until the firearms unit gets there.' He held the radio up to his lips.

'DC Mackintosh, you are not to follow DS Jackson, do you understand?'

'But what about Nell, sir? She's on her own.'

'That's the choice she made, Constable, but I'm giving you a lawful order, and I repeat: do you understand?'

Carla almost couldn't bear to hear Paul's response; a lawful order was as high as it got, you disobeyed a lawful order from a senior officer and you might as well hand in your warrant card to HR the same day. But how must he feel, knowing Nell was going in while he just sat and watched?

After a short pause, Paul replied. 'Yes, sir.'

Bremer put the radio back on the desk and folded his arms. Carla didn't say anything while he stared at a blank wall.

'I know what you're thinking,' he said, not looking at her.

'DS Jackson can disobey an order if she wants to, but I'm not losing Paul just because of her stupidity.' He stared down at her. 'I'm not losing both of them, Carla.'

Nell entered the house silently through the back door. Baton outstretched, stab vest securely pulled around her chest, she scanned each room as she entered. With downstairs clear, she moved to the bottom of the stairs, pausing as she heard voices: upstairs, door to the left, immediately at the top of the stairs, two voices, both female. She moved slowly up the stairs and onto the hallway landing, then moved along the wall until her hand was on the door handle. She took three deep breaths, steadied her hand, and walked in.

Sixty-four
Now – Mary

There is a sound. It doesn't come from the beach. I tense. The tears stop. I grip the metal in my hand.

'It's OK, it's just the wind,' Joanne tells me.

But it isn't. The lights flash outside like a black and white movie and I pull myself up. I hear footsteps on the stairs, each one a burst of gunfire, then a face appears at the door. I know that face. How do I know it?

'Eve Graham, put the gun down.'

I feel Joanne move from my side, but I don't care. I'm too busy trying to understand why they think I am Eve.

'Come on, Eve, give me the gun.' The face has a hand now and it's reaching towards me. I look at the gun, then back at the hand.

'Nell?'

Her face is relieved. 'Yes, Eve. It's me.' Her hand gestures towards the gun. I look at Joanne, cowering in the corner of the room. Why did I let her live?

Our lives, Aoife's and mine, were set out before us from the moment we met. Or from the moment we were born. And even if we'd stood a chance, Alf's arrival put paid to that.

I'm tired of being angry at the world for letting him near us. I'm tired of the guilt that's consumed me ever since and the longing I feel to make it right.

I look at Joanne. She looks like Aoife, small and waiflike, with eyes that make you feel you've known her all your life and all the others that went before it.

'I'm sorry,' I say.

And then I pull the trigger.

Sixty-five

The pain took a moment to take hold, but when it did Nell grabbed her shoulder, thick, warm blood pumping through her fingers. Joanne screamed and crouched down next to her, eyes on Eve.

'Get out,' Nell hissed, 'get out and hide.'

Joanne didn't move as Eve walked towards them. Nell pulled herself upright, back against the wall, wincing with the pain of moving.

'Get out,' she repeated, trying to form thoughts, trying to judge how long she could contain Eve so Joanne could hide. But Joanne refused to move, as if fear had soldered her to the floor.

The room began to falter. Nell felt Joanne shift away, causing Nell to fall sideways, the movement seeming to shock Eve into action, as if only then remembering she was there. Nell tried to sit. She needed to get to Eve, get the gun.

Beneath them came the sound of a door being smashed open. Eve was standing over Joanne, so close she'd have no chance of survival if Eve pulled the trigger.

Officers shouted words Nell knew but couldn't hear. The gun was still two feet from Joanne's head. Steps on the stairs, voices loud, urgent . . .

'Room clear, room clear.'

This room isn't clear, she wanted to shout; *this room has a gun and it's two feet from Joanne's head. Two feet.*

Nell tried to kick, but her leg no longer belonged to her – useless limbs connected yet disconnected.

A black helmet appeared at the door, gun outstretched, a second helmet behind the first, a second gun outstretched.

'Stop or I'll shoot,' the helmet said.

The room shrank further, the floor pulling Nell down as if into bed. Before she shut her eyes, Nell knew three things:

The helmet's gun was four feet from Eve.

Eve's gun was two feet from Joanne.

A gun went off as Joanne screamed.

And then Nell knew nothing.

She was on the floor, an officer pushing hard on her shoulder. She could hear shouts from downstairs.

'It's OK, the ambulance is almost here.' The officer's voice was gentle. She stared at his eyes, blue like the sea, his reassuring smile.

'Eve?' Her voice came out like a croak. She swallowed but even that movement made her wince.

'Got her.'

'Alive?'

He nodded. 'You did really well.'

'Joanne?'

The officer's expression told her the answer. She felt a tear roll down the side of her face and down the back of her neck. Then she noticed the uniforms in the corner of the room where Joanne had been crouching. She tried to pull herself up. What were they doing? They looked frantic; discarded first-aid wrappers littered the floor around their feet.

She looked at the officer.

'It's not looking good.'

Nell felt a surge of hope. 'Let me see her, please?' She couldn't bear the thought of Joanne dying with a violence matching that of her birth. The woman deserved so much more from life than she'd had so far. Nell pushed herself upwards. 'Please,' she said again, and this time the officer relented.

Joanne's face was covered in blood from the hole in her stomach. She was making desperate grabs for air, her eyes fixed on the officers as they tried to find enough material to stop the blood pumping out of her.

Nell took her hand and gently stroked it while the officers worked.

'Hey there,' she said.

Joanne tried to move her head but only managed her eyes, which grabbed hold of Nell and begged her to help.

'I can hear the ambulance.' But she couldn't – where the hell was it? 'It's going to be OK.' She gently squeezed Joanne's hand. Joanne's eyes told her she didn't believe it.

'You've got to think it will – you have to fight it.'

Joanne's eyes looked up to the ceiling. It took a moment for Nell to realise she was trying to talk. She pulled herself closer and leaned down.

'Is she dead?' The words barely a whisper.

'No, they got her.'

'Jail?'

'Yes. She'll go to jail for a very long time.'

Joanne attempted a nod, then winced.

Nell stroked the hair away from Joanne's cheek and held her hand tightly. Ambulance sirens got louder. 'Can you hear that?'

Joanne was staring at her. Mute now, her body focused on surviving.

Nell watched the heartbeat in Joanne's neck slowly fade, each gentle thud slower than the last, before it finally stopped as the paramedics arrived at the door.

Sixty-six

The main entrance to the hospital was brightly lit and the darkened windows above blinked machine lights, like reflected stars. Carla parked by the maternity wing, its entrance dark, as if babies were never born at night. As she walked past, the chill of the night a welcome reprieve from the weeks of heat, she thought of Baz and of the answer she was going to give him.

Carla continued left to the front entrance, where smokers gathered around the base of a tree, underneath a sign saying *No Smoking*. Ten feet away stood Ian Fowler with a man she didn't know. He caught her eye and hate seemed to reach out and touch her.

She kept her head down but the man next to Ian called over to her. 'Carla Brown. Got a quote for the *Oxford Mail* about how Thames Valley Police persecuted a young woman to her death?'

He stubbed his cigarette out and walked towards her, iPhone held forward as if to record her.

'No comment,' she said, pushing at the revolving doors.

'Really? No comment when a woman who was wrongly convicted of killing her own baby was killed by the very woman who had testified against her?'

Carla glanced at Joanne's husband; even in the shadows his face was grave and broken. The journalist's anger seemed to radiate for the both of them.

She wanted to say she was sorry. She wanted to walk up to Ian and tell him that to his face.

'No comment,' she repeated, entering the small glass cubicle and willing it to revolve.

Bremer had been watching through the floor-to-ceiling glass window. 'Well done.'

Carla didn't feel like thanking him.

'Remember, never say sorry, not until the case is closed and people are in jail.'

'The coward's way out?' she said, instantly regretting it. Bremer let it slide.

'How is she?' she asked after a moment.

'Argumentative. Wants to get out already. Hates being fussed over. So, very well!'

Carla laughed. 'I'll get her some grapes to really wind her up.' She looked over at the M&S shop. Gerry was somewhere above them. Lying in some bed down a myriad of corridors, past countless swinging doors.

'He's on floor five,' Bremer said.

She gave him a small smile. 'Not sure I'll go and see him.' After all, what would she say?

'You should. It will do you good. He's going down for a long time – it may be your last chance.'

She nodded. He was right. She'd lost the nearest thing to a father figure she'd ever known, so the least she could do was say goodbye.

The lift took Carla to the fifth floor and tiny signs directed her to Gerry's ward. Nurses were chatting at the nurses' station, not bothering to look up as she walked past one bay after another, bedsides beeping, patient belongings scattered across movable cabinets, wipe boards scribbled with words dictating what could be eaten and when.

Gerry was the third bay down and furthest from the corridor. Half a curtain was drawn across his bed, light from the television printing colour onto its light blue material; the table by the foot of the bed, empty. Because, of course, who was there to bring him food now?

Gerry's eyes were closed, his head heavily bandaged, face pale and sallow. She took a seat by the open window, glad of the light breeze, and took his hand. It was warm, sweaty. She held it for a few seconds, remembering the Gerry she'd thought she'd known, remembering the jokes he'd made and the warmth he'd shown her. All of which turned out to be a lie.

She squeezed his hand until his eyes flickered open.

'Hey.'

He looked at her, surprise showing in his face before it was wiped off by pain. He managed a slight smile and a squeeze of her hand in return.

'Thanks for coming. I didn't think you would.'

'I almost didn't. Bremer persuaded me to.'

'Ha. Never thought I'd have anything to thank that man for.' He closed his eyes with the effort of speaking. 'I thought once you'd found out my lies you wouldn't want anything more to do with me.'

They sat for a moment, Carla's hand on his.

'Why did you lie?'

He opened his eyes. 'It's hard to explain.'

'Try.'

'When I first met Mary she was terrified. And in my own way, I was too.' He closed his eyes. 'My mum had abandoned me at birth and I didn't get the best foster homes, so when I joined the police it felt like I'd found a family. I wanted the same chance for her. In one instant I made a stupid choice and all the ones I made afterwards stemmed from that.'

He paused, eyes still shut. 'I'm not trying to make excuses. Just to explain.'

Carla nodded. 'Go on.'

'So we picked a new name. Eve.' His breathing was heavy. 'So she could still have a bit of Aoife with her, and it was fine for years. She worked hard to make a good life and her achievements astonished me. Her ability to do anything she put her mind

367

to.' He opened his eyes and looked at Carla. 'Whatever happened and however wrong it was, she is a force of nature.'

'Why a pathologist, though? Surely it would have been better to keep her head down rather than run head first into a role that put her in daily contact with the police?'

He leaned back against the pillow. 'I suppose we thought hiding in plain sight might be better. Also, I'd transferred so was already pretty visible, and it just seemed OK for her to be the same.' He shifted awkwardly, wincing at the movement. 'And after a few years she became the Eve you knew. She wasn't Mary any more; she was following her own map, not being directed according to ones other people had drawn for her. I think for a while we forgot Mary ever even existed.'

'She did though.'

He closed his eyes again. 'I know. I didn't face it for a long time, but gradually Mary came back.'

'When did you start to notice the lines becoming blurred?'

'It happened gradually. About ten years ago I started to notice she would become confused; she'd be convinced Mary was coming back, as if she'd forgotten she was Mary.'

'Ten years, Gerry. That's a long time to deal with shit like that.'

'I love her,' he said simply. 'I love going to the cinema with her, walking across Port Meadow and picking up a pub lunch the other side. I even enjoy bickering with her just because we enjoy the banter. The best thing that ever happened to me was finding her.'

They sat for a while, holding hands, and Carla thought of

Connor and Alf Waites. She wondered if the latter regretted not taking Mary down with him, and she supposed that had been another stress always hanging over her – wondering if one day he would.

'Did Mary kill Connor because she couldn't kill Alf?'

Gerry looked up, surprised, and she worried she'd woken him.

'I gave up long ago trying to work out what drove Mary. But when Joanne found us it was like a trigger and everything just spiralled downwards. I think seeing Connor there with Kelly-Anne just brought out memories of Alf and what he'd done to her. She wanted to punish Kelly-Anne for her role in Georgie's death while punishing Connor for his actions that killed their baby. But really she was punishing her fifteen-year-old self.'

'I'm not sure Kelly-Anne is going to see it that way. The poor woman has been accused of murder.'

Gerry was pale. He reached for a glass of water, hand shaking. Carla leaned over and steadied it.

'She tried.' His free hand gripped her arm. 'She wrote the letters to unmask herself and I gave them to you in the hope it would. She couldn't just admit her past, so she was looking for someone to do it for her. I begged her to get help when I realised she believed she was speaking to Aoife, but she always refused. The letters were our last hope.'

Carla took her hand away. 'You should have told someone, Gerry.'

'I know. And I'm sorry.'

Sorry wouldn't bring Joanne back.

'We really wanted children, Carla, but each one wasn't meant to stay with us.' He gave a little laugh. 'No wonder, really.'

She stayed silent.

'Then when Joanne came back she felt like it was Aoife returning and she couldn't face the physical manifestation of what she'd done.'

They sat in silence for a few more minutes until Carla stood. 'I have to go now.'

'I know.'

'I lied to my team for you, Gerry. I put myself between you and them because you mattered so much to me and I refused to believe you could be anything other than a good man. And then you lied to me and manipulated me.' Her heart pounded with each word. 'That's the worst bit. You used me to protect yourself.'

Gerry tried to reach out for her hand. She pulled it back and shook her head, emotion getting in the way of words she wanted to say.

'I'm sorry,' he said.

They sat for a few seconds, listening to the beeping of machines and the chatter of the nurses. She took his hand.

'I know you are.'

He pulled her hand to his face and held it to his cheek. 'Promise me you'll look after yourself?'

'I promise.'

He smiled, and she returned it.

'I have to go.'

Gerry let go of her hand and nodded. She tried to ignore the tears in the corners of his eyes.

'Bye, Gerry.'

'Bye, Carla.'

She gave him the biggest smile she could manage and then, desperately fighting the urge to cry, turned and left.

Sixty-seven

Nell woke to find Paul asleep in the chair by her bed. She couldn't decide if that was a welcome sight or not. Her shoulder ached but the pain was bearable, thanks, she assumed, to the morphine drip in her arm. She lay still, listening to the regular beep of the machine next to her, and tried not to picture Joanne's eyes as she died.

Nell put her hand to the bandages wrapped across one shoulder and thought instead of the flashing images: the ambulance siren as the medic worked on her, the fluorescence of the hospital lights as they rushed her to theatre, the urgency of the doctors' voices.

The heart monitor beside her quickened its beat. She remembered the hand of the anaesthetist pressing down on her throat so she wouldn't vomit and then choke on it. The look on their face as they pushed the anaesthetic into her veins until they faded out of view.

She couldn't breathe. She grabbed at the bedcovers, desperate for air, but the panic was crushing it out of her. Shit. *Breathe.* She tried to sit and reach the phone on the table by the foot of her bed, but the heaviness of her shoulder pulled her back. She still couldn't breathe. She didn't want to die. She'd survived. *Don't let me die.*

'Shit, Nell.' Paul was by the side of her bed, his face close to hers, before he was swallowed up by darkness.

Bremer was staring at her when she next came round. He smiled. 'You scared us there for a minute.'

'What happened?'

'Panic attack.'

Jesus, was that all? 'I thought I was dying.'

'Serious things, panic attacks,' he said, studying her. 'But we can help. I'll call the force counsellor as a starting point and—'

'I'm not going,' she interrupted.

Bremer put his arm on her hand. 'Yes, you are, Nell. You're a good cop and I want you back on the team as soon as possible. And if that means you're going to have to suffer a few sessions with a shrink, so be it.' He pulled back and glanced at the door. 'Carla's almost here with grapes. Be nice to her. She's just seen Gerry and is a bit tearful.'

'I'm always nice and why the hell did she bother doing that?'

'Closure, Nell. It's what emotionally intelligent people do.'

Nell rolled her eyes. At least that didn't hurt. She clicked for a hit of morphine, then looked at her bandages. 'Will it get better? I mean, will I be able to work again?' It suddenly occurred to her she didn't know the extent of the damage. What if she was retired on health reasons – what the hell would she do?

'You'll be fine. I've grilled the nurses within an inch of their lives and they have repeatedly confirmed you'll be fine. You'll just be a DS with a dodgy shoulder.'

She leaned back in relief as Carla appeared holding a bag of grapes, followed by Paul carrying a tray of three coffees.

'None for me?' Nell asked.

'Caffeine and morphine will make you high as a kite.'

He wouldn't catch her eye. She remembered pulling rank on him. Clearly he wasn't going to let that one go anytime soon. Shit. She was going to have to apologise. Not her forte.

'Sorry.'

Paul glanced at her. 'Forgotten.'

Bremer looked between them. 'Very touching,' he said. 'Now, let's have a quick debrief before we let Nell rest?'

Carla sat on the end of Nell's bed. Paul took a seat by the window.

'The biggest thing we're going to have to manage is the press. They will crucify us for this and we probably deserve it. So brace yourselves and don't give any comments.' He looked pointedly at Nell. 'Don't bite.'

'I'd never bite a journalist, leaves a nasty taste.'

'And then we'll have the court case. Eve will obviously remain in prison until then.'

'Will she and Gerry be tried together?' Carla asked.

'Doubt it. There'll be multiple charges brought, so I imagine they'll keep it simple to avoid overloading a jury.'

Nell watched Carla process this. Was she picturing Gerry alone in the box, worrying for him? Or hoping he got everything coming to him? She concluded it was probably a bit of both.

'But with Eve,' Paul said, 'who exactly will be in the dock, if you know what I mean?'

'Eve or Mary?' Bremer asked.

'Yeah. Are we charging her as Eve or as Mary?'

'Mary. That's who she is. Eve never existed.'

Nell pitied the jury having to untangle it all. She still didn't get it and she'd met both Mary and Eve, but as the former had left Nell with a permanent reminder of herself, it suited Nell just fine that it would be Mary who got to spend her remaining years in jail.

Joanne's face flashed up again. Nell felt the breath catch in her throat.

'You OK?' Bremer was looking at her, his face full of concern.

She nodded. Took a breath, grateful for the feeling of air down her throat.

'Let's leave the debrief.' He picked up his coffee. 'Rest. Don't think too much. And if you start to panic, pull on the cord for a nurse.'

'Yes, sir.'

'Don't be belligerent, Nell.'

She laughed. 'I called you sir.'

'Exactly.' He beckoned for Paul to follow. 'See you shortly, Sergeant.'

Carla remained on the bed.

'God, give us a sip.' Nell pointed to the coffee cup.

'No. You don't need any more adrenalin in you.'

Carla looked pale. Tired. The red lipstick was on, but rather than hide her fatigue, it just served to highlight it.

'You OK?'

'Mostly, yeah.'

'What's happening with Baz?' Nell asked.

Carla looked out of the window. 'He left me a note.'

'And?'

'I haven't read it yet. What with everything that's happened, I just haven't wanted to.'

Nell pushed herself up in the bed. 'You got it on you?'

'Yeah. Why?'

'Hand it over.'

'Nell, now really isn't the time.'

Nell held out her hand. 'Give it.'

Carla hesitated before reaching down and taking the letter from her bag. Passing it over, she then cradled her coffee in her hands, watching as Nell took the page from its envelope.

Nell looked at her. 'Ready?'

Carla nodded, so Nell began to read.

Dear Carla,

I know I left abruptly and that must have upset you. I'm sorry for that. I haven't gone for good, but I need time to get my head together and I felt if all my stuff was still in our flat I wouldn't have space to do that.

I think, by now, you will know if you want children and if you want them with me. We have been together for over ten years now: we left school together, went to university together, and now live together. I can't understand a reason why you don't know yet whether you want children. Is it because you want a career? If so, you can still have that. Is it because you feel you want to explore the world a bit? If so, we can do that too.

I suppose what I'm trying to say is, we can fit the baby around whatever you want to do, but I don't think I can compromise about having one.

Will you read this and think hard about what you want and then let me know? I don't imagine it will take long to decide, so I would really appreciate hearing from you as soon as possible.

All my love to you, my lovely,

Baz

Nell put the letter down and rested her head on the pillow. 'That's good, yeah?'

Carla, staring out of the window, gave the smallest shrug.

'Come on! Give the man a break. It was a sweet letter. Hell, it almost brought a tear to my eye.'

Carla smiled at her. That was better. God, Nell wanted a cigarette. Spotting a wheelchair in the corner of the ward, she nudged Carla's arm.

'Hey, Brown, fancy recreating *The Great Escape*?'

Carla followed her nod. 'Seriously?'

'Seriously.'

Carla glanced at the corridor, then back at the chair. 'OK, Jackson, you're on.'

Outside, Carla rolled them each a cigarette, lighting Nell's before handing it to her.

'Do you think Bremer's going to hang around?' she asked.

Nell took a long drag, enjoying the sudden rush to her head. 'What do you mean?'

'Well, now he's got a good result under his belt, do you think he'll move on up?'

'Maybe, but I think he'll want one more case with us, just to prove it wasn't a fluke.'

'Do you want him to go?' Carla asked.

'A week ago, I probably would have said yes, but now ...' Nell shrugged. 'I don't think I do.'

'Me neither.'

She watched Carla look around at the other smokers, huddled in their groups. 'What's up?'

'There was a journalist here when I arrived. Just didn't fancy bumping into him again.'

'What did he want?'

'A quote.'

'Well maybe it would be useful to have a pet journo. Save us getting a kicking in the press every day.'

'Maybe we'll become famous and they'll make films about us – the next Cagney and Lacey!'

Nell's laugh turned into a cough and when she'd finished, she found Carla's face full of concern.

'You had me worried back there for a minute, you know,' she said.

'For what, coughing?' But Nell knew that wasn't what she'd meant. 'Look, if it hadn't been for you, we wouldn't have even known there was a firearm. You had my back and I won't forget it.' Nell stubbed the cigarette out without finishing it. 'You're a good cop, Brown.'

'I'm not a cop, Jackson.'

'You know what I mean.'

'I do,' Carla said, and Nell watched as she blew smoke up into the crisp night air.

Epilogue

The judge is summing up. I am sitting in the wooden box they have assigned me and I'm waiting for the jury to assign me another. My husband is in the gallery, leaning forward. He clutches his hands between his legs as his eyes flick between the jury and me. The bandage is still on his head and whilst he has explained to me why he has it – why he may not be able to visit me for a while – I still struggle to understand anything other than that Mary hurt him, but why she did I still don't know.

'Mary Balcombe has been accused of a crime of the worst sort, murder,' the judge is saying, and it takes me a moment to remember they mean me. I have given up explaining their mistake and instead have resolved to suffer their foolishness until I am able to prove otherwise.

*

It takes four hours for the jury to decide my fate and the look on my barrister's face tells me this is not a good thing. Hushed conversations follow, between my husband and her, before I am escorted back to the courtroom between two blank-faced prison officers, both of whom smell of sweat.

I am reminded to stand as I wait for the jury to inform me of their judgment on me. I think of Joanne. She was never as I imagined, far too delicate to have come from such hate, and as I picture her I feel a deep sense of pain; she had hardly begun her life – for what age is thirty-five? – and I was never able to love her like a child should be loved. If the jury want remorse, they've got it, because I could not regret more my inability to mother her. But how can a child who hasn't been mothered learn to do so herself? It sounds like an excuse, I decide, but a fire rages in me to tell me I'm wrong – it's not an excuse if it's the truth.

The foreman of the jury stands. The judge asks him if I am guilty of killing Joanne Fowler.

Aoife's child.

I hold my breath, begging them to understand it wasn't me, that I would never kill the only child who lived to draw breath after so many others tried and failed.

'Guilty, Your Honour.'

Someone shouts from the gallery, someone cheers, and the jury's faces merge to become one giant blinking eye with a finger below that jabs at my chest, pushing all the air from my lungs. I grasp the sides of the box and bow my head, sucking in the lost air until I am fit to burst with it. Then I stand and let it back into the room.

'I DID NOT KILL OUR BABY.'

Acknowledgments

As it's taken eight years to get here, I have a lot of people to thank, so brace yourselves for a Gwyneth style Oscar acceptance speech.

Clare Mac. Can you believe it? Turns out all those years of ranting over email about ChipLitFest was worth it. Long may our rantings continue. Fanny Blake, I honestly don't think I'd have made it here if it weren't for you and Womentoring. I'm endlessly thankful for all you taught me. To the first crime writers I ever really met – Steve Mosby, Eva Dolan, Mark Edwards, Chris Ewan, Stav Sherez, Martyn Waites – thank you for your constant support, and to Mark Billingham for being the legendary quiz master. Thanks to Rosy, Emily, Jessica and Laura (don't argue about the order) for always pushing me forward and believing in me. Thank you to my Wilkes family and the

Gordon-Browns for being almost as excited about this as me. To the Hanborough Massive for your encouragement (and drinking abilities), and the women at Ox City Council, and Mike, for making the job so much fun. Thanks also to Dom for the last minute name steal (Roger this is my atonement for all the Ox Mail articles). I often write in pubs so I also need to thank The Yeoman in Freeland, The George and Dragon in Hanborough, The Chequers in Cassington and The Kings Arms in Woodstock, and thank you to The Three Horse Shoes in Hanborough for your late night whiskey when it all got a bit much. To the residents of Freeland and Hanborough, thank you for electing a crime writer to represent you; it's an absolute privilege.

Almost finally (but not quite) thank you to Becky for taking me on and believing in me. You'll never know how much the words 'oh yes, the admin bit? I'll send you over a contract,' meant to me! To Emily and Sonny, editing with you has been the most exciting part of this whole journey. I've learnt so much and enjoyed it all – except the copy-edit bit (thanks for bearing with me over my 'that' breakdown) but I'm thankful for the copy-editor's thoughtful comments, as well as to the designer of my cover, which is brilliant.

And my real final thanks go to Nell, Abe and Betty, for eating cereal when I was on a deadline and to Martin for clearing up the crumbs when they did. This book is as much all yours as it is mine.

Follow Merilyn online

🐦 **@nellbelleandme**